VALLEY OF THE
THOUSAND SMOKES

VALLEY OF THE THOUSAND SMOKES

A North–Western Story

by

Dan Cushman

III

W

cop. 3

Five Star
Unity, Maine

Five Star Western
Published in conjunction with Golden West Literary Agency.

November 1996

First Edition

Five Star Standard Print Western Series.

The text of this edition is unabridged.

Set in 11 pt. Bookman Old Style by Warren Doersam.

Printed in the United States on permanent paper.

Library of Congress Cataloging in Publication Data

Cushman, Dan.
    Valley of the thousand smokes : a North–Western
story / by Dan Cushman.
       p.   cm.
    ISBN 0-7862-0663-2 (hc)
    I. Title.
PS3553.U738V3 1996
813′.54—dc20   96-5873

VALLEY OF THE THOUSAND SMOKES

A North–Western Story

Chapter One

There was a big Tom Flynn and a little Tom Flynn, but the big Tom Flynn, five feet nine, was little Tom Flynn's father. Little Tom Flynn was six feet and about two inches. This was considered quite a joke up in the Border Country where Red River — the Red River of the North — crossed the U. S.-Canada boundary: Minnesota and North Dakota on the south and Manitoba to the north. The Flynns played no favorites and took homesteads on both sides. It was perfectly legal, once an Englishman always an Englishman, and shouldn't it work the other way, too? It worked out *real* well because folks found that they could not only take homesteads but vote in the elections, too. Everybody behind the counters in the courthouses said it was only fair — they paid taxes, didn't they? So you ought to have a say as to how it was spent. And they would be handed cards to tell you who to vote for, if so inclined.

There was a whole flock of towns where everybody knew everybody else, places such as Pembina, Dufferin, St. Vincent, and Gretna, or Gretna Green. People visited Winnipeg, Grand Forks, Minneapolis, and St. Paul. The wheat went mainly to St. Paul and the big water-powered flouring mills, as far up the Mississippi as a boat could get. It was the famed Red River wheat, hard wheat unmatched for fine breads. So much for that.

When little Tom Flynn graduated from high school, or Latin school as the older people called it, he decided to give college a whirl. He had been working in his Uncle Frank's livery stable, U. S. side, the office part, and his Aunt Frances, who had a circulating library up in Roseaux City, Canada, said he was just diddly-winking his money. He was making good wages, better than fifty per month, plus tips, and what he ought to do was save some and go to college. So he laid some aside, and his Uncle Frank was good for a hundred (a bachelor and all that money he'd netted on the gold mine stock at Bullfrog, Nevada), so he went down to *Le Lycée de Fleuve Rouge et le Sacré Coeur* in Grand Forks on the Dakota side. It was a French school but had come around after about fifty years to teach mainly in English. So little Tom Flynn, six feet two, bought a large brown leather suitcase and took the cars down to look things over.

It was summer. The regular term hadn't started, but there were some classes. The rooms were often filled. Teachers brushing up on the new methods, completing post-graduate work, but Flynn didn't think too much of it. They were mainly at work on things he had no interest in, and the students were often a little old. Fellows his age told him, if he wasn't a Catholic or didn't admit to being one, he'd be in luck. They had all these Holy Days, novenas, and this and that, but only Catholics had to attend. Being a Protestant, he'd be in or out . . . well, "like Flynn."

Flynn could see little advantage in laying down the money if he didn't attend. And then there was this *smell* when they got up to leave. It was the old varnished oak chairs, seats revarnished about once in every three years, new varnish over old, and hence the *smell* building

8

up from years and years of people that were now long in their coffins, the smell of their hind-ends being resurrected. The upshot was he went on to St. Paul and Minneapolis, the Twin Cities. St. Paul was the old town and Minneapolis the new one. St. Paul was the capital. St. Paul was mostly Catholic, and Minneapolis was Protestant. He liked St. Paul better because of the old-time joints, and cowboys who came with the cattle trains, and not a lot of jim-crackery electric bulbs spelling out **Cafe**. He saw the shows and visited the houses of pleasure with some new acquaintances — they were going to the university — and he rode the streetcars which were changing over to electric power transmitted by a wire overhead. However, the city became tiresome. There were too many people, strangers who hurried all the time and wouldn't stop to talk. He took a tour of the blue cheese caves — and imagined he smelled mold all night, it had so impregnated his clothes — and the waterfalls and dams and the biggest flour mill in the world.

Tiring of the Twin Cities, he rode the C. M. & S. P. railroad to Milwaukee where he visited the Schlitz Palm Garden, which was said to have been moved by sections up from the World's Columbian Exhibition in Chicago and refitted with scarcely a stone disturbed. It was, as advertised, a bewildering grove of palms in green containers with vines of growing plants, a marvel to behold. He was given a flagon of Schlitz beer free.

It was on Lake Michigan, so he bought a ticket first class on the Michilac Excursion Boat which would go via the celebrated Sault Ste. Marie locks and be lifted to the level of Lake Superior. He got acquainted with a very pretty and very sad young woman who had lost her husband to typhoid fever. He tried to comfort her, saying a fine-appearing young lady such as she was would have little trouble finding happiness once the clouds rolled by. He'd thought of the expression himself, and liked it.

His hope and confidence did seem to have an affect on her, and she wept on his chest, and they went ashore at Green Bay where the boat put in. They ate at a restaurant called Lido's, trout and some sort of fish roe, and had some champagne at $4 per bottle, and she wept all over his chest again, and they went back aboard where he comforted her still more, but in the morning she was gone. They stopped at Marquette, on Lake Superior, and she must have gone ashore. What's more, she had taken all of his money, except for some cached in the suitcase lining, along with his seventeen-jewel Hamilton watch, gold chain, and even his pants — but the pants were found later. She'd carried them out to go through the pockets and had dropped them behind a chair.

His ticket was gone with his wallet, and Flynn thought he was going to have to fight the captain to continue his voyage. It led to quite a row. A lot of people were around, taking Flynn's side, and finally he lost his temper and held the captain by his ankles over the side. He weighed a good 160 pounds and could easily have been dropped if he'd struggled. In fact, a lot of fellows were yelling that Flynn do that very thing. "Drop him!" Someone had even learned his name. "Drop him, Flynn!"

Of course he didn't do it, but he was worried later because the ship was to put in at a port up on the Canadian shore, old Port William, and he might do it there, so he mentioned he had relations in Canada, and one was a lawyer in Port Arthur, right close on, and he intended to report the whole thing since the steam-boat line was responsible for his property and his safety. The stop was made without incident, and he was carried on to Duluth, where the captain came ashore, shook his hand, and said he hoped there were no hard feelings. They had both lost their tempers but should understand each other's positions.

All Flynn had by then was some small change in his pocket. He wondered what he could do to earn enough for a ticket home. He didn't want to be forced to telegraph collect to Uncle Frank, his best bet in emergency. He was saved from having to do this by what seemed to be the damnedest piece of luck! He saw a sign:

Drivers Wanted.
Dock to City Dray.
Top Wages.

He grabbed it, of course, explaining his livery stable experience with horses of all kinds, and — a double piece of luck — the manager was known over in Pembina. They had several mutual acquaintances, so he was signed on at the high rate of four dollars per ten-hour day!

"Been down to Chicago?" the man asked, and Flynn, just for something interesting to answer — no mention had been made of the bereaved woman — said yes, he had just got back from the Boer War in South Africa where he had served with the famed Irish Fusileers. Actually he intended it to be sort of a joke because the war had been over for some time. But Lord Winston Churchill had been lecturing about it in Chicago and was said to be harried by the Irish because of his British nationality. Every time they got to hooting, Churchill would bring up the Irish Fusileers, a small contingent from around Dublin, to save the day. And so the jeers would have to change to cheers. They never figured out a way of deriding Churchill without including the fusileers.

Apparently the manager hadn't heard of Churchill and maybe not the fusileers, but he'd heard plenty about the war and Flynn, being a returned veteran, was put on a solid footing. War experience fell right in with the job. His quick employment at high wages was due to a drayman's strike, the new Dray and Transport Workers International, and the driver was a real target, seated there, even though the seats had been lowered and the freight, which was mainly trunks and other baggage to the hotels, so placed as to give maximum protection.

Next morning Flynn set out, and the union was waiting, all rested for the encounter. They hooted, threw things, and waved signs such as — **Eat Hearty While Children Starve** — but he got by without any close calls. There were police posted, and his seat was set low, the baggage high. This had its drawbacks, however, because it shoved his face right in the horses' hind-ends, and he'd never realized how often a horse had to arch his tail and let those stinking brown quarter-circles of manure roll over the cropper. A cropper is the folded spheroid of leather that passes under the tail, holding the harness in place, the most revolting fate leather can have, a vile hangman's noose. Flynn hoped that if he were ever to hang, as some had predicted when he got in trouble, they wouldn't think of using a cropper. Dry they weren't so bad, but before half an hour passed they were reeking. Still, he stayed where he was, on guard from the bricks,

12

rotten oranges, and other projectiles.

Flynn might not have stuck with the job longer than it took to get carfare home, but the strikers made him so damned mad. Here is an example. They would not only hurl rocks but also gather cheesecloth bags of fresh manure, weight it with a rock, urinate on it, and fling it by a piece of rope. At least that was what one fellow did, and Flynn was waiting for him. He wrapped the reins, leaped off, and took after the miscreant, a response that so surprised him that Flynn got him by the collar and, damn, if it wasn't a boy of about ten. And scared! He thought Flynn was going to break his neck or something, and he was bawling, his eyes begging Flynn for mercy.

Flynn said: "Son, that was a great shot. It deserves a reward." Flynn held him with one hand and wiped the urinated manure off his neck with the other. "Take this," he said and gave him a quarter. The kid didn't take it right away. He thought it was a trick to grab his hand and break his wrist, because Flynn was about strong enough to do it. "Go ahead. Take the two-bits. Why did you do that? You're not old enough to drive a dray. Does your dad belong to the union?"

The kid shook his head and finally thought it safe enough to pocket the quarter.

"Are they paying you?"

He shook his head again. He was still scared.

"Why are you doing it?"

"I dunno. Jus' fer fun, I guess."

"Listen, son, that's no way to have fun. You deserve to be paid for it. You start a hoodlum's union. Then go around with a committee and tell those cheap sons of bitches in the drayman's union to pay you your rightful day's wage. Will you do that?"

"Uh-huh," he said.

The rest of the gang was about fifty yards away waiting to see what Flynn was going to do with his captive and, when he went back and got in the seat, they came up closer to stare.

Flynn didn't quit. He was stubborn and vowed he'd stick with it. When he was washing himself in the water spout, another driver pulled up and asked why he'd let the kid go?

"Because he's got nerve. And imagination. Mark my words, he'll be an inventor some day. He can go to work for the munitions makers."

"Used to his kind in the Boer War? Those Dutch pretty tough?"

"I don't want to talk about it."

The fellow said: "Well, that's what Pa said about the vets in the Civil War. Got bad enough they didn't want to talk about it."

Things let up a little as the union fellows got to finding jobs on the lake. Flynn remained mostly on the hotel routes, hauling baggage from the docks, easy to load for protection, and the better hotels often sent a guard to see to it none of the guests' baggage was fouled. What Flynn disliked most was having to answer questions about the Boer War, that particular piece of fiction having clung to him, so he got to spending a lot of time in the library reading about it and about Duluth, about how it had been founded by David Greysolon, Sieur du Lhut, in 1679. Duluth was the ultimate anchor of the French Company in Montreal, the outfit that fowled its own nest by arresting two fellow Frenchmen, independents who came in with a huge cargo of fine furs,

Medard Chouset, Sieur de Groseillers, and Pierre Esprit Radisson, generally known merely as Groseillers and Radisson, a pair like Montgomery and Ward. Groseillers and Radisson were released without the furs worth a fortune and carried their plea to Paris where nobody would listen, and thence to England where they *did*. England had just buried the Puritan leader, Oliver Cromwell, without suitable decency then, when the new king, Charles II, was crowned, celebrated by digging up Oliver Cromwell and putting his body on the city dump. At any rate Groseillers and Radisson got a much better hearing in England. A new hope gripped the country with their new king and, when the English were told about all the beaver, black fox, and mink country that lay open by water via the North and Hudson Bay with endless forest, rivers and lakes westward, they were in business again. In fact they had the king's brother as partner and so was born the good old Hudson's Bay Company. Situated on the western shore of the Churchill River, the English were content to take their ease while employing Crees, a tribe stretching from the bay to the Rockies, whose long trains of trading canoes carried not the cheap junk of France and Spain but the best Sheffield steel. Indeed, they carried the best of everything, for the Indian did not ask for whiskey, not until later. As nearly as Flynn could guess, the first thing the Indian wanted was a knife, one with a big, long blade that held an edge, Sheffield steel to cut up moose and buffalo, and next an iron or bronze pot, a great big one to cook this meat in and to replace his former hole in the ground, lined with rawhide, heated by hot rocks dropped in and fished out, hours on end. And muskets! Long steel muskets with plenty of smooth bore length to use all the power that gunpowder had, although it's doubtful that the Indians ever had to stack beaver to a rifle's height. Meanwhile the English took their ease and turned the loading over to the Crees and long, long strings of trade canoes, one after another, loaded with the best, going and coming back, farther and farther, finally to the great wall of the Rocky Mountains.

It really stirred Flynn, reading about it, and about Jay Cooke who had financed the Civil War, and how he had chosen Duluth as his starting point for a railroad to the mouth of the Oregon, great river of the west — "where flows the Oregon and knows no sound save its own dashing!" But old Jay went bust, with end of steel at Bismarck, Dakotah — named for Otto von Bismarck of Germany but with no strength attained by it. It had to be steamboats from there to the gold fields and loss of Canada to the whiskey-trading Yankees had it not been for the new Army of the West, the North West Mounted Police, that Ottawa planned to supply by steamboat via the Sasketchewan, known as the Missouri of the North. Only this river proved too swift. It promptly smashed the steamboats. Hence St. Louis and the Missouri had to serve. The R. C. M. P. was supplied with American arms, Colt and Winchester, and it was too bad for jolly old England!

The whiskey dealers were chased out, and the R. C. M. P. almost froze. They were a riff-raff at first, ill-clothed, ill-housed, and they would desert in platoons, getting over the U. S. boundary often with frozen feet that had to be amputated, so the gold and cattle camps of Montana Territory were filled with legless men, pushing themselves around on dollies. But finally they worked things out, built the Canadian Pacific to save British

Columbia from seceding, and boomed with the wheat lands of Red River and the gold of the Klondike. What a story! Flynn tingled at it. By the gods Flynn wanted to be a Mounted Policeman! There was a picture in one of the books, a Mounted Policeman in his flat-rim hat, scarlet jacket, and Flynn could just imagine himself so garbed, a long leap from that dray!

"Why not!" said Flynn, mounting to his place behind the horses' croppers. "Why, I'm a veteran of two wars, the Boer and the Drayman's!"

He quit. As a veteran he figured he had a good shot at starting as a sergeant. That's how he saw himself, all six and two of him, straight as a Blackfoot lance, in his scarlet coat and flat-brimmed, four-way dented hat. He went to Chicago for a rest, bought a Civil War medal for his Uncle Frank just as a joke, and some Boer War stuff at a place that sold medals and papers of every sort, even a Victoria Cross that was like gold but with a $22 price tag that stalled him. It would have been fun walking around flashing it and telling about Spion Kop and how Kitchener himself had pinned it on him. "If you're going to lie," his Uncle Frank had once said, "make it a big one, because otherwise it won't be believed, and you'll lose respect."

Chapter Two

Anyhow, his family had learned where he was. He'd written, dressing up the facts a little. He explained how it was to his aunt who had the circulating library in Minnesota-Manitoba, smack on the line. She understood common sense things better than his folks. He rested for a while and renewed old acquaintances. "Oh, I got in on the drag end of the Boer War in Nineteen Aught Two," he told them and showed his fusileers' medal.

He gave his Uncle Frank the Civil War medal he'd bought with a portrait of Lincoln and a quote from the President's second inaugural address because his uncle was so down on Lincoln. "This just arrived in the mail," Flynn told him. "Seems to have been mislaid. See, there's a quote from the late President on it."

"By God!" said Uncle Frank. "It's just what I need to pin up my underwear."

But he knew Flynn had bought it as a joke. The "late war" was his favorite subject — not the Boer War of 1900-1902 but the Civil War, the War Between the States. Uncle Frank had made an enemy of nearly every Northern partisan in the region by telling how Negro slavery was a plot by England. The English had made fortunes out of Caribbean sugar and, when the market was ruined by Far East sugar, they were left with all those Negro slaves on their hands, hungry, wanting to be fed, so the Wilberforce brothers, one a bishop and the other a member of Parliament, got them set free, making it sound great — slavery no more anywhere in the British Empire! What they did was fob them off on the U. S. A.! Well, it was profit all around because they were said to be able to raise cotton to supply the English cotton mills, but soon the New England mills were the worst slave owners of all. He had read a book that proved it.

Then Lincoln got into it, was elected on the slavery issue, a minority President — a three-way split. "I wasn't old enough to vote, one year short, but I'd have *voted* for him!" Uncle Frank said in his laconic, clipped manner of speaking. "Even though he wanted to free the slaves by force, which meant war. Anything for a vote. No word against the cotton moguls in Connecticut. Or in England. Only the poor devils in the South with their chains clanking. Naturally the slave states objected, fearing they'd lose their money. The Southern states' leaders were actually in New York, trying to borrow for individual state treasuries. No idea of war. Oh, some hotheads, yes. But they could have worked it out. Then the hotheads hung old John Brown, sent Lee to do it, a Virginian, anything that could get things fired up. The country was a powderkeg, and every word Lincoln spoke made it worse. He had to go through slave country to get to Washington, Maryland. Sneaked in! He was in disguise! Dressed up in a Mother Hubbard and a sunbonnet! Then he asked Lee to head the Union Army. After fixing things so there wasn't a chance he'd accept. Captured Lee's home and plantation. Made a graveyard of it. Revenge! Then Charlestown harbor and that fort . . . Fort Sumpter. A hothead Texas senator named Wigfall went down and

19

pulled the lanyard on a cannon. Knocked some bricks out. Well, who was in command at Sumpter? A Northerner named Abner Doubleday who claimed to have invented baseball. Did he shoot back? Yes, but not at Wigfall. He cut loose on this resort hotel on Charleston harbor. He had wanted to sign for his dinner the day previous, and they wouldn't accept his signature!

"So the Southern states gave up trying to borrow from the Northern banks and went home. Lincoln had everybody laughing at him. The papers had cuts showing him in bonnet and dress and, to save face, he marched off to take Richmond, Virginia. And was he in for a surprise! He wasn't fighting any Black Hawk Indian war *then.* Those Virginians practiced military like we do croquet. Up here everybody was asked to enlist. I did. I admit it. Not old enough to know better. Lied about my age. It was a lot of fun drilling, marching around. Got seven-fifty per month and all expenses. That was a good bit of money at that time. But I soon got sick of my bargain. I'd hate to tell what I went through. Worst part was seeing what a poor bunch we had for officers. Swagger around. Rode horseback. Pose for the newspaper photographers. And God, how people were coming into the country! Emigrants. Couldn't speak a word of English. Settled in Illinois and Iowa. And California, where they dug gold. We died while the damned foreigners grabbed up the land. Lincoln said grain would win the war. Comstock Lode. Millionaires by the score. California, Nevada, Montana, Colorado. Pouring out money for the North and did old Abe spend it! Millions! Billions! But even that wasn't enough. He had to print greenbacks. Copper mines up in northern Michigan. By God, he spent it all. Instituted the draft. Riots. Irish didn't mind fighting, but they wanted to eat a little of our beef and potatoes first. Worst generals in the world, both sides. Lee! Why, he marched up into Maryland *twice.* Where was he going? To Canada? Never said. Had to do something. Invade the North! News headlines back home. No shoes, finally. Only the tops. Gettysburg.

"That's where I got my wound, at Little Round Top in western Maryland, just below Pennsylvania. Lee had the idea Philadelphia would rise to support him. Or Maryland! Of course he had to retreat back to Virginia. Left his dead behind. Let us bury them! And that damned fool speech Lincoln made at the battlefield! I didn't hear it! I was in a hospital. Flies everywhere. Regular gut-wagon. I read it later on. 'Fourscore and seven.' Why not come right out and say eighty-seven like he was at the auction sale? He had to fancy it up. And all that about how the country was dedicated to the proposition, that about men being equal. Created equal! Well, maybe, but if he'd look at his Constitution he'd see that it had a black man was equal to two-fifths or three-fifths of a white man! It's set right down. Some *equal!* And the Indians! They weren't worth much of anything. Driven out of the Carolinas. Sent packing to Oklahoma. Even Sam Houston was mad about that. Went up to Washington dressed like a Cherokee, and Jackson sent him off to the West, where he run the Mexicans out of Texas. All that before Lincoln.

"And the generals he had! But back to that foolish speech. 'Brave men who struggled here!' Why, we hid behind rocks, anything we could find, but it looked like Lee wanted to get it over with, so he just marched across this big field and got his men shot. He might just about as well stood them up against a wall. Executed. And

21

how he wanted to finish the work we'd *nobly* begun. We were hid behind rocks. I was and got hit anyhow. And that part about 'the government of the people, by the people, and for the people . . . !' He stole that! A fellow showed me. It came from the front page of the old Wycliffe Bible. 'This book is for the education of the people, by the people,' and so on. Stole it! Fobbed it off as his own! It was plagiarism. Ask your aunt with the books."

Flynn said: "I heard that Edwin was not the greatest Hamlet in the Booth family."

That stopped Uncle Frank cold. "Well, I see what you mean, and I don't know I'd go that far."

"How's your old battle wound?"

"Fine!" But he wasn't through with Lincoln and the damned Republican government. "Wounded, couldn't work. Bullet still there. Those Army doctors couldn't do a thing. Doctors! Couldn't make it in private practice. Had to wait for a Democrat to get elected to get my pension. And a doctor that could do something. Army doctors! The worst! Finally at my own expense I went down to Minneapolis, and there was this big, tall, raw-boned fellow with saber scars. He had attended Heidelberg. They fight duels there and get scarred to show they're not afraid of pain, or blood . . . their own as well as yours. Don't do things to you they won't to themselves. Well, he got me stripped and poked around. And he made me bend this way and that way. Big, long, white fingers. Poked real deep while I breathed and bent this way and that, and he'd put blue and red X's and O's here and there, after which he laid me down and did a lot of figuring. Got all the things so he was satisfied. Sort of like solid geometry from the outside.

"Then he gave me this long needle full of something called lime of coca. It benumbs. And pretty soon he just ran in a thing like an ice pick and found what he was looking for. But mind you this! *Not* where it hurt! I thought he was away off, but he came in with some long tweezers and zing! Out it came! But not from where I expected. He knew by my moving where it was. He had it, a slick, greenish ball, like about a Forty-Four caliber. All thick-coated slick and green. It's down at my room in the old house by Skinner's Springs. I'll get it and show you."

"I'd like to see it," said Flynn. He was serious.

"Sometime when you're over there I'll show it to you, though it looks different, the green gunk all dried. I'll spit on it. Bring it back like it was." He laughed and went on: "I'll own, it scared me a mite when I saw those saber scars. Here, I'll show you my scar."

Flynn had seen it before, but Uncle Frank undid his shirt and opened his underwear from the front and showed the scar which was only about an inch long. Also the wound, from Little Round Top, much older.

"Hurts me once in a while, down in here, but hell, at my age . . . !"

"Uncle Frank," said Flynn. "You are a proved commodity!"

Anyway, Flynn was home, in good clothes and spirits. He shook hands with everyone and sat around his aunt's, reading books she had saved out for him, especially *Moby Dick* by one Herman Melville which he'd heard talked about, and he read and read and learned more about whales than he ever wanted to know.

Chapter Three

Flynn read many books from his Aunt Frances's library, among them *The Last Days of Pompeii* by Bulwer-Lytton, Bart. (He could never understand what Bart. stood for — it couldn't be *bartender*.)

His aunt said: "Oh, Thomas, *really*," when he called him "Bart" as if it were his last name.

He read Morgan's *Freemasonry Exposed*, which his aunt kept hidden away, and had a pretty fair time with *Taking the Bastille* by Alexandre Dumas, which he pronounced Doomas and she said: "Oh, *now* you're trying to be *funny*," but he really wasn't. So he bought a book called *Pronunciation Made Easy*, with an appendix on yellow paper — The Five Hundred Most Mispronounced Words — that seemed to have just about his whole vocabulary. He used it and devised all sorts of clever ways and means — Dumas was pronounced *do* and *ma* illustrated with a picture of a little boy calling his mother — and similar stratagems. But the best way he learned was to attend the theatre when people such as Maurice Barrymore were on tour, especially if they sold paper copies of the play that he could sort of memorize beforehand. The real trouble being there wasn't a city closer than Winnipeg to which a good actor ever came.

When he read aloud to his aunt from books such as *Lorna Doone* that had a lot of rhythm in it, she would

24

stop him whenever he ran into something. "Your trouble, Thomas," she insisted, "isn't that you mispronounce so many different words. You mispronounce the same words over and over."

She made a list of these words and fixed them up in rhyme for him to memorize. It was a wonder how she could do it. But then she got an even better idea, killing two birds with one stone as it were, and made him read things like "The Raven" or "Annabel Lee" and had him repeat them out loud until he got every word right. She even had him learn three whole pages of "The Fall of the House of Usher" and declaim them. "Nothing like Poe for *rhythm*," she ventured. "And *cadence*." When she dealt him Oscar Wilde who had become the *fin de siécle* scanda*l par excellence*, she made him say it right out in genuine French, telling him not to mumble.

"You get to do it by *rote*," she said. "Your tongue gets in the habit! That's right. And poetry makes it easy, because of the meter and the rhyme. With poetry you just turn your mouth loose and let it ramble. 'The Fall of the House of Usher' is like poetry because good prose has meter. It's easier to say it *right* than to say it *wrong*."

"Well, dog my cats," he said — which he'd learned from Huckleberry Finn — but still referring to Oscar Wilde.

"Yes, but he did a lot of harm with that book," his aunt told him.

So Flynn was soon saying:

> **" 'I never saw a man who looked**
> **With such a wistful eye**
> **Upon that little tent of blue**
> **Which prisoners call the sky.' "**

"Fine," commented his aunt. "You see, good speech has nothing to do with the rules of grammar. What you do is read something out loud, or to yourself out loud, as if your tongue were working, and sooner than you know you'll go all day without making a mistake."

"Like ducking when somebody throws a rock at you," suggested Flynn.

"Correct!"

And that was how he learned, by reading out loud to Aunt Frances. The damnedest thing was that poets like Poe and Tennyson and Kipling didn't work if you pronounced them wrong. They just didn't.

> **" 'When the Himalayan peasant meets**
> **the he-bear in his pride,**
> **He shouts to scare the monster,**
> **who will often turn aside**
> **But the she-bear thus accosted**
> **rends the fellow tooth and nail**
> **For the female of the species**
> **is more deadly than the male.' "**

"Yes," responded his aunt, "but you don't *believe* that, Thomas!"

"I heard a fellow say that Kipling never got chosen poet laureate by Victoria Regina on account of his poems."

His aunt picked that up: "It was mainly because of his 'Lonely Old Widow at Windsor, with the heavy gold crown on her head.' "

"Oh, I say!" said Flynn. "That's a bit of all right."

"It was a bit of all wrong for him," said his aunt.

So Flynn read poetry over and over. The rhythm kept

making talk easier.

His aunt told him: "After all, Thomas, there are only about one hundred thousand words in the dictionary. I've heard that foreigners come here and get by quite nicely with only two hundred."

"All the rest is only frosting?" he queried.

"Not exactly. But you get the idea."

And that was how Thomas Flynn learned to speak the English tongue — *correctly.*

It wasn't long after having accomplished that that he began thinking about the future and presently he made up his mind.

"What I think I'd like to do is see the West," he announced to Aunt Frances. "And, you know, they let you do it at *government expense!*"

"What are you talking about?"

"Joining the Royal Canadian Mounted Police."

"Just like *that?*"

"It's been on my mind for weeks. Well, when I really did get to considering it was in Duluth. I thought: 'Here I am, driving a dray and in danger of my life. Why not?' "

Anyhow the decision gave him an excuse to visit Winnipeg. He walked around a block about twice and sat for a time on a bench in Assiniboine Square, a fine stand of trees giving beauty to that section of town. The government buildings were across the way with the Union Jack, the flag of England, flying and the Canadian national emblem one length beneath it. To Flynn this showed which came first. If it didn't bother people in Winnipeg, it was still a challenge and an insult in Quebec. Quebec considered itself a *conquered* country and by God and *Mon Dieu* the French-Canadians let nobody, not even the Governor General himself, forget it! And here were these two flags, the Union Jack and the Canadian variation, flying in that order with no second thought given.

There was a sign:

Recruitments
Walk In.

The door was open. Not a soul was in view. Flynn stood for a time at an oak counter, highly polished, until somebody looked in, retired a moment, and came out again. It was a man about as tall as himself wearing a sergeant's stripes with added insignia indicating years of service. The man was about fifty. Advancement seemed slow indeed.

"Sergeant Gibson," the man stated.

"Yes. Sergeant. . . ." — he almost said Sergeant Flynn, checked himself, and added: "Flynn, sir. Thomas Maxwell Flynn. Duluth."

He should not have said *Duluth*. He should have said Boundary Creek, which was the nearest post office to his father's farm, on the very border between the U. S. and Canada, population thirty-five.

"Well, only temporarily," Flynn elaborated. "I had just arrived and, after a long absence, well, I did stay for a time. The breeze from Lake Superior, you know."

The recruitment sergeant looked interested. "I couldn't help noticing your sun tan. You can see right where your hat stopped."

"Helmet."

It had in fact been a helmet. Flynn had bought himself a Derby hat, about two sizes too large, and filled it with flannel cut in long strips. He had hunted all over to find some flannel approximately the same hue as the hat. This gave him a feeling of comfort when he saw those hoodlums hiding in alleys. Actually, the Boer War hadn't entered his mind, not then or now.

It only came up when the recruiting officer remarked with solicitude: "Talk of your useless, dirty wars! No, not the Boers. I mean, they had something on their side. But the Kaiser. What they were doing was laying down their lives to establish the Germans up in Rhodesia."

"I think the Boers realized it, too, toward the end," Flynn agreed. "The Kaiser has always been haunted by the spirit of Otto von Bismarck, but he's no Bismarck. Such things are more obvious here than down there is my guess. You have a better perspective from a distance. There's too little time for global strategy when the ambush bullets are flying." Flynn changed his tone. "Little wonder I felt my spirits cooling off. The great piney forests. Even Red River. That's my old home. My uncle served in the Civil War. You could stand on our homestead and urinate across into the dear, old U. S. A. . . . which itself seems moved by the same imperialism in Cuba. And now, I hear, the Philippines. Why do our neighbors prize the Spanish empire? It certainly has meant nothing to *them*. Still, what do I know of global policies? The closer one gets, the farther he is away. Things appear plainer up here in the Dominion that never do down in the caldron. It was why I decided, after turning my back on a good education . . . *Le Lycée de Fleuve Rouge et le Sacré Coeur* in Grand Forks, that I might break into something more to my temperament in the R. C. M. P. I hope I can qualify . . . possibly with a sergeant's rank."

He had several identity cards, one of them a *faux* passport he'd purchased in Duluth when he had a notion to visit Europe but found his cash in hand insufficient.

"Oh, yes," said the sergeant. "Yes. Well, these will serve for identity, were any needed, which it is not. Your deep sun tan is sufficient. Just a moment."

He was gone for several minutes and returned with a man who, from appearances, had just risen from a nap. He wore the scarlet jacket and epaulets of an inspector. Flynn did not quite catch his name. He started to salute, checked himself, and said: "Habit," and they shook hands. Flynn's hands were still in rough shape from Duluth but had started to smooth out.

"Inspector Jerome, this is Flynn . . . Thomas Maxwell Flynn," Sergeant Gibson introduced him. "Lately, Sergeant Flynn in the Boer War, sir."

"You bear the color of warmer lands," the inspector observed.

"Do I? I was flattering myself on becoming Caucasian . . . make that Celtic . . . again," Flynn explained. "Irish Fusileers, you know."

And so it went. The two men retired and the recruiter, reëmerging, said the usual bout of camp could be dispensed with in his case and a place would be found for him, if he agreed. He was to be sent west, to Fort Saskatchewan — "near the bright lights of Edmonton, there to await a more permanent assignment."

Things were not booming at that time in the recruitment area. The addition of a sergeant, still bearing the sun tan and bruises of war, was an unlooked for bit of good fortune. At least that was the impression Sergeant Gibson seemed to convey. Flynn was ushered into Inspector Miles Stockwell's office. Flynn came to what he hoped was a proper attention but not in uniform did not salute.

"Flynn, you come at a good time," the inspector concluded. "No, don't salute. Wait until you see whether you like the uniform."

It was meant as a joke, but Flynn said directly and seriously: "The uniform of the R. C. M. P., sir, is admired by services throughout the world. Of course. . . ." He broke off.

"What were you going to say? If an exception, now will be your last opportunity. I warn you, it will go hard for you after taking the oath." Despite the words the tone was all in good humor.

"I was going to remark, sir, that the combination of uniform and background, forest, plains, mountain, and snow, as ever pictured, is what is famed and admired throughout the world. Your handling of the great gold rush is everywhere considered *masterly*."

Flattery? A danger no one wanted was the praise of the self-serving but, damn it, for Flynn this was the *truth!* They had handled the gold rush. Kept out the undesirables. Established law. Prevented starvation.

"I served in the entry regions, the Chilkoot and White passes, for two full seasons," the inspector related. "We now try to limit boundary service to one year, although the main problems have been ironed out. Most of the fatalities were due to that mad so-called Inside Passage about which I'm sure you'll get two earsful when you get into the region, so I needn't expound. You will have charge of, I believe, seven recruits as far as Regina. There our inspector, or superintendent, will give you further instructions. You will be measured for a uniform. We always think it's best to travel uniformed, though it's not absolutely required for a period of forty-five days.

31

Part of our Northern experience made that difficult . . . in other words, at the outset we needed more men but couldn't properly clothe them. We were buying what we could from . . . this is no joke . . . the Yukon Commercial!"

Flynn answered (correctly) that the Yukon Commercial was U. S. owned.

The inspector chose to ignore that comment. "You'll have a minimum of four days here," he continued, "if you would like to visit anyone, even your home. Didn't you say it was Red River? . . . well, that's only fifty-odd miles. Ah, Red River . . . the wheat that built the West!"

Chapter Four

"I'm afraid you'll have to leave in uniform," said Sergeant Gibson. "I'll have you conducted to the warehouse." He had a look at Flynn, front and back. "Attention!"

Flynn almost clicked his heels. Thank God he'd had some training the summer he'd been sent off to ranger school, the great advantage of living with a foot in both countries. The Dominion Youth Agency had the idea that all youths sixteen to eighteen of the white race would benefit, as would the forest, from six weeks in the wilds. A foppish English lieutenant from Sandringham had had them marching around, doing the common maneuvers, fitting them for parade duty if not to the benefit of the wilds. Hence Flynn knew the common parade stance, how to imitate the lieutenant's accent, and to exclaim: "Oh, I say! That's jolly good!" — and things of a like nature.

"Oh, yes," Sergeant Gibson continued. "Those are good shoulders. We'll fit you without trouble. If not, we can squeeze out a few pence for some tailoring. We have an old merchant tailor, semi-retired, whom we hire on occasion."

"I average out."

"Oh, that's the devil of it, Sergeant Flynn, nobody averages out. I was telling the chief the other day that I thought perhaps it would be better to make all jackets stoop shouldered with a slouch, slightly askew . . . but to which side, that was the question!"

It was a intended as a joke, so Flynn laughed. "What answer did you receive?"

"The one I deserved. He said we'd have them all looking like those drawings one saw of storming the Bastille. You're not French? No. We have to be careful about demeaning the French. Oh, we get a few, and some good men, too, but never a French national that can march. And don't say, as I heard a man say a while back, that he'd rather have men who could storm the Bastille than shine on the parade ground. But, of course, we're the *Mounted* Police. You ride a little? We do still ride in parade, though where you're going the riding is chiefly on the water. You'll be needed at Fort Saskatchewan, above Edmonton. Above the Fifty-Fourth . . . well, above the Fifty-Fifth anyway . . . the boat becomes dominant. Our force moved steadily northward since almost the grim beginnings. The gold, you know. And the tar. Petroleum, we like to say. But gold, *toujours* is gold! The gold, gold, gold!"

"I suppose there was quite a rush to the service after the Klondike."

"No, we had trouble keeping men on duty rather than working the rocker. And the points of entry . . . which amounted to any place anybody could find . . . in order to climb. Chilkoot! We had a dozen Chilkoots. But we saved a lot of lives."

"Rescue? How did you communicate?"

"No, not rescue. Making sure they damned well had their supplies, and I don't mean whiskey. Potatoes! Had to be kept from freezing. And cranberries. In the North the cranberry has to be the king of foods, durable, solid, and the prime number one preventative of scurvy. Scurvy and the rest killed more than the raids and gold combined. And their Soapy Smiths! Our men at the boundary saved more men than the Salvation Army." It was a pretty good remark. "Food. We made them take a ton of food. A British ton. Oh, flour and bacon, beans, sure, but we made them take potatoes and keep them from freezing, if we could, and cranberries!"

"Scurvy?" Flynn asked.

"Right! Orange peel, lemon. Those little Chinese beans were good. Bean sprouts. A lot of that we learned on the job. Naturally you could do nothing about the mine shafts, the fifty or hundred feet down through frozen ground and the black cough. Don't get me started. I have a feeling you'll get North, sergeant. White Horse will be the great city of the North, not Dawson, but don't tell Richardson."

Flynn figured Richardson must be in command in Dawson.

After seeing the police tailor Flynn got his free issue. He had some money and Jim Sikes, a pool room owner, sent him to an old Jewish fellow named Sol Goodman because he could buy a few things of his own, really tailor-made. "Tell him I sent you," Sikes said. So he did, and Goodman knew what he should do without asking, furnishing what was the service material only better, regular issue and dress scarlets both.

Flynn felt that Mr. Goodman sort of took to him. He knew what to do without asking. The high command never noticed the slightly better material and tailoring, only a fellow looked better. And once Goodman had the measurements, and knew where to set the knees on his dummy, all Flynn would have to do was stay the same

35

weight and send in for anything he wanted.

Goodman asked the damnedest things! For example: "You wear maybe Vici kid shoes?" or "You wear riding boots?" Flynn wasn't sure he could rule out either, and asked why, only to be told that Vici kid and riding boots both made men change their postures, the extreme softness and gleam of the one, and the underslung heels of the latter. Also, when reordering, Flynn should have himself weighed, just as he was, without coat or hat. He weighed himself on the tailor's scales and had it set down at 174.

One thing led to another. After getting those tailor-made clothes, Flynn's suitcase would never do, so he bought a new one and a portfolio to carry under his arm. His drayman's experience here stood him well because he learned pretty much to judge men by the luggage they used. He had noticed that the best-appearing men always carried large, flat cases and perhaps one alligator-skin valise. So he bought the large, flat suitcases and a portfolio instead of the valise.

"Now, don't get to showing off," Aunt Frances cautioned Flynn. "If you do, they'll take you down in a hurry."

"With that praise, my cup runneth over."

"Well, praise is one thing you don't need."

"Thomas Maxwell Flynn, Bart. That's for *bartender*."

"Don't crow, or it's where you'll end up."

But she was proud of him. And gave him a limp leather book. "A prayer book that just suits you."

It was a new edition of the "Rubáiyát of Omar Khayyám." Flynn opened it at random and pretended to read: "Thou preparest a table before me in the presence of mine enemies. Thou annointest my head in oil. My cup runneth over."

"That's *with* oil," Aunt Frances reminded him. "And don't roll your eyes. It makes you look like a cretin."

Flynn had to look up cretin, which was worse than he thought. He thought it was like moron, but the dictionary said cretinism was "a peculiar endemic disease accompanied by imbecility."

Anyhow she got rid of Omar Khayyám because she had had to keep it in the back room because of the religious, some of whom were good patrons and not to be offended. She admitted as much when she said: "Oh, I'd given up on you a long time ago."

"Well, thanks," said Flynn. "Thank you very much!"

Sergeant Flynn, in scarlet, left with six recruits by day coach, and one more recruit was picked up at Portage la Prairie. Regina was the main stop, and Flynn spent two days at sort of an instruction school. Winnipeg must have telegraphed because he was honored by being taken to a modest affair at a rather good hotel by the superintendent from Battsford, which was some distance away, who wanted to talk to him about the African troubles and whether Flynn could give him any news about this fellow or that, friends of his. Flynn, of course, could not, but chiefly Flynn had wanted to get away from his post for a while, to the bright lights of Regina — its hotels, beautiful women, and for once a first-class dining room. Flynn felt composed and secure in his made-to-measure scarlet and promised to carry this greeting and that to the superintendent's comrades of the colors in Fort Saskatchewan, a buggy ride north of the gold rush mecca — as was the joke in Edmonton. At the hotel in Regina there were women guests, some of them the superintendent's relatives — wife and two daughters — who gave Flynn flattery and pleasure, managing to dance the polka, schottische, and the new Paris *galop*— accent on the last syllable — with which Flynn was none too familiar, but quick to learn.

"For a new sergeant, not bad," the superintendent remarked at the *soirée's* close. "A whole night and not one ruined slipper, not one mashed toe!"

The following day Flynn reached Edmonton where a military van waited to carry him north the five or six miles to Fort Saskatchewan. Of the recruits only Flynn left, although the van carried two constables, apparently long in the service. Flynn guessed he was lucky to get rank early, because a constable was a constable, always, it seemed. They occupied the one side, giving Flynn the facing seat to himself.

Flynn introduced himself, and they introduced themselves as Polk and MacDonald. No first names. Apparently it was just *Constable.* However, one did add: "Special Service. Carpenter."

"Well," said Flynn, "we wouldn't want the roof to leak."

It wasn't much of a joke, but they laughed as though he was Weber and Fields rolled into one. So it seemed that a sergeant, of his grade at least, was a man of importance. Flynn wondered if he should be wearing the scarlet jacket? He decided to ask.

"I wouldn't know," said MacDonald. He seemed to think it a bit strange that Flynn would have to ask the question, at least of him.

"I've been away a bit," Flynn clarified. "The Boer War, you know."

It drew the proper respect, and the driver looked back from his elevated seat with a new interest.

"I guess they flew hot and heavy down there," said the driver.

"The war is one thing I don't care to talk about," Flynn said.

He was actually quoting Uncle Frank, but Frank would say that and then go on with a lecture about the English who turned their slaves loose when sugar failed, knowing they'd be taken by the United States' cotton farmers, millionaire plantations, many New England-owned cotton goods manufacturers, and all the rest of it.

Flynn liked Edmonton. It had seen a huge boom when it was promoted as base for the Inside Route to the Klondike. Actually, though, there wasn't any Inside Route, only some old fur trails. Certainly nobody ever really got to the Klondike by means of it, but belief in it led to a boom in farm lands near Peace River and development of the tar sands, which proved to be a form of petroleum, peerless for roofing and pavements. For hundreds of English dudes who came to go north and fish two railroads had been surveyed as far as Peace River, and there was a revival of interest in the old U. S. to Russia telegraph line with only the forty-odd miles underwater at Bering Straits, in anticipation of another break in the Atlantic Cable.

Flynn was invited to dinner at the inspector's and danced with all the girls — not stepping on a toe — and went with a party of four, including the inspector's daughter, to see a touring company at the National Theatre. William Gillette was appearing in his peerless portrayal of Sherlock Holmes, which the great thespian had adapted himself for the stage. Flynn had an idea that the inspector's daughter rather took to him, with his new-tailored uniform and his air of far lands, though he resisted any temptation he may have had to talk about places like Pretoria, so lately in the news.

Men from the thick of the fighting naturally never liked to talk about it afterward. The memories of blood, dust, and flat Pretorian stones hot enough to fry eggs at four in the afternoon were too much. "Ah, this Northern air!" was Flynn's way of talking about his recent experiences. "I can't describe the *smells* of that land. And to fight for it, die for it! You find out Kipling was right, like him or not, as was the late Regina's privilege.

> **" 'And the end of the fight**
> **Was a tombstone white**
> **And the name of the late deceased;**
> **And the epitaph drear**
> **A fool lies here**
> **Who thought he could hustle the East.'**

"Of course South Africa isn't the East," Flynn added. "But it amounts to the same thing. It's not England, and it's certainly not America. No, it's something better not talked about. I was born sort of straddling the line. Canada and the U. S., that is. My Uncle Frank was in the war, and really had it in for Lincoln. And England."

"England!" She could hardly believe it.

"Yes, Bishop Wilberforce. Or his brother in Parliament. Claimed the sugar plantations went broke, hence England freed all the black men, stopped feeding them. They were sent north to pick cotton. He claims it's what started the Civil War. He was wounded at Little Round Top. Gettysburg. He said Lincoln went there and gave the biggest fool speech of all time. Of course, he wasn't in much mood for oratory. Carried a bullet way inside until this Prussian doctor with saber scars located it

40

by nerve reflex, but when he had the exact location in he went, with a razor sharp forceps, and pulled it out. He had these saber scars from college, and that gave Uncle Frank faith to let him go ahead."

"He got it?"

"That far in!" Flynn measured off a good six inches. "Our own army doctors claimed it couldn't be removed. Took him no more than one minute once he located it by anatomical triangulation, solid geometry, you know. Radius square times *pi* is as far as I ever got."

"You're just being modest."

"No, modesty isn't my style. You notice I'm just a sergeant. But I went and had my clothes made by a tailor. I was told by some old Northerners the Mounted would dress me down in a hurry, but here I am taking the commandant's daughter to see Sherlock Holmes!"

She was really pretty good looking, if you overlooked a few things like having crooked teeth, but he had no time to progress in any courtship because next day he was in her father's office being shown a lot of maps, some of which he was told to keep — and, by God, not *lose*, if he didn't want to wake up some day a corporal. The inspector laughed when he said it, but Flynn didn't take it too lightly. He could see that this was a country where you might get lost and never be found — all the hill ranges looking so much the same, and timber, level fields and more timber, a real scarcity of landmarks.

Flynn departed north by coach — actually it was a wagon full of supplies, with a sort of hooded passenger compartment up front, where the driver sat and had a view. There were farms and farms, very green, just about the greenest farms Flynn had ever seen, and they raised a lot of things he'd never heard of, such as red rye grass that bore small seeds. The driver knew all about red rye grass, every inch, and wasn't a smart-aleck, as many are with tenderfeet, but said what it was, how it could be harvested for oil like flax in some years and other years, when things weren't just right because of too much rain or an early frost, how it went into silage. This was the Peace River Bloc, he said, southern section. It was considerably better for grain than the Peace River Bloc, northern section. However, up north they raised fine horses and cattle and, as soon as the railroad was finished, it would make all the difference. The railroad as surveyed would cross over the Rockies and reach the Fraser River just at the Big Bend.

Flynn mentioned having been given a roll of maps thick through as his arm, but the driver said: "Yes, that may be true, but it's such a big country. A map doesn't do much but satisfy your curiosity. You have to take it one piece at a time. Like you lived in Chicago. You been in Chicago?"

Flynn had been there when he bought the medals, but he said: "Can't say I know the town."

"You go to one part of Chicago, it's all foundries. Then it's the stockyards. Pretty soon they make machinery. Middle Chicago was all brewing until the fire, when, I'm told, brewing moved to Milwaukee. Then you have the lake shore, mansions, big stores. And so on. A man can live half his life in Chicago and not know the other parts exist."

"Canada is a lot bigger than Chicago," Flynn suggested.

"Not to me it isn't. I get lost in Chicago a lot quicker than here. Anyhow, this Peace River country is all surveyed off into townships and sections. If we get lucky and find the boats running, you can change over to steam at Fort McMurray. There's a police station there at McMurray. You'll know by the smell if the wind is anywhere near north. Tar pits. That's as old as any place in western Canada. The Indians used it years before even the two companies came, smearing it inside the boat seams. Worked as caulk and glue both. You ever been tarred and feathered?"

"Not yet," said Flynn.

"Just a joke, Sergeant. Just a joke. Well, tar and feathers comes off a boat hard as it does off the skin and takes some of the boat with it. Cracks sometimes in icy water. But better than pitch. They saw off young pines to gather pitch, but this tar is better. Best boats use tar with a little melted pitch over it. Well, that's neither here nor there. You aren't going to caulk any boat. However, the oil companies are all in here drilling around for oil, and settlers come for a hundred miles to get it for mending roofs, and so on. These geological fellows talk in the millions. Millions! They talk in the *billions.* Bit on the extreme, and the tribes have a lawsuit down in Ottawa. Bet you never thought you'd live to see the day when Indians would be hiring lawyers."

"Well, they're citizens of Canada."

"None older! But what they claim is we *aren't.* Pretty good joke, hey? We send them to school and that's what they learn! The French are responsible for that. Quebec! Anyhow, you'll smell Fort McMurray long before you see it, wind what it is. Good police house. Not a headquarters. The police don't care for the smell." He laughed to show no offense. "No fools, the police. They don't want to be in the middle of every squabble over tar, and they have a natural site up north at the landing. Athabasca Landing. That's where you're headed, I guess?"

"Temporarily."

"It's always 'temporarily' . . . except for the inspectors. There used to be one up at Athabasca Landing. That's where the English dudes go. Lake trout big around as a fat woman's thigh!" He laughed. "They catch the trout, right enough. Lake trout. Put up one hell of a battle. But they mostly came up here, or to Athabasca, for the big spiney pickerel. The dudes, Lord this or that. Nobody's actually caught one of the big ones, but they've seen the bones in among the highwater driftwood. Spines that stick out from the back long as a paring knife. And sharp. Some people say they don't exist, but I've seen the spines. One time there was this fellow . . . he was a cousin of the king . . . said to have had one on the line and saw it break water, but he cut the line off. The fish did. They have rows of teeth like a circular saw, only narrower, of course, and more curved in shape. That's why they're never caught . . . they saw off the lines. Anyhow, the dudes come all the way from England, trying to catch them."

Flynn laughed and said: "Indian boatmen are the guides? I'll lay money *they* see them all the time."

"Oh, sure. It's money in their purse! Not unusual to see camps of twelve English lords and twice that number of guides, cooks, Indian canoemen, spear fishermen. Regular damned expeditions. The Indians see a scad of whitefish about a foot long frozen in the shallows, still alive, and they break the ice and get the fish. Best dog food there is. One or two good whitefish makes a dog's supper. They swallow them whole. And still alive. You'll see it if you winter. The dogs swallow a whole frozen fish. Near choke getting it down. Two or three, maybe. Then they lie and wait, and the fish thaw and start to flop inside, and the dogs roll around and yelp. It's fun to watch. Best dog food in the North. Absolutely fresh. Of course the Indians eat them, too. By the thousands, given a hard winter. Farther north, all salmon. Smoked. Catch the grease drip and bottle it. Skin flasks. Worst smell on earth, that salmon oil gone rancid. Smell the whole village for miles when the wind's right."

"What do they use it for?"

"Lamps, perfume, medicine."

They drove on into a ground-disturbed country, moderately hilly. There were hundreds, thousands perhaps, of black-streaked excavations, many partly overgrown by bush.

"Season starts in June, even earlier," the driver commented. "Those are Indian claims. They date back to earliest times."

It reminded Flynn of the mining towns in Nevada, which he'd visited with his Uncle Frank. Frank had bought this considerable block of gold mining shares in what was called Consolidated Bullfrog — a thousand shares. He suspected names such as "Treasure Trove" or "Golden Reef," and Consolidated Bullfrog offered at about forty-one cents a share, actually forty-one dollars per hundred shares — the least quantity the broker would sell in order to keep out the small fry. A brother in Minneapolis talked it up, showed how it was right down near Goldfield, famed for precious metals. Anyhow, when the stock went up to around six dollars, Uncle Frank decided to go look at it, see it on his way to San Francisco. Flynn was about fourteen years old, and he took him along.

Flynn was gangling enough to get in a saloon with adult company, and they were standing there in Bullfrog at a bar, having a beer, a flagon for Uncle Frank and a nip for him. Nobody raised an eyebrow to a boy of fourteen in a saloon having a nip of the foamy, not in Nevada. Well, they were there, and this fellow came around, saw they were from back East, smelled of the train, and he offered Uncle Frank a candy sack with about two pounds of ore in it. It was quartz, with iron oxide and gold lumps sticking out like warts on a tree toad. Wanted to sell it. Prospector, he said, and couldn't afford the refining. Hence real cheap. Frank forked over something like ten dollars for it. Gold was twenty dollars per troy ounce at the government price. The sack, it turned out, once pounded up and melted out by an assayer, yielded $200, or thereabouts.

"You were probably buying your own gold," Flynn said, and Uncle Frank agreed.

Frank had his thousand shares at home, and Flynn congratulated him because it looked like it would go up and up. It had gone up fourteen dollars more by the time they looked at the Mining Board in San Francisco. So Uncle Frank just sold it all. He had to get his shares from the East. That is, he had to get the shares certified as being in escrow. He made a mint of money on it, but good gosh, Flynn said, with gold sticking out of it like that . . . ! But Uncle Frank said: "Yes, and there's 'Niners to take it . . . highgraders." Flynn asked if mine workers couldn't be searched coming out, not allowed to carry dinner buckets and things like that, and Uncle Frank said yes, then they would just come to a rich streak and hide it. Cover it with muck, figuring to come back. "More'n one way to skin a goat," he said. "Never buy anything that looks too good."

And Uncle Frank had been right. The stock went up

well above where it was when Frank sold out, but next they knew it was down to a couple of dollars. The pay streak had run out — a good share of it in dinner pails, Uncle Frank concluded, or covered by muck down there a thousand-odd feet. "Never play aces in another man's game," he told Flynn. "I bought it because it was a give away, cheap. Sold it high. Cupidity said: 'Hold it, see if it hits five hundred.' But pretty soon you're just holding the bag . . . empty."

So they stayed in San Francisco like nabobs, saw the shows, ate pounded abalone steak at the Cliff House, all on the mining profits. Uncle Frank was advised to buy government bonds, but he declined, saying: "It's been downward the dollar ever since they learned to print paper." He would rather put it in flour mills, electric power, railroads. "Can't carry much flour out in a dinner bucket," he advised. "I wouldn't buy U. S. government bonds. They're printed on paper. Paper costs ten cents a pound. Two percent interest, my eye! What if Bryan gets in? Silver! They'll just print more money. A dollar's only worth what it'll buy."

"They can give me some more money whenever they like," other people would say.

When Uncle Frank did go and vote for Bryan, it was because so many in their part of the country were into wheat, and the price was too low. Frank took a lot of joshing about it. Did he have some silver mine stock? "No," he said, "I voted for him because of his Cross of Gold speech. He earned it. There's a new day dawning. The Democrats got me my pension. I've always voted Democrat. There's too much money in the rich man's hands."

Minnesota went for McKinley over Bryan, despite the

wheat farmers. Flynn was still too young to vote.

"Solid South for Bryan," he said to Uncle Frank. "Why are they all Democrats?"

"Because they don't let men of color vote. Don't let them ride on the Pullman trains. Jim Crow cars. It's all Lincoln's 'new birth of freedom!' "

Chapter Five

At any rate the Goldfield and Bullfrog districts in Nevada had the same look of pockmarked dumps as McMurray, only the dumps in Nevada were rusty white, and these were gray and black. These so-called tar pits had big, glassy black veins and sometimes in hot weather even flowed like a real thick molasses. The Indians had long dug tar to caulk their boats, coming for it hundreds of miles. They had had tribal claims and fought with bows and arrows. Now a lot of white men were buying in, drilling for oil. No luck so far. Just tar. It broke up easiest in winter, like broken black glass.

"The hotel is set away from the main stink, which is bad now because they build fires to get the tar running," Flynn's driver remarked. "Get a room on the west side, if there is one. This is a busy time, mostly north of here."

It had been a long day in the wagon — and days in the North were *real* long anyway. They had slept a while at a place called Fifty Mile House and went all the next day before catching the smell of the tar pits. Actually it wasn't so bad; the wind was from the west, and Flynn could sleep. The police house had a message for him by telephone, saying he was to catch the boat upriver to Athabasca Post, a new establishment just south of the lake where the two big rivers almost came together, the Athabasca and the Peace. He would get further orders there.

It was a fair-size steamboat, with bunks for twenty. Most passengers went on across the lake. As it turned out, Flynn never did get to meet any English dudes, or see if they'd caught the rare trophy pickerel with the spines long enough to make squaw needles. But he did see the smoke of their camps away over to the north and east. He was to go up the Peace by way of Fort Vermilion, one of the oldest trading posts in the North. "It's a feather in your cap, Sergeant!" That's what the fellow on the phone had said. Flynn hadn't known whether he was joking or not. He was a corporal, so Flynn assumed he was serious. Having already gained the strong impression that being a sergeant was something, he knew, if he weren't of the nobility, he was at least in the *working* force, and a sergeant in the R. C. M. P. was truly a man to be reckoned with!

"Where?" Flynn distrusted the phone. It kept crackling and being interrupted. He wanted to make damned sure. It was a big country.

"Vermilion. Up Peace River. Where are you now?" The corporal didn't wait for Flynn to answer. You had to make use of the phone while it worked. It was always shorting out due to the damned porcupines. They climbed the trees where the wires were strung to get to the sap. "Sergeant? Listen, you have to get above the narrows, north side. North Landing. Or Peace River Landing. See your map. That will be right on the Twenty-Ninth base line latitude on your map. There's so many ports up there. . . ." The line had got to howling. It must have been the damned porcupines again.

"Hello! Hello?" Flynn said. Always keep talking was

the cardinal rule on the phone lines.

"Yes, hello, Flynn. You have the location?"

"I'm looking at it right now. The Twenty-Ninth is right on the west arm of Athabasca Lake."

"Right! Ask where the steamboat puts in. It may have changed. Fellow named Grumphausen runs it. Yes, Grumphausen. They'll know where he takes freight and passengers. He runs up the Slave River, too. The trader at North Post will know. Anybody will know because they have to get freight, or load on freight. . . ." The line had started to howl again. When it stopped, the corporal was still talking. "Tell him by God to take you, make the run, or he'll lose his contract. Sometimes, if there isn't enough freight, he'll try to skip a trip. He's all right, but you have to act tough. Grumphausen. If there was ever a man rightly named. . . . Tell him you'll call the inspector, and he'll lose his contract. If you haven't a boat, call the Agency. Don't give those Indians any money. The Englishmen have them spoiled. Transport for the police is part of their contract."

There was a trader outside. He saw Flynn and came in. "Where's George?" He was talking about Constable George Demming who had charge of the post. "Well, he must be at the Agency," the trader concluded. He knew all about Grumphausen, and where he stopped. He said he'd take Flynn and his dunnage, that Grump would turn over any freight he had bound for the south. He had the transfer contract.

It was plain to Flynn the trader wanted to be friends with the R. C. M. P., especially with a man of a sergeant's rank. He seemed disappointed there was nothing for him. He had ordered this and that and some treaty goods. He assumed Flynn knew what he was talking about,

51

and Flynn let that stand. The trader tried to get some-body on the phone and failed. So he loaded Flynn's gear, and they set out by canoe with two Indian paddlers and got across some rather big water to a small trading village called North Slave and the dock Grumphausen used. There was even a building and the padlocked dock had a sign reading: **Property W.T. Grumphausen**. There was a roofed building for boat dockage, and the sort of things boatmen accumulate, cordage, packing, old cans of white lead, axes and hammers with broken handles, and just plain steam engine junk. There was fuel, mainly pitch pine, and a sign reading: **Dockage For Rent, See W.T. Grumphausen, Prop**.

There was a small store that served meals, and Flynn had tea and canned corned beef with crackers. The Indian woman asked if he wanted to sign, but he asked how much? She left for a while, coming back to say: "Fifty cents." He paid it. Eventually Constable Demming arrived and greeted him. He had been over at an English camp. He asked if Flynn had been charged for his dinner and, hearing he had, proceeded to give the woman a lecture in her native tongue, whereupon she tried to give Flynn back his fifty cents, but the constable said: *"Meyo, meyo,"* meaning something favorable in the Cree tongue.

"We try not to spoil these people," the constable told Flynn. "They get a monthly stipend for police and police guests. You won't have to wait for Grump. I saw his smoke up north."

"Just in time!"

"No, he'd have waited. There are three other boats on the Peace, and it's in his contract. He's supposed to pay for your food and lodging for up to a week. If he hadn't come, or you'd missed him, you could go by United. There's a lot of business on the Peace. A lot of farms up there. And freight for the mission at Hay River. They get goods from the Port Nelson brigade, too. From the west. Oh, this is a busy country up here, Sergeant. White Horse and Edmonton will have to watch out."

"What's at Hay River?"

"One of the oldest places in the land. Old Russian stone church, onion steeple and all. Sisters of Mercy are there now. Indian mission. Quite a town, really. Bigger than Nelson. School, hospital, stores, H. B. C. post, the whole business. They get things from White Horse and from the MacKenzie, too. Lot of trade on the MacKenzie. Longest steamboat route, except for the Yukon. There are two or three towns up there on the Arctic shore. Old-time whaling country. That MacKenzie is one great river. Steamboats to Port Laird almost at the Sixty."

The Sixty was the sixtieth degree of latitude, northern boundary of the western provinces. Only the territories and the Yukon were farther north.

"Any whaling up there at the mouth of the MacKenzie?" Flynn asked.

"Damned right there is. And you can smell it in the summer. Oh, not here. But the Mounted has its last post up there, pulling back a hundred miles or so to get out of the smell. We have a superintendent inspector, flock of constables. It's an extra pay assignment. Port McPherson. Hardship. Run their own traplines. Depends on who's in command. God! . . . that's a big country."

"Me, I'd like an assignment at White Horse."

"Who wouldn't? You know, that's the most prized assignment in the North? Sergeant, it looks like you were in for some luck."

"How's that?" asked Flynn.

He saw the smoke from a steamboat. It had just started to turn black. The skipper had tossed in some old hair, or other dark-burning substance, a signal from afar that the steamboat was coming.

"Say, that's quite an idea," Flynn observed. "The smoke signal."

"Wait a second, and he'll blow doughnuts with it. See? There it is! He gets it going good and then blows some steam from the boiler. Like blowing smoke rings with a cigar." Then the steam from the whistle started, and in a second or two the toot-toot-toot! "Yes," the constable said, "it's Grump, all right!" as if he'd known him for years.

It was a small sidewheeler with a vertical boiler and a tall black stack. The size and height of the stack was way out of proportion with the craft, but there was more than the stack, part was boiler and vertical steam pipes, an economy that gave good deck space, a walkway all around, and a cabin and cargo hold. Grumphausen was towing a rowboat, a two-ended skiff, that could be rowed either way, hardly a boat the whalers would use but fine for the river. When you wanted to go the other way, all you had to do was switch yourself, and it was done. The skiff could be used for extra cargo, which was covered with a tarp.

He came in and docked, had a look at Flynn, made a quick appraisal of his character — *who* were they putting sergeant's stripes on now? — and came in against the dock very easy so as not to damage the sidewheel housings. They were sheet metal, and by the looks of them they had taken about all they could.

"All aboard!" he started to yell even before tying up.

"All aboard the steam-lightning express!" But he came ashore, went to the outhouse, washed and lathered himself, and shaved in front of the store mirror.

He was very easy to know. He said his name, told how to spell it, and no, Grumphausen didn't mean backhose in German! "I do have my mouth all set for a bottle of that good Vancouver beer!" This was a joke because no liquor was allowed on an Indian reserve, which this technically was, and Flynn could see it was a joke he'd make use of frequently. "You the new commandant at Fort Vermilion? No? The inspector has been gone so long I thought they'd sent a replacement. The corporal is all set to have hot rums all around for the new inspector, but you're a sergeant. Haven't had a sergeant there in, well, two years."

It took him no more than half an hour to eat, refuel, load the new cargo aboard, and try to get through on the telephone to somebody in Dixonville, only to learn the town had no phone line.

"That where you have that widow you were chasing?" the constable asked Grumphausen.

"You keep a civil mouth in your head, or I'll have you busted to dog tender." It was the lowest post the R. M. C. P. had. "Well, time is money. I got a cargo of . . . ! Well, what do I have? I'm nigh empty. What cargo you got? One sergeant and dunnage. The mail? All right. Who are these for? More prunes for North Vermilion?"

Actually, there were groceries for all along the river, making finally more than two-thirds of his cargo. The boat hauled freight and express all the way to Peace River, the town, although it was closer to Edmonton by road from the southeast. They set out, whistle tooting, and tooting, and tooting. Everyone came forth to wave

55

good bye. Flynn was the only passenger, though there were four bunks and a folding cot in the cabin.

"All ship-shape," said Grumphausen. "A sailorman has to be neat and tidy. Matter of space. True on this boat, true on ocean liners. Now you look at this pipe." It was a real short pipe, so loaded with burning tobacco it almost burned Grumphausen's nose. "I bought it short to conserve space. Small things all added up do big things make. That's a quote from some place."

"Never got the habit myself," said Flynn, "except when I was about eleven, and Ma gave me a whaling."

"Served you right. Pipe like this not only saves ship space, but it gives you sort of two smokes in one. You draw the smoke in, and then it puffs out the bowl and you breathe that through the nose. Get it going and coming. Saves a real pack of money over a lifetime. Also, every other kind of a pipe I had always got knocked by something and fell in the river."

He stopped for two more passengers. Both Indians. Half fare. They didn't even have that, so he said all right, they could work their way, but they'd have to sleep on deck.

"They got the money, all right," Grumphausen told Flynn. "Government gives it to them. But they know you can't turn them down. Make them stand on that side and it balances the boat. Downwind side. They eat so danged much fish. Comes out in their skin. Oily skin. Sometimes I let one fall in, fish him out, but he gets a bath. Fellow tried to sell me a squaw one time. Ten dollars. He had two squaws, and they didn't get along. This squaw he tried to sell me wasn't more than twelve years old. He started out at twelve dollars, one dollar per year, and came down. You married? I figured not.

Mounted policeman gets to be a sergeant, though, he gets married. They put him in some small town. He becomes a resident. This Indian girl, sort of broad-bottomed but pretty in a way. But you know how they are, always apt to run away and go back to the hutch. They eat too much fish. Salmon is the worst, too oily. They smoke it for winter. Not many salmon here. Lake trout. But the *smell* is there anyway. And they're lousy, you know. Never yet saw a squaw you could delouse. You know when you find 'em about twelve to fourteen, they're nigh on to being pretty, but in five or six years they look like all the rest."

The steamboat was small but surprisingly roomy. You could sleep inside if it rained. It had a whistle Grumphausen had just installed, and he was quite proud of it, blowing it at every opportunity, whenever he came to a bend, as though he expected another boat to be coming. The engine burned pitch balls, which were made of pine sawdust from the mills — pitch secured by topping the trees, waiting for the spring season to make it flow, then mixed with sawdust to make balls.

Grumphausen told Flynn: "Wear gloves or the pitch will take the skin off. Come cold weather they get hard enough to bounce on the floor. You toss one in and God! . . . how it would burn! No ash, just *heat*. But you have to be careful not to add too much too fast. The pitch will get away and run down to the ash hopper, a waste and a danger, because it might run out on the deck, and good bye boat!"

"Did that ever happen to you?"

"Not to me," said Grumphausen. "Did to a fellow I hired one time. He got the boat ashore and just skinned out for parts unknown. Afraid I'd shoot him, I suppose.

Pshaw, I never shoot anybody, Sergeant. If I did, some fellow like you would have me in irons on my way down to Edmonton. You know they can hang you in this country if you shoot an Indian? Quicker than if, for instance, I shot you. Well, maybe I could shoot somebody like Survay."

"Why is that?"

"Well, that's because you don't know Survay. He's been looking for it. He took a shot at one of those English dudes back at the lake, claimed they cut his nets. He's so damned big and mean. And the way he looks people are afraid of him. You'll meet him before you're through. The thing I figure about Survay is he gets to looking at himself in the mirror, and it's like a wolf showing his teeth. Did you know, if you get a dog to show his teeth at himself in a mirror, he'll go half crazy?"

"Never heard that." After waiting a while, Flynn asked: "What about Survay? How does he spell his name?"

"With the 'a,' not the 'e' like a geologic survey. He's only about six feet and an inch and not so broad, but powerful! He has this whole side of his face black-speckled, like you had a handful of that tar sand, hard and crushed, about like a number three good load. What it is, and this will stump you, is black gunpowder. He got in this quarrel over on the Yankee side when they were getting out spruce for the Yukon boats. They built some real big boats, ships really, and took them through the rapids, too. Well, he was playing poker with this American fellow from down in San Francisco. And they were both in this pot pretty heavy. Either this Yank dealt seconds, or else Survay wanted to make it seem he did, because they got to jawing at each other. Pretty soon Survay stood up and went for him over the table, but

58

what he didn't know, this Yank had a Derringer pistol, double barrel, one load of lead, and the other powder only. They do that when it's dangerous to kill a man. Some places they hang you right off. Anyhow he had the barrel loaded with real coarse black powder. Regular squarish pellets. Size of barley. Or bigger. Heavy, good load. It hits you all of a sudden and will leave you all baffled where you are. And it sort of got Survay alongside the face. It went under the skin and seemed to follow the endodermis . . . that's what the doctor called it . . . followed the endodermis under the epidermis. The skin seems to be in layers. Well, it spread and did quite a job. Whole neck and jaw and the side of his face, but skipping his eye. Ripped his ear half off, but they sewed that back. It fell off for good, finally, about two years later. About half of it did, the rest stuck up like a pointy-eared rabbit. He was in bandages for a month or longer, but the doctor couldn't do a thing without skinning him on that side, or he'd never have lived. They told him down at Juneau, at the hospital, not to fret, it would stay sore but slowly go away. But he was like a tattooed man. The black powder never did go away. It just spread out and looked worse. One time I was over at Watson Lake . . . I had a boat there . . . and Survay showed up. God, he looked mean. You'd never in your life guess what caused it. There was this one time he lit a cigarette over a lamp chimney. He leaned over and lit it, and *crack!* He let out a yelp and sat down cross-legged, holding his face. The lamp had set off one of those pellets of black powder."

"Why didn't they give him the chloroform, or a big dose of laudanum, and burn them all off?"

"Doctor said no. Too dangerous. Skin might all come

off. Besides, he's so damned mean. Suggestion like that would set him off. If he caught somebody staring at him, like a stranger might if not warned, he'd demand: 'What in hell's name are you looking at?' He's got an absolutely ungovernable temper. Come right after you, maybe. Other hand he'd get to drinking and show off. He could sharpen his axe with a stone until it shaved like a razor. And he'd hold that axe over the coals in a stove, or maybe over the lamp chimney, a big double-bitted axe, until the edge was red hot. Act like he was going to shave, looking in the mirror, and, *pop!* . . . he'd make those grains of powder go off. Show his strength. Never burned himself. At least not much. 'How you lak get shave?' he'd ask. Imagine! Those grains of powder . . . after all that time!"

"I hope *I* don't have to arrest *him.*"

"I do, too." Grumphausen took the remark seriously. "Thing I'd do is hit him from behind with one of those shot-filled leather saps . . . they'll knock down a moose . . . and then put the handcuffs on him behind his back."

"Don't tell me he's one of our citizens at Vermilion!"

"He comes around now and then. Has a gold mine somewhere. He buys powder and caps, fuse, you know, the usual. Pays right up. I'll say that for him. And you know he has a sense of humor? Playing cards, he may roll a cigarette and set off one or two of those pieces of powder that gets to itching, or do it for a joke. Fellow asked one time: 'Surv, what would you do with that San Francisco sharper if you caught him?' Well, he reached out and grabbed this fellow and lifted him right off the floor, arm's length. Then he says: 'You feel that? I break his back!' "

"Think he could do it?"

"You *better* think he could do it!"

"What does his gold look like?"

"Like gold."

"I know, but fine dust? Got real nuggets?"

"I have an idea it's a hardrock claim."

"Find out what it assays and I'll make a guess where he gets it."

"You know your gold, boy?"

"No, but I can send a little out to somebody who does."

There was an assay office in Edmonton, and those fellows always knew. Flynn remembered being with Uncle Frank in Nevada. The fellow in the assay office would take one look at a sample, tell you where it came from, and guess the value. He'd assay it and always came close.

Flynn had done a lot of thinking about being a policeman and decided that in a country sparse as this he could know everyone there, and the most important thing to know about anybody was *how did he earn his living?* What he thought of doing was getting a clothbound book of blank sheets and writing everybody down, age, sex, nationality, and how did he earn his living? You couldn't do it in Duluth, or Winnipeg, but you could do it here. Indians excluded, of course. Indians always pretended that they didn't "savvy," unless it happened to put money in their pockets.

Flynn spent two days on the little steamer, mostly listening to the skipper, who was fun to listen to. He even tried out his British accent on Grumphausen. It added class, but did it go with the name Flynn?

They reached Vermilion, R. C. M. P. on one side, trading post on the other. "Well, here we are!" said Grump. "It don't look like so much, but it's one of the oldest posts in the North. Old company post . . . both old companies, H. B. C. and Montreal . . . and, I hear, by traders before that! The Russians got here long before, from the other side. It was a great fur spot in the early days, not so much beaver but fine marten. That's the Russian golden ermine, prized by the tsars. Mink. Otter. And the damned wolverines to add interest."

"Any trapping now?"

"If there wasn't, Vermilion wouldn't be here. Most of what you hear about gold in these parts is just glitter. It comes to the top of the pan."

"How could that be?"

"Mica. *Mica.*"

"Oh," said Flynn, feeling foolish.

He knew what mica was. It was split in plates for stoves and, when it was fine, it often looked like gold but cluttered in the pan. Mining country. He should get a book and read up. He imagined he'd have plenty of time but maybe not. Maybe he'd be mostly on the trail. Plenty of fresh air. Snowshoes. Toboggans and sleds. Malemutes, Huskies. God! . . . he had a lot to learn. He thought, as the boat followed the endless river, how some of that fresh air would have been when he was backed up to the croppers in Duluth!

"I see the flag isn't raised," the skipper said. "Inspector can't be here. Corporal McCabe, lazy bugger, nothing to do and all day to do it in. He's seen us and is raising it now. Give him what-for! You'll probably be in command."

Flynn had the idea he'd more like to feel his way to begin with.

"This country would be a regular damned Eden but for early fall," Grumphausen went on. "Rain, twenty hours of sun in summer. Grow oil seed, sheep, gardens. Trap all winter. Good fox country. Wolves hard on sheep, but there's a market for wolf skins. Dogskin overcoats. Grass that high, but it won't cure because of the rain. Well, rain makes it grow. Can't have it both ways. I'll take you in first. Don't tip those Indians. They'll just get to be pests."

They came in, thudding against the massive old dock. There were Indians on the fort side, carts and wagons on the other. The cable was being raised by block and tackle, swinging, dipping, touching water, and going up inch by inch. It was used for what looked like a one-wagon ferry from North Vermilion. He sensed an animosity between police and storekeepers. Always was, always would be. No Indians were allowed on board. Grump helped with the dunnage. He shook Flynn's hand. "Well, don't let 'em whoop you up!" he said.

Chapter Six

With churning sidewheels and a hard rudder the boat got across the river without need of the cable. The crowd there seemed chiefly interested in who had come to the fort. Flynn let his things be carried, and it grew to be sort of a parade, himself and the Indians to the police house, which was obviously very old but in good repair, and the flag was up. The corporal, he supposed, had hustled to do it but now waited inside and would act surprised. He must have been notified by telephone. Whenever the phone worked, they used it all the time. It was the police phone, not the Dominion's, and the police kept tight rein on its own.

There were dog pens in the back, and a half dozen dogs were raising a great commotion at sight of the boat or him. He distributed *backsheesh* as they did in the novels, against Grump's advice, and walked in. Only one of the Indians, a tall half-breed, followed. Flynn learned he had something to do with keeping the dogs.

"Hey!" he yelled like a returning prodigal. "Sergeant Flynn reporting!"

The corporal appeared with a half salute. He was medium short, powerful of shoulder.

"Michael McCabe. Flynn, is it now?" A good Irish brogue, only partly assumed. "Corporal McCabe. You shouldn't spoil those Indians with money, but what's

64

done is done. Besides, I am outranked. You are of this moment in command, if your assignment be permanent. The inspector's still gone. You'll find that here the lower ranks are seldom consulted by the upper ranks, but that's life. Begorrah, you're a big man! Tall and look at those shoulders on you! Now, this is *infra dig,* if you get my meaning, but were the inspector here I know of experience he would expect that you be welcomed suitably from the official bottle. So, in his absence and to his health, will you join me?" He had already opened a cabinet and taken out a bottle, nearly full, of H. B. C. Scotch whiskey, the Five Crown, twelve years old at the bottling. "The pure malt Scotch. Not to compare with our Irish whiskies, but I am but a corporal."

Just a little bitterness there, but Flynn was good at overlooking such things after Duluth. He and McCabe, Irish to the core, could join in their attitude toward the inspector, British, ever absent from the post. The room with its desk was newly picked up, a hurried order of sorts, but Flynn sensed that the corporal was pleased it was not the inspector.

"Sergeant Flynn?"

"Yes?"

"To repeat, it is the Inspector's wish, his *command* (were he present), that you be greeted with all courtesy and hospitality. A drop, therefore, and a toast to the service and her Royal Majesty. . . . Ah, no, no longer. We now have a king." As he talked, he got two glasses, wiped them on a piece of rough toweling, and poured what was a generous but not unseemly amount of whiskey. It saddened him to see the amount gone from the bottle. "Well, there is more at hand, at that scoundrel's post across the river. And as this is an *event.* . . ." He set Flynn's glass for him, decided it required a drop or two more for an equality, then he set the bottle back in the exact place he'd found it. "Yes, where was I?"

"You were toasting the king."

"Two Irishmen toasting the King of England! Well, we're a forgiving race."

Flynn thought of giving him the line about being with the Irish Fusileers who, ever in the nick of time, saved things at Mangesfontin and Spion Kop but decided it would be unwise. Keep it up and he'd be found out. Of course, the war of Duluth, his view of it from under the cropper, could be given the saving grace of humor. "To His Majesty, the King."

"To the King and to the R. C. M. P. . . . long may they wave."

The Scotch was excellent and just what Flynn needed, although not a drinking man. They sat afterward and exchanged small talk. He saw the corporal eyeing the bottle.

"May I buy one back?"

"Well, now! That *is* thoughtful of you. Whom should we toast?"

"The inspector. In all courtesy. It is his bottle."

"Yes. But I believe a replacement could be found across the river. The man owes us one, to be truthful. There are certain charges that could be brought. I told him I was only waiting for my superior, and you would most amply fill the bill."

He didn't go into detail, but Flynn thought perhaps he had been selling liquors to certain of the Northern races for whom it is unlawful. They had one more. It was enough to make a person relax, to give thought to the situation, and to check to see whether the boat had set forth. It was tied to the trading dock, goods unloaded, fuel being carried aboard, but no toot-toot of departure.

"I've had some trouble with him." McCabe was referring to the trader. "His being across the river puts me at a disadvantage. You see our problem here. There are French, who buy liquors legally, while Indians cannot. Yet most of the French have Indian blood, Cree as a rule, but Indian. You have to make certain decisions. Decisions of Solomon."

"I can see how that might be."

"And, of course, the Catholics take their potion at the Holy Communion. No price suffrage, brother. You can see the problem."

"I can."

"What we can do, if he doesn't have more of the H. B. C. pure malt of this age, is pour in a fitting substitute? There are a number of brands. The Glenfiddich is quite suitable."

"I'll want to pay him my respects."

"If you do, offer to pay him. But I would expect him to do the right thing, and he will if he has the idea your arrival has anything to do with the allegations being whispered."

"No, that would be bribery, and we can't have it."

"Right you are! Wait for him to offer as a gift, a welcome to North Vermilion. His name is Burlingame. Burley, they call him. An Englishman, or one of those Yankee mixtures."

Flynn would buy the whiskey, H. B. C. if he could, with not the slightest intention of accepting a gift — a bribe, really — since it would be a very poor manner to launch forth so. A bribe curses the man who gives it and him who takes it — or *he* who gives and *he* who takes? Flynn's grammar was still shaky, but this was a quotation from Shakespeare. Yes, Shakespeare. It is 'the mightiest of the mightiest,' but in reference to the quality of mercy, as he recalled. What he vowed to himself to do, when he had the opportunity and the money, was to buy a complete Shakespeare or a selection — he would write to his aunt. What better way could man spend his time in the Great Loneliness, as they often called the North?

"I'll pay him a visit. In courtesy."

"Do that."

"Cheers."

The liquor had eased things considerably with this corporal who, much longer in the service, might resent him. But the man had plenty of experience in a service where advancement was slow or not at all, and he now set forth to give Flynn the benefit of some of that long experience. He started with the female sex and the affliction of loneliness on the young of body and mind. One had to be careful of the Indian women, many of whom with a husband's consent — even encouragement and outright solicitation — offered their body for hire. Such situations are easier got into than got out of — no pun intended. It was pretty fair, whether intended or not, and Flynn laughed until tears formed at the corners of his eyes. The corporal was encouraged.

"Ah, there is no humor like the Irish! Do you know, while the subject is at hand, the main difference between an Indian woman and an Indian chief? In actions, that is?"

"I can think of several, but. . . ."

"The main difference, my years have taught me, is quite simple and based on the laws of physics. It is this . . . an Indian female in the age of mature judgment always urinates facing the wind . . . while her male counterpart learns by experience quite the opposite, as do we. Why, my own father told me: 'Mickey, me boy, always piss with your back to the wind.' Of course, my own father intended that as advice not in the physical but the intellectual, problem-facing sense? Swimming against the tide, and all that."

"Right!"

"But here in the necessary act of relieving the bladder only . . . you see what I mean? In fact, I made up a bit of poetry on the subject." He struck a pose and then recited:

"High on a windy hill
The missus pisses."

Flynn had to laugh; he really did. "By the gods, and in all honesty, that's pretty good!"

"You think so? You really think so?"

"I do."

"Well, the Irish are a poetic race. Sentimental and poetic we are. It's the chief reason we've survived against our enemies, the Danes, the Romans, the damnable British, against them all. Down in the States, in spite of their 'No Irish Need Apply,' we today control the governments of their great cities, New York, Chicago, even Boston! I was reading it in the newspaper, owned by a Yankee and the paper not liking it a little bit! Corrupt, they called us, but we controlled the councils, the police, and the firemen."

Flynn said: "And they counter with the Masonic Order, a Scottish Rite. Nothing against the Scotch, or their whiskey . . . pure malt. There's another Masonic rite, also. The Grotto, or some such name. A great many priests of the church joined the Masonic Order in Italy, until the Pope banned it."

"You don't say!"

"Oh, there are many fine masons, Corporal. They were at the forefront of American freedom during the Revolution. There are masons and masons. On the other hand, my uncle, who has been interested in the West . . . mines, an investor . . . and history, says all too many men with names such as O'Connell and Murphy were hanged in the early camps. But then came a great rush of Irish north from the U. P. to the rich gold camps. Many came early, wheeling their goods in a barrow, called 'the Irishman's carriage.' All the long distance from Utah. And look at Butte Hill! Richest on earth. Irish millionaires. Things changed in a hurry, *then!*"

"That's good news! So there are Irish Catholic millionaires."

"Oh, yes. Quite a number."

"And they came in wheeling their things in a barrow?"

"Indeed, they did. Oh, the masons sang a different tune then. It was, 'Hello Pat,' and 'Hello, Mike,' and, 'Did you lay a wreath for poor Robert Emmett today?' The Irish martyr, but he was a Protestant!"

"No!"

"Yes indeed. And Wolfe Tone as well."

"And priests in Italy taking Masonic orders. I never dreamed."

Flynn said: "Your poem, now. How was it?" He heard the corporal repeat it and gave it some thought. Indeed, pondered, before he said: "If it was *facing* the wind, then it should be included in the rhyme."

"You know, I thought of that, and I have a second version.

> **"Facing the wind,**
> **Upon a hill,**
> **The missus pisses."**

"There!" exclaimed Flynn. "Now you have it! Do you know what's special about that rhyme? You have managed to condense *so much* in *so little space!* And you have created what my aunt (who owns a rental library) would call a *double diphthong.*"

"Have I now! It was pure chance. What, pray, is a diphthong?"

"It consists, I believe, of two vowels occurring together and pronounced as one. The vowels are a, e, i, o, u and at times y, as you need not be reminded. The 'i's in succeeding words might be considered a double diphthong and the 'e's, but it's the repetition that gives it so much strength!"

"Would your aunt think there might be a market for my stuff? I have heard there is real gold to be struck in poetry."

"Well, yes and no. Alas, poor Oscar Wilde! A better poet never put pen to paper, but he was Irish, and we know what the British *did* to him. A false charge brought by a nobleman. He resented Oscar's friendship with his son, Lord Alfred Douglas. You've read of it."

"Yes, too much of it. It shows what happens to an Irishman . . . Wilde *was* an Irishman!"

"And the father of two children. Son of a famed Dublin medical doctor. Ah, the British never forgive the Irish for invading their land in a literary manner." Flynn struck a posture and recited:

> " 'I never saw a man who looked
> With such a wistful eye
> Upon that little tent of blue
> That prisoners call the sky.' "

"He was in prison at the time?" McCabe asked.

"He was, and also, this will stir you," Flynn answered, striking another pose:

> " 'He did not wear his scarlet coat
> For blood and wine are red,
> And blood and wine were on his hands
> When they found him with the dead.' "

"Blessed be God," said McCabe, "it would break your heart. I'm afraid my trifle would not measure up. . . ."

"Wilde himself wrote many a light verse. And your poem, while brief, points out a physical fact which most have never thought of. I know I hadn't. It's something to ponder."

"There is good pay in poetry, eh? I mean, I wouldn't expect any great amount . . . but who would print a rhyme on that subject?"

"Why, there are frank bits of a biological nature printed all the time. This is the Twentieth Century, man! Cromwell and his Puritans have been still these many years. The public is ready for you!"

"I couldn't very well say it was by Corporal Michael

McCabe of the R. C. M. P. I'm afraid the commissioned officers might not be pleased."

"A pen name, man, that's what you need. A *nom de plume!* Just sign it 'McC.' But as for money? In truth, poets are wretchedly paid. They have to settle for fame. But this . . . the biological *fact!* It's something the public should think about!" Again he struck a pose and recited:

> **"Facing the wind,**
> **Upon a hill,**
> **The missus pisses."**

Just hearing it, you might try it first on some periodical such as *Everyman's Magazine.* Writing for men, they will be struck . . . don't misinterpret the word by the reverse situations of man and his mate."

"By God, I'll do it! I'll just sign it 'McC.' "

"Send the return postage. Just address the return to Barracks, Fort Vermilion, and so on. Oftimes writers suffer repeated rejections. Even the best of them. But be not discouraged. Think what Wilde suffered . . . imprisoned, forced to leave his native land, and spend his last sad years in Paris. The French, more tolerant. Rimbaud and Verlaine. You will join a select circle."

"So there might be money in it!"

"Not a great deal. Writers, particularly the poets like I said, have to content themselves with fame and glory."

"Oh, that's all right. We're Irish. We sing the songs. Even in the great potato famine it is recorded on the books that we kept right on sending our quota of food to the English."

Chapter Seven

Flynn did not long rest easy in Vermilion. A telephone call came through, quite sharp and clear for a change, relayed from Fort Saskatchewan and hence not to be taken lightly. Any number of relays were required in such a long call, and it was rare the voice you heard was the one that had started the call. Telegraph was more certain, but the officers liked to have their own voices heard, if possible, at such a distance. Flynn studied the map, 400 miles by river and nearly 350 overland — hardly a place in the States could match it.

"Survey map? Survay?" He couldn't get it out of his mind they were talking about Black Jack Survay, the fellow with the big black lumps of gunpowder under the skin, the man who would take the double-bitted axe, shave with it, and once in a time or two get one of the powder pellets to pop with a trail of smoke if he heated the axe first in hot coals!

"Black Jack?" he shouted. "What are you talking about?"

"What are *you* talking about?" the voice crackled back. "I said Hay River Post! It may not be on your Geological Survey map. The Indian agent there will tell you what's wrong. A man got shot, so take a medicine kit. Borrow a horse from somebody in Vermilion."

"If it's that steamboat man," McCabe was saying, "tell him. . . ."

The telephone responded: "Is this the corporal? Has Sergeant Flynn arrived?"

"Barely warmed his chair. This is Flynn speaking! Got here four days ago."

The telephone started to rattle and howl at him, but he stayed there in hopes it would come back. It did but with a different voice. The relay had failed as it was being repeated from God only knew where. "It's no use," the voice said. "There must be an electrical storm."

"Where are you?" asked Flynn.

"This is Murray at Peace River. I'm getting it on line number four. The line to Lake Clare is grounded, but I get it from High Prairie. His relay is out, but his phone works."

Every time a call went out, people all along the line picked up to listen. When that happened, only one telephone call per week might get through, though not always by the same route. All telephones were a gamble, here and in the great cities.

"Are you on the line with the inspector?" asked Flynn.

"No, but I have his message down. Some fellow was reported shot at Hay River Post. That's north and east. . . ."

"I know where it is." It was hard to keep from shouting, although he knew you got through better in a controlled, measured voice. The high vibrations always rattled. "Man shot at Hay River Post. What else?"

The commissioner suddenly came back on the line. The voices mingled.

"Commissioner? Sergeant Flynn here. I got your message. Hay River Post. Yes, I got it. Afraid there's been trouble with the railroad survey crew?"

Apparently, from what he gathered, there were two railroad surveys trying to finish before snow fell. There was the one from the south up Sifton Pass and one from the west — those damned Yanks who had a line from Juneau through Taku Pass! They had a franchise only to the hot springs, but once started they kept going. The phone howled and rattled.

"Get off the line!" The voice, from the authority in it, evidently was the commissioner's.

"Sergeant Flynn?"

"Yes. Fort Vermilion."

"What's this about a surveying crew? I want you to get up to the sisters' school and hospital at Hay River."

"I know where it is. I'm looking at the map right now. I'm in Vermilion."

"Good! Somebody has been shot. White man. I just got it the long way around but not from any survey crew. I have no idea except it seems to have been a white man. There's a town named Assumption. That's nearby, but the hospital and school are a mile beyond the old Russian stone church. There are a dozen little camps around Hay belonging to fishermen after whitefish and lake trout and this Catholic mission school and hospital."

"Camps of English dudes?"

"No, they're over at Athabasca. That's the opposite direction. Stop talking and listen to me. A white man has been shot, and he's in the sisters' hospital. That's at a town called Assumption. Get that, *Assumption.* They set it up as an Indian mission a long time ago. They have a hospital but no doctor. They have some nursing sisters there. Assumption. You'll see the tower of the old Russian stone church. You could get to wandering around those damned lakes for a week. Go to the church and the sisters are close by. Mile or so. Quite a town there. Should be busy, getting ready for winter. Trapping season. Fishing for dog food. All right?"

"Yes, I'm looking at Assumption now." He had the brass dividers and was measuring. "About eight miles south of Hay Lake, south edge of the Indian Reserve."

"Right! You can't miss it. Not too much timber. You'll see the Russian church. Hire a wagon off one of those farmers. Fellow name of Straw is all right. Farmer. Ask that corporal at the fort. Don't pay any dollar a mile. Some may try that if you're new, but Straw is all right."

"I measure it as just a hundred miles cross-country."

"Some of that country is surveyed and has roads. We have to get somebody there. Pay with a warrant and do it in indelible pencil. Keep a carbon copy. We like to know who is doing what and what he's being paid. The sisters are all right. They'll send us a bill. Corporal McCabe will show you the warrants for transportation. You'll have to sign as temporary in command. Listen . . . ?"

"Yes."

"That's not Hay River on the Great Slave Lake. This is Hay Lake. About One Hundred and Nineteen and Fifty-Nine, actually just short of Fifty-Nine on your map."

"Right. I'm looking at it now. North-west by west about one hundred miles. It looks to me as if our survey land goes only ten-twelve miles."

"Well, don't depend on the surveyors' flags. These farmers move them around to hog more land."

"And I don't think I'll get any wagon for ten cents a mile!"

77

"Who said ten cents? Do what you have to. Cheers."

The line started to rattle again. "Porcupines?" said Flynn.

"Wrong time of the year. Hell, Sergeant, this is a good connection compared . . . ," and his voice trailed off. He stayed on the line a while, and others started coming on wanting to know what was going on? Flynn handed the receiver over to the corporal. He said: "I have to get across the river. Do you know anybody named Straw? Jack Straw? The inspector says he's all right. Hundred miles to and back, two hundred miles. I'll have to sign a warrant. You know him?"

But the corporal was now talking with somebody, apparently at some other post. After a time the corporal turned to Flynn: "It's been on the Athabasca line, too. Seems there was some trouble up in the territories, Fort Laird. That's the final steamboat post on the MacKenzie. From Kitty-Gat, not Cat-Gat! On the Delta. The great stink. Summer and steamboats come down the Mac-Kenzie for better than a thousand miles."

"River miles?" asked Flynn.

"No, by the gods, cut-across miles. Fifteen hundred river miles. Look at your map. Shows all the ports. Fort Laird is the final one. Twelve hundred miles from the Delta. Old whaling stations. The big stink. Whalers have been coming in there for two-three hundred years. No exaggeration." He hung up, continued talking, following Flynn around. "Great fur country. Our last port is away up there, Fort McPherson. Big layout. Thirty or forty men. Has an inspector or superintendent. Lots of police run fur lines of their own. Long winter patrols. They get extra pay."

Flynn got outfitted while the corporal was following

him around. The inspector evidently thought the trouble had originated east of the MacKenzie. Flynn said so, and the corporal answered: "Hell, man, you have no idea. This is a big country. If he was shot at Fort Laird, well, that stands to reason. It's the last steamboat port on the Mac. It takes a whole season to make one run up and back. And there's the Valley of the Thousand Smokes. That's where some old Frenchman is sort of a king. *Père* Brissaud. Supposed to be two hundred years old. You hear such stories in the North. Crazy camp country up there, land of the midnight sun, the Northern Aurora, many electrical storms. A compass is no good whatsoever. You have to get your bearings from the stars. The damned North Star is practically overhead. Those survey fellows will shoot the stars to give you the date, and the time of day or night." Flynn was now hunting the closets to complete an outfit, bedroll . . . rifle. "It's a fact! A compass points as much east as north and then goes absolutely north at times. The eastern territories have hundreds of hot springs and even geysers, like Yellowstone, sulphur springs."

"The hell you say! Geysers!"

"Indians go up there to cure their boils. They get terrible boils from filth, lice, and fish oil. Sulphur springs cure them. The Indians named it the Valley of the Thousand Smokes because of the geysers. The hot springs warm the ground, so the Indians build very big, thick-roofed houses. Because the warmth comes from below little fire is ever needed. But it's worth a man's life to go over there. Damned Frenchman!"

Flynn had finally outfitted himself completely while the corporal got onto the subject of the great stink. "There are whaling stations all along the Delta. The stink comes from the whales. There's nothing like it on earth in hot weather. You can smell it from three-four hundred years back."

"Whoa! Columbus came in Fourteen Ninety-Two."

"I wouldn't put anything past those whalers. They never tell where they go and sometimes probably don't know themselves. It's a great sea for whales, the Arctic, and they've always pulled in there. There's always been a settlement. It freezes hard in the winter, of course, but summer! I've heard the first wind of it would stop a skunk cold in his tracks. Fort McPherson's our last post north, two hundred miles south and it's still too close."

"One whaling station?"

"One? They got them scattered for a hundred miles along the Delta."

"People live there?"

"Sure. Can't wait for the thaw. All kinds of whale bone, ivory. Worth a pack of money. I been told their sense of smell gets accustomed. Chemical change. They leave and think something is wrong."

"Ivory? Whales?"

"No, walrus. And fossils from the great hairy mammoths of long back. Ivory resists all decay. They find tusks big as your thigh and fifteen feet long. Worth a mint of money."

Flynn, outfitted with clean underwear and the rest, fresh wool socks and fur-lined, rubber-lined, rubber-coated boots. He now also had a rifle. The post had been equipped only with the corporal's .30-30 Winchester and the inspector's target rifle — which was actually a target rifle only in that it had a hairing, or set trigger, plus the main trigger, the love of his life, Flynn supposed.

People didn't like to have their pet guns used, but if so, it shouldn't have been left there. It was a .45-70, a lot of gun. He took it and a box of cartridges with three missing. He loaded the rifle and dropped a couple of extras in his pocket. He also decided to take the side-arm and latch-down holster, part of the uniform. If it was a sisters' mission hospital, school, or something of the sort, he didn't want to walk in looking like Wild Bill Hickok. The corporal was saying: "The inspector will nosebleed all over the place if you put any gouges in that pet rifle of his. Didn't they have you stop at the armory back in Fort Sask'?"

"No, they didn't say a word about it."

"I suppose they didn't want to chance anything with a damned Boer War veteran. They shoot them on sight over there, according to what I've heard, all from ambush. Farmers . . . toughest enemy you can find. They fight for their homes. Isn't that right?"

"I had some pretty fair stuff thrown at me, if you want to know. Cluster stuff. And it would burst right in front of your face, if you stuck your head out."

"You've been around all right! You've had it hot, now you'll have it cold. We take pride in *not* shooting people up here. When a corporal got ambushed, or someone tried to ambush him, he found himself up for investigation for shooting back! Killed a fellow. They gave him a transfer, after suspension."

"Damn it, I'm not going to kill anybody. And I'll not lose the inspector's gun or put any nicks in it."

"I just wanted to tell you."

Flynn got across the river and was in luck. The farm kid named Straw was in with a team, the shortest and shaggiest team Flynn had ever seen. It was the Jack

Straw, naturally, the police inspector had mentioned. He was about fifteen years old, was loading groceries, and jumped at the chance of driving Flynn to the sisters'. That's what everyone called the Catholic Sisters of Charity, he told Flynn, sisters, out at the Catholic mission school and hospital on Hay Lake, actually *Sainte Terese de Bon Dieu.*

"Dollar-fifty a day too much?" asked the kid. "Team, wagon, and all?"

"Is that cash on the line, or will you take a police warrant?"

"Police warrant is good as gold far as I'm concerned."

"It's a deal then. Don't let all these guns fool you. I'm not expecting trouble. It's just the rules." Yet Flynn really didn't know a damned thing about the rules. Why hadn't they given him some police training? Well, he supposed the recruiting sergeant thought it would be done, and the inspector thought it had been done, the grand *soirée* in Regina, and all.

The country north and west was all surveyed farm land but apparently damned big farms, a section each Flynn would have guessed from the few fences and signs of habitation. The boy talked.

"Grass mainly. High as your waist. Long summer days. Plenty of rain. Not much night. But about when it ought to cure, the rain comes along. We cut it and make heap silos. Tarps, logs, and moss. You spray it with this stuff. Gets to stinking pretty strong, but the stock goes for it. Horses, cattle, sheep. Wolves were bad for a while, but the government hunters got 'em pretty well shot out. Gee whillikers, I'd a-done it and sold the hides! Still do, when they're prime. Ma makes cheese, butter, and so on. Sells it in at the store, and to you fellows

82

at the fort. That's how I know we took warrants. Good as gold. Indians get warrants, but they're a different color. That's so they can't buy booze. Pa says nothing doing when it comes to booze for Indians. He ain't going to jail for no Indian."

"Good for him!"

They had mid-afternoon dinner at Straw's farm. Jack's mother wouldn't take money, but Flynn left fifty cents where she'd find it. He knew by the smell she made butter and cheese. Game was plentiful and fish. They had homestead-smoked bacon, cut a quarter inch thick, and four eggs each. And she put up a box of pasties, or meat pie, for a supper. They had to sleep in the wagon and put up the tarp because it might rain. Next morning they breakfasted on hot tea and leftovers from supper.

"This kind of weather . . . it gets to be old stuff after a while," the kid told Flynn. "Ma makes berry pies. After a time berries sort of turn to wine. We smoke a lot of fish. Catch some through the ice. There's a law about shooting deer, but you fellows don't enforce it. Least-ways, I hope you don't, me saying what we do."

"Wouldn't make any difference what you said, you have to commit the act and be convicted first," Flynn said.

"The main trouble we have is cash money," the kid went on. "We get food a-plenty, but cash is the problem. However, you can make a mint of money if you get a good lay in the tar sands, that is if you get lots of tar and little sand. In hot weather it runs like molasses, but when it freezes down, it's more like coal only harder. Pa says it's like anthracite."

"How'd it pan out for you? I understand the smell is very bad."

"Not bad in the winter. In spring the Indians come

to get it in skins and use it to pitch their boats. But you're right. There's this blue sort of stink over everything. That's why we got out and went back to farming. Hadn't missed much. We've got cattle, and sheep, and horses now. And how things do grow! But we don't get the late summer sun."

"You ought to combine with Arizona. Down there they say that rain is all that hell needs."

"Well, sun is all we need. We get it all summer and plenty of mosquitoes and black flies, too. Things grow great, but they don't . . . say, there's the mission, a way off. See the steeple. The Russian church. School, church, hospital. No priest, only what they call a suffragan brother. We're Methodists ourselves."

"Ought to be Baptists."

"Say, that's pretty good! Total submersion." Then he changed the subject. "We have dogs. Sell 'em in town for sled dogs. Feed 'em frozen fish. Swaller 'em whole. Never should let a dog in the house."

"Man's best friend."

"Maybe, but Pa says no. Pa says a dog will follow the man who feeds him. Have a dog, one feeds him, other doesn't, both men move away. Both say, 'Come along, Shep.' He'll foller the one that fed him. Pa says there's no gratitude in a dog."

"How about women?"

"He hasn't said."

Flynn could see the top of the little domed Russian church on high ground, so he stopped, got out his dress uniform, shook it, rubbed it with wool to bring up the nap. Now with his scarlet jacket and good pants he pulled straight the brim of his hat. He had shaved, shivering, at breakfast time. "How do I look? Pass muster?"

"Gosh, whillikers. You're really somethin'!"

"Feel better, too. Clothes don't make the man but they do make you straighten up and remember." Flynn wished he had a mirror. Those chevrons on the scarlet coat . . . he could glance down and have a view of those, of kingly size, tailor-made like the jacket and not service issue, regulation but fine silk and gold. Flynn reconsidered then said: "Clothes don't make the man, but they sure help."

"Gosh all whillikers!" said Jack Straw.

Junk, trash, a rabble of empty huts came first and then the real houses. They were made mostly of sawed, unfinished lumber. Some were of logs, some of poles, but there also were Indian lodges, low tents with heavy skins and without form. There was a street of businesses dominated by an old, two-story, log H. B. C. trading post. Sleds and toboggans were all out for the winter season, leaning against walls, bottoms out, many newly waxed, some with the peculiar, changing luster of graphite over the wax. Graphite is the slickest of all substances and very resistant to wear. In fact the wax would wear off and still leave the graphite on the steel or wood.

They soon were leading a procession of Athabascans. Taller than most Indians and very erect, these proud people had close-set eyes, noses that seemed larger, higher in the bridge. When faced toward the quarter, such a nose would shade one eye from snow glare.

Flynn thought of Survay, a half-breed three-quarter, or four-fifths, a mixture dating back to Old Russia and the peoples before that heritage was lost in time. They had first crossed the Bering Straits before the Spanish were in Mexico and produced an unknown mixed-breed, *un homme du nord* as the French called them. Ships in those days searched for the Northwest Passage and found ice floes that carried them almost to the pole. The pole was known as the land of *le grande mirage* where one saw ships floating upside down in the sky. Such stories were legion along with tales of electricity, northern lights, spectacular displays of color. There were strange electric accumulations at the Magnetic Pole which shifted around with the globe's grand magnetism. Surveyors using this magnetic means had to adjust for a new declination every year. All the world was electrical energy of one sort or another. These reflections caused Flynn to break out into poetry.

" 'O, that this too, too solid earth would melt Melt and resolve itself into a dew.' "

"What's that you say?" asked Jack Straw.

"Oh, this aunt I got runs a lending library. She's always sending me books I ought to read. Crazy stuff. 'Have ye seen the white whale?' "

"Nope. Never did see a whale."

"This was a whaling country before anything, at the mouth of the big river, the MacKenzie."

The old Russian church, with its dome, was on the highest knoll. Snow had drifted over the steps. The sisters did not use it. They occupied a long frame building, simple steeple, cross, but they had no imitation onion like the Russians. The small drift of snow across the walk had been cleared for Flynn's arrival.

"Want me to wait?" asked Jack Straw.

"A minute or two then drive over there . . . seems to be a shed. Keep your eye on the Indians. They pick up things. There's a girl motioning to me. Wait over by the shed."

Flynn wondered about his revolver, deciding to keep it on but latched down, under the skirt of his jacket. The girl waited at an opened door. Flynn went up the walk, the steps, touched his hat brim in salute. There was a stove inside, providing a slight warmth, the smell of the summer being burned off. The girl followed Flynn inside, looking scared. She was a half-breed with a religious-looking cap but no hood, none of that white-lined black tunnel by which sisters shut out all view of the wicked, wicked world and where they could be alone with God.

Flynn turned to the girl, clicked his heels, and gave another half salute. "Officer Flynn, Northwest Mounted Police."

The girl led him to an office, rapped.

"Come in," said a voice in an English-French accent.

Flynn bowed, saluted the sister in her white habit, and said: "Officer Flynn. I was summoned. Thank you for receiving me."

The nun answered and stood. Her name was Sister Jacques de Bon Dieu. As a received guest, Flynn removed his hat. "I have heard there was an occasion of violence."

"Yes, an unfortunate thing. A man has been killed. We are. . . ." She changed that. "We have been led to believe that he was a runaway thief. Killed in the pursuit. We only know what are the obvious facts and what little we were told."

Flynn took a wild guess. "We have been led to believe that a man named Survay was involved."

The nun hesitated, and Flynn knew he had touched a nerve. Finally she said: "This we do not know, but the name has been mentioned."

"I see."

"We have been told the victim was an escaped thief, that he was wanted, and at last died in the pursuit. We have no doctor. We know only the obvious facts. His throat was badly torn. There were many bruises. Two Indians brought him in as directed by a young woman, a Marie Brissaud. They came by toboggan in such snow as we have in the north and east. We know only what has been told us and the obvious wounds. Our duties are only medical and religious."

She really kept hammering that home to Flynn. He had the feeling she had rehearsed it. That was fine with him. He liked to know where people stood. He could have said he operated only within the law but didn't. He did not know exactly what the law provided, except in the broadest limits of keeping the peace and collaring people who disturbed it or injured others in a serious manner intentionally and not in self-defense. This, he knew, was judged on very liberal terms up here in what some called "The Great Wolf Howl." The police were spread very thin, and courts were few.

The sister opened a door and led him chilly-swish down a hall. Another door opened, and a girl stepped out. She had been waiting and listening, had known a policeman was coming, had known for minutes, watching from a window. She was light-complexioned with cream-blonde hair that was not native to the land. Flynn would have guessed her to be about sixteen, maybe eighteen, although nineteen was possible. She wore moccasins of some gray material, high as Indian women favor, with rosettes in pink, white and green beads made distinctive by sprays of colored and flattened quills. Flynn noticed

88

the rasp-whisper of the moccasins on the floor, a sanded white larch with splinters. Even though the floor had been varnished and waxed repeatedly, here and there an edge of the hard larch grain came through. The very quiet and stark severity of the room made one notice. She wore some sort of perfume. Perhaps her things had been laundered in a special soap. Even Castile has its smell. Youth and age have a smell. Goodness and evil have each their smell. Flynn had long ago given up cigars, and cigarettes unless the English oval type were available. At times he smoked an Indian cigarette, rolled of shredded dry red willow bark, which is actually a red-bark dogwood, and made one sleep in peace when the pain of long, cold travel lay in his muscles. The Crees smoked it, and the Crees generally knew what they were doing. Never deal with a Cree, he had been told, and expect to get the better of it. So much for that. He deferred to her, a bow in full courtesy and an understanding which he didn't yet possess. His eyes rested on the bedsheet with a form under it. It seemed rather short for a man's body.

The sister gestured with authority, and Flynn was obliged to lift back the sheet that covered a still form in the very hard, flat bed. He realized, by the unresistant bed, that he was in the hospital mortuary. The girl, with barely a whisper of her moccasins, started to leave, but Flynn with a gesture had the sister stop her. The girl seemed very frightened. "Now, now," he said. "You will feel better. I may have questions."

The sister, who brooked no nonsense, gestured for the girl to stand still. Flynn had uncovered the body, not hesitantly but honestly and all the way, head to feet. He was just a bit startled to find him naked and moved with deliberation, for there is something tangible that leaves the body as the spirit leaves. He asked the sister to help him turn the body over. It was quite rigid. Nothing is so bad if you go ahead and do it. Flynn did not much mind the cold skin.

He took care not to change expression. The nun had no trouble at all. In fact, she seemed a bit impatient with Flynn's deliberation. Faith had its uses. To her the important part of the boy had flown away. What Flynn wished to examine was the deep wound in the neck, blackened from hard blood, and so deep a bit of bone was exposed. His neck had been broken. He had died instantly, or nearly so. The flesh was torn outward, perhaps with the rolling motion. He had been attacked by a great fanged beast. The marks were on both sides, showing the outline of the creature's jaws. That his neck was broken could be seen by the displacement of his head.

It was grotesque and the words came so naturally to Flynn that they were almost spoken: " 'Good heavens, Holmes, these are the teeth marks of some gigantic hound!' " The words came from a book by Conan Doyle, *The Hound of the Baskervilles*, lent to Flynn by his aunt. Since the Minneapolis paper mentioned "The Current Tour of William Gillette in his famous portrait of Sherlock Holmes" that he'd had the luck to catch in Edmonton with the inspector's own party, Flynn had read the book twice, although Aunt Frances had asked him to return it promptly because everybody was asking for it.

Flynn said aloud with the proper lack of emphasis: "I believe these to be fang wounds inflicted by some large animal, most probably, in this land, by a hound, a wolf, or a very large Husky. Logic dictates this last. He was taken from behind while running. The attack carried him forward, hence the snow burns, now turned more white than red, but some of the blood congealed. The weight of the animal and the strength of his jaws most certainly broke his neck vertebrae, probably severing the spinal column. Death must have been instantaneous. The question that one of my profession must in duty ask is this . . . was the attack intentional? If by a malemute, because of its owner or the one who controlled him? He seems to have been somewhat mauled and torn afterward. If the animal was not restrained, or if someone gave the command, it is my duty to make every effort to learn his identity."

Flynn was addressing the frightened girl. He had heard of only one dog by name since coming west, and north, and that was the one owned by Survay, the man who had been horribly blemished across the card table by the American gambler's double Derringer, .44 caliber, leaded in one barrel at least with coarse black powder. He had this dog, *Mach de Fer*, and men speculated about even the master's own safety. Perhaps the dog was only waiting his chance and one day . . . *Mach de Fer*, Flynn had been told by the skipper, meant Jaw of Iron in French. He asked the question abruptly, and it touched the girl like a hot wire. *"Mach de Fer?"* he said.

"Iron jaw . . . literally, jaw of iron," she whispered in reply.

"Yes," agreed Flynn. "I believe *M'sieur* Survay owns such a dog. The dog is quite famed, even notorious, in the land. Was this boy attacked, while running, by *Mach de Fer?"* The girl did not answer. "Did his master attempt to stop him?"

She seemed stricken, and she merely stared at Flynn.

He did not care to torment her. It was by any count the most painful task he had faced yet in the service. Until now he'd pictured his life as merely striding around, in uniform, to the admiration of all.

"Will you help me turn this boy back as he was?" Flynn asked the nun. He got no answer, but she did so. "Why was he pursued, *mademoiselle?*" he addressed the girl.

"He stole some articles," she answered simply. She was doing a good job of maintaining control. "He was a guest. He took pearls, and pearl shell, and ivory worth a considerable amount." Her voice was quick but little more than a whisper. "He would have left on the boat, but it did not arrive at Fort Laird. It was held at Nahanni, perhaps."

"Were the articles recovered?"

"Yes. I do not have them. They were sent back."

"To *Père* Brissaud?" That was the man at the Thousand Smokes. She did not answer. Then: "To *le Vallon?*"

"I'm not sure. I never want to see them."

She wouldn't look at the cadaver, either. Flynn closely examined him again. His skin was so *white.* Good God, he really seemed to be no more than a boy. Eighteen years old at most. The sister was talking in very rapid French now and being answered in the same language by the girl. About all Flynn could understand was *"Non, non!"* The nun was really putting her over the jumps!

Flynn was staring at the boy's poor, limp phallus and the thick foreskin. The Rabbis circumcised all boys at a certain age. Uncle Frank used to tell about Joshua and how he had the whole tribe lined up and circumcised before setting off to take Jericho, and it formed a regular hill of foreskins. "Bible says so," Uncle Frank had insisted. "Must have been a feast for the crows and magpies. They'd get one stuck in their throats and have to wheeze through the hole in the middle. And *painful*, walking through the brush. Glad to get to the river. River Jordan. Looked forward to it to cool the member off, but Joshua had God lower the river. There was no mercy in that man. It wasn't like that Nevada desert . . . Bullfrog, where they dug the gold . . . Joshua had God make the sun stand still. Hot! You can imagine! No wonder they took Jericho . . . with God's help. Bugles blew and the walls fell down. Then they killed every man, woman, and child who lived there. People who had never done them any harm. He never knew how a rabbi does a circumcision, but Joshua used a stone knife. That's why I'm not strong for the Bible. Got the Koran one time. Much superior. Lots of poetry."

Imagine such thoughts at a time like this! The mind is indeed a treacherous thing. That poor, damned kid! That great, white, fatty dollop of foreskin made him seem so awfully dead, and cold, and pitiful. The deep gashes along his neck had turned black. His head was off to one side, neck broken. At least he died mercifully quick.

The sister was firing questions. *She* should have been a sergeant. Flynn caught the word *fordeau* and knew it had something to do with pack or burden. He resolved to get a book and learn some French, though most of the French one heard was among Indians who spoke a *coyotié* French, full of English, Cree, and Algonquin — Spanish, even. Many Mexican traders came up all the way by the Mississippi and the Missouri. The sister seemed to have got what she wanted from poor, scared Marie.

To help a little Flynn said: "It was very thankless of him to steal from *le grand Père* Brissaud after all his kindness." He might as well say it. No arrests could be made in this quarter. The girl had no part in the young fellow's death. It was Black Jack Survay with the black-peppered face and that damned man-killer of a dog. One day somebody would go out in the pen and shoot him and everybody, including Black Jack if he realized it, would be better off. Those dogs get to hate their driver more than any other man or beast, and one day Survay would have his back turned and *zing!* — that dog would spring and have him like he did the poor, limp kid, yes, a blessing to one and all.

Flynn was relieved to learn from the nun that Survay had vanished. Now he didn't have to worry about taking him into custody — and on what charge? Owning a dangerous dog? That didn't prove a thing. Escaping thief? Survay was French, quebecois. Nobody would pin a medal on him for dropping that in their laps! He'd just leave it all as sort of open-ended in his report.

However, Flynn did stay for the funeral. The boy was buried as a Catholic — conditionally. Marie prayed and never lifted her eyes, saying her beads. It was lonesome, sad, that cold, cold earth. The suffragan brother read the mass, sprinkled the holy water. All conditionally because no one could certify that he was a Catholic? Flynn could only think at the last — thank God it was over.

Chapter Eight

Flynn offered to return Marie Brissaud to Fort Vermilion. They'd have along his driver, young Jack Straw, as a chaperone. The sister superior at Assumption didn't think much of it, a girl driving off with two men, but she needn't have worried. Marie — or *Père* Brissaud, master of the Valley of the Thousand Smokes — was possessed of some far-flung influential friends, and news of her whereabouts and the tragedy had reached Fort St. John on the upper Peace. Flynn had to find the fort on his map. A brigade — that is what they said, a *brigade* — was already on its way. The brigade from St. John would take Marie to Summit Lake and the Railway Surveying Camp. Another railroad would take her north from Prince George, over the Sifton Pass, newly named for a government minister bringing settlement to the West, and eventually to White Horse, the Klondike, then via the New National Northern east and west from Edmonton, through the Rockies, to the Pacific at Prince Rupert, below the lower wall of Alaska! Canada was, by the gods, taking no chances about the Yanks grabbing north-western Canada! The gold country — and copper, too — was extending itself with new discoveries every year. It was to be as big as South Africa or bigger. Anyhow, there were a number of surveying crews in the district in more or less fixed camps and a brigade from one of these was already on its way to fetch Marie Brissaud.

There was a local police house, empty but good enough for a camp until Flynn could make sure that his charge was safely on her way, with two sisters of the order to give the young virgin ample protection from any lecherous males on the way to her destination and one sister to watch the other coming back. The nuns always traveled in pairs. The Catholics had a permanent mission at Fort St. John, which had communications with Quesnel — or God knew where (when talking about British Columbia, you're talking about a very large area). At any rate there were Catholic half-way houses, or Hundred-Mile Houses, all along the way to the final destination on the Canadian Pacific with its sleeping cars, dining cars, observation cars — and a Wall Street debt larger than some small European countries. The railroad was in turn supplying farmers, mostly "Bohunk-speaking" mid-Europeans, to complete the divestiture of the poor Indians and make Canada *white*. The luxurious parlor, sleeping, and dining cars of the Canadian Pacific would provide Marie Brissaud with unusual safety and luxury, either to Vancouver (which was rapidly becoming a British city) with, of course, rather a mild British climate or any of the cities of Quebec in some one of which was her actual home.

Flynn said to young Jack Straw: "By the gods, that fellow up there amid the Thousand Smokes swings some influence!" The kid couldn't understand it. Why that country up there in The Barrens was the end of nowhere. But Flynn said: "That stuff he was supposedly stealing doesn't look like Fort Saint John is the flat-broke end of nowhere!" Still, Flynn puzzled about man in the image of the devil, Black Jack Survay. "Ever read the Bible, kid?"

"Ma does some at night, but I don't much take to it."

"I pose as no authority, but somewhere in it there is a section about Lucifer. He led a revolt against Almighty God."

"He *did?*"

"Don't ask me why. They were supposed to have just about everything, but he wasn't satisfied. He got a lot of angels and archangels . . . there's a Russian city named Archangel . . . well, they got together and started a revolt, and that's how there came to be a hell. God needed a place to cast them into. They're the fallen angels you hear about. 'Better be first in hell than take orders in heaven,' was what Lucifer said. And, of course, he and his followers were all cast down. They couldn't win . . . since God was all powerful, you see?"

The kid, who wasn't as dumb as he looked, sat there driving with his mouth hanging open and said: "I guess that's why we come up to a country like this. Pa says he'd rather run his own place as he pleased than hop around and take orders at twice the pay."

"Right! That's why our ancestors came here from Europe. You see where that puts us. Your pa, and the Yankees, you and me . . . it's what we asked for. The kingdom of hell! You have to scheme to get in. There's nothing worse than being homeless. However, there is a dog named Cerberus with three heads at the entrance to hell, guarding the way. The people who want to get in have to have a sop, or a piece of meat, to toss this dog. They toss it over and, when he is diverted by the meat, or sop, one head fighting with the others, I suppose, in they go! I asked my aunt who runs a circulating library and is very widely read . . . I asked my aunt about it, and she said this came mainly from a book named *Paradise Lost* by Milton, a very famous English poet. There's also a *Paradise Regained*, only nobody much reads it. There's just not much interest in golden streets, hymns all day, and the like. I figure Hades must be something besides just lakes of fire. Maybe horse races, casinos, faro games, and the girls upstairs, but you're not old enough yet to hear about those things."

"Oh, I've heard about them. Plenty."

And that was how the conversation went as they drove on, hour after hour, sometimes with a light snow falling and sometimes with an autumn sun coming through.

"Smell those leaves!" Flynn exclaimed after a time. "Some people like spring the best, but me, I like the fall."

"I like winter best," said young Jack Straw. "I like to run trap lines. This year I'm out for mink. I ordered some traps from Montgomery Ward, size one and a half. I ain't got a permit for beaver. Pa says mink's the thing in our parts. Number three is for otter. Pa says he knows where I can get some second hand. A second-hand trap is better than new, if not rusted weak anywhere. The older a trap is the better, provided it's been cared for. You should never oil a trap or put rustproofing on it, because the animals will smell it, even after a year. You ever do much trapping, Sergeant Flynn?"

"Just gophers and stuff. Rather fish and shoot ducks. Mainly I worked around town. Livery barn, pool room. Cut school one whole week and shot pool. Pa took me out back to give me a hiding, but he just lectured and told me to yelp a couple of times for Ma's benefit."

Jack Straw thought that was pretty funny. "How come

you got both U. S. and Canadian citizenship?"

"My family took homesteads on both sides. We were called double dippers. Some people didn't get any good land at all and resented us, talking about a lawsuit, but they got nowhere. My Uncle Frank, who had the bullet wound from Little Round Top, couldn't work hard, so he hired me."

"Guess you have to work for what you get."

"That, or be smarter than the next fellow. With most people it's a matter of work. Tramp all day on a trap line, for instance."

"Or join the Mounted and travel all over protecting other folks' property!"

"Right. You hit it right on the head!" Flynn laughed and added: "Oh, you can inch a little here and there."

But he didn't mention his Boer War experience, or how he'd gone and had his uniforms tailor made out of material just a bit better than the government issue, although he got value received. It didn't harm the service one single bit to look a bit better than was the standard. At the theatre in Edmonton, in that beautiful tailor-made scarlet that fit him just so, it made him *want* to sit straight! . . . thus he was benefiting the service and himself at the same time! In other words he was giving *more* for amount received. Yet, it was a subject he didn't take up with young Jack Straw. After all, advice was never worth a damn. You always had to do it on your own.

Corporal McCabe had the headquarters building warm with even a baked trout, sizzling hot and ready for serving.

"I saw you coming with that kid and his Siwash team,"

he told Flynn. "They're pretty good horses for this country, now that the wolves are shot out. You know they get in a circle, like buffalo, and fight off the wolves with only their heels out. Heels are horses' chief weapons. All horses came with the Spaniards. Shows how they learn survival. Northern horses get good with their front hoofs, too. What happened at the lake? Fellow all right?"

"Oh, he's dead. He was dead when I got there. Stiff dead. Eyes still open. Sort of slits of blue. Blue eyes. It gave me such an awful feeling. I'd never make much of an undertaker."

"You'll get used to it. You get used to anything."

"He was so young, but he'd stolen stuff and lit out with it. I had no way of telling who killed him. It looked like a dog, probably that hound from hell, *Mach de Fer*, but it can never be proved. I would have had to run down Survay, arrest him, and get the sisters to be witnesses and everything. How would you ever hold a trial out there, surrounded by the great empty? I never thought when I got into this how damned far everything is in the event of trouble. Some day you may have to take him in just the same, to White Horse or Edmonton. It'll cost a mint of money, but English rule demands English justice. Only in this case you'd never get your witnesses together, including the French over in that Thousand Smokes country."

"Yes, they stick together, the French. They hate the English worse than the Irish do. They've got sulphur springs and geysers up there. They even have them in Iceland, you know. The Indians go over and treat their diseases. Hot water, naked, run through the snow, and sit in a sweating house. Some of the springs are sulphur. Said to stink awful. The Indians get these terrible cases

100

of boils. It's hell for them. I've seen Indians covered with scars, all from cases of boils. The hot sulphur water acts on boils. You're supposed to drink it, too. I think it's the filthy clothes the Indians wear, year after year, and, like I told you, their lice. Yet, it's strange because, if you get dirty enough, the lice leave you. That's a fact. Teamsters are said to sew themselves in their underwear."

Flynn's mind was on the dead boy. "He was so damned young!"

"A cup of strong, green tea is what you need," McCabe said.

It was strong, right enough! And the ever-Irish joke: "When I makes water, I makes water, and when I makes tea, I makes tea!"

The Mounted kept moving Flynn around. He was stationed four months at Vermilion amid snow, cold, and the corporal who kept writing poetry and watching for the mail whenever the boat arrived — or, when the river rose, the sack that came in on the sled weekly, which meant perhaps every two weeks because things were always happening. One time the post office at McMurray burned down. All the mail was saved, but Corporal McCabe would not believe it. He was certain it had burned, and they were trying to ease peoples' minds, because he always got four issues of *The Irish Mail*, a weekly newspaper, and that month he'd received only three.

"They'll lie to you," he told Flynn. "Never admit making a mistake. They lost *The Irish Mail* and they probably also lost my answer to the letter I wrote to the paper regarding my poem . . . you remember the one?"

101

"Distinctly," Flynn assured the corporal, "and I could repeat it in all versions. A very memorable piece of work. But all is not lost. You can do it again and send it to someone else."

"I could send it to *The Irish Mail* again, but what would they think of me? I'll wait a while."

Then the Mounted summoned Flynn to Fort Nelson. His way took him again to the mission where he visited with the sisters and the suffragan brother, still there in place of a regular priest. He was still hearing confessions, giving Holy Communion, and performing other duties. He wanted to baptize Flynn, when he learned that he was of no particular religion, but Flynn declined, saying the bishop back in Regina had rather agreed to usher him into the Church, and he didn't wish to disappoint him.

Flynn went on to Fort Nelson, an old-time post of the Hudson's Bay Company, and found the police house empty and cold with not even a supply of wood chopped. He had to do the whole thing on his own, putting it in shape, sweeping out the packrat litter, and found it congenial to spend most of his time with the factor at the post. One good thing happened to him. The factor took a look at Flynn's dog string with a practiced eye. He knew malemutes and just chanced to have attained ownership of one hell of a lead dog, a trifle mean and headstrong but nothing that would go for a man's throat. The dog by name was Nanuck, or Nanook, after his famous predecessor which had in fact fathered the father of Nanuck.

"You'll need a strong hand, Sergeant, which I would guess you have, judging by the pride of your bearing . . . and I would part with Nanuck for one hundred fifty dollars, cash. I could hold him till the spring fur season and get at least half again as much."

Flynn had a look at the brute. He was on the broad side, a sign of endurance rather than speed, and that, said McTavish, the factor, was what would pay out in the long run. So they closed at the sum of one hundred dollars, a nice round figure. McTavish didn't want to hold Nanuck any longer with the season getting on. It would be July or August before the big auctions, and he could use the R. C. M. P. warrant as so much money when he mailed his credits through to the bank at White Horse. That was where the late winter supplies were coming from, not from Montreal as in the old days. Yankee suppliers might or might not please him, but they provided only the best once they found out you would accept nothing else.

Flynn traded two other dogs, which were in need of rest and healing and some proper food, and secured animals that had run previously with Nanuck, hence setting the tone not to tear him to pieces, as dogs will, when a new lead dog has the wrong smell.

"They can tell strange dogs by their smell," McTavish affirmed. "What they have to eat and all. It will make it easier for you, Sergeant, and you will avoid many of fights and consequences, such as being ripped to ribbons with your guts hanging out, a very bad thing."

Flynn thought this was a good deal for him and said so.

"It will take you a while on the trail," McTavish reminded him. "But they'll shake out with little waste of blood, having a pair like that to set the tone. In fact, I'd advise you to trade me your present leader and that way avoid any true struggle for primacy. A dog string is not a kingdom, where prince follows king in regular order, but one to be proved in blood, and Nanuck will have two at least who know him, and you'll have little trouble."

"He's no *Mach de Fer*," Flynn observed.

"Oh, that damned lead dog of Survay's! Believe me, that dog will kill him some time, and it will serve Survay right. If there was ever a half wolf that should be removed from the traces, that's the one!"

"A sort of brotherhood of evil."

"Partnership conceived by the devil, you mean. I won't have him in the camp. Not that black-pepper French 'breed or his hound from hell. That *fer* stands for *fire*. *Chemin de Fer*, the baccarat game, okay, but they mean railroad. In French *Chemin de Fer* actually means road of *fire*, not road of iron, no matter what they say. *Homme de fer*, that's the devil. Some day that big 'breed will turn his back at the wrong time, and his hound from hell will see his chance. Jump him! Break his neck if he gets him right. If Survay lives, he'll be lying there, unable to move. I've seen the day when they've shot a man mercifully, when he's been left in that condition, rather than strap him to a board and take him out to rot away in some Vancouver hospital."

Chapter Nine

Survay, Survay, Survay, spelled with an "a" not an "e" as with the Geological Survey — it had been written on the wall with pencil with an "a." Small matters are often large in importance, so Flynn had been told in the semi-yearly training course. The name in pencil on the wall — Survay, not Survey — the dead trapper had printed it very boldly before his body was dragged out to be devoured by the hungry beasts of the land. Now there was just a skull with eyeholes looking over the snow, no jaw, just some teeth and the skull.

Flynn was on his long tour, or route as they called it in the Army. He took two a year just to make sure the country was still there. He used Cree snowshoes, the long ones, touring shoes not the short bearpaws the trappers liked, but they made him go spraddled footed. Long travelers favored the long ones, and Flynn was a long traveler. He was still a sergeant. He had gone to the training school but came away a sergeant. Advancement *was* slow in the R. C. M. P.

He wore a sailcloth parka with edgings of wolverine guard hair, dark, blacktipped. Sailcloth was hard to come by and growing harder in the age of steam. He had gone to the coast to find it. Old sailcloth, beaten by the ocean gales, made the best of all parkas. He wore Indian snow glasses, made of wood with tiny holes. The police-issue glasses transmitted cold in, or his own heat out, and gave him a pain between the eyes. He drove a dog string, led by Nanuck, the best damned lead dog in the North. Nanuck was mean, strong willed, and figured he was wiser than his master. On and on they went. Flynn turned a shoulder against the wind.

SURVAY — put down firmly in pencil on the wall, the last effort of a dying man inside about two feet from the floor in a cabin up there in the Oosta Hills, the famed mink trapping grounds. The finest dark skins in the North were claimed, of course, by Brissaud, master of the Valley of the Thousand Smokes. And Survay, the height from the floor where a wounded man would crawl and print it, Survay, not Survey, Black Jack Survay with an "a."

At the summer police school they came down heavily on the little things. How often it was some trifling thing marked the crime in what might seem an accident, a trifle. Flynn had been — how long? — four years now in the service and still a sergeant. If there was not the slightest hint of advancement, well, the corporal had told him as much. "Once an Englishman, always an Englishman," Corporal McCabe had said. "And once a corporal, always a corporal."

Survay, Survay, Survay — someone had written that on the cabin wall in coarse black pencil before the wolves, lynx, even the mice, had devoured all of him, all but the bones, and some of them as well. The hungry land. . . . A hunch, he was driven now by a mere hunch. Little things were most often important. Watch out for the little things. "A single hair divides the false and true. . . . 'And upon what, prithee, may life depend?' " It was Omar who had asked, Omar the tentmaker, and Flynn's parka was Omar's tent. " 'Call me Ishmael.' "

Flynn's reading had been constant, books sent by his aunt he had ordered, rented, at his insistence or chosen on a visit, when his aunt would be sure to say: "Oh, Thomas, I could depend on you finding *that!*" Well, it was not, quite — she kept it in the back room, so you could draw your conclusions.

Flynn kept going. He had became entranced with moving. On and on he went, as if dreaming while asleep. It was so full of sound and form that it was like dreaming inside the sailcloth, with the wind and snow, the wolverine hair, long and black tipped, blowing over his face, screening the view.

"Nanuck, damn you!" He pronounced it Nan-*ook*. At every chance the big lead dog would assert himself by snapping at one behind. "Moosh!"

Flynn unlimbered the whip, and it made a frozen snap, always just missing the dogs. " 'Call me Ishmael!' " The desert was a desert of snow, a desert of sea. " 'We hunt the white whale!' " — it gave Flynn the shudders, Captain Ahab's megaphonic answer to the captain who was searching for his son after the great storm, while Ahab was hunting the whale that would destroy him. . . . Flynn had never become so tired of a book nor had one hung on so long in his mind, some event constantly coming to life, as here in the snow. Brissaud, *Père* Brissaud. He thought he owned the whole damned country, including through Black Jack Survay the mink-trapping grounds up there in the Oostia. Brissaud country. The Valley of the Thousand Smokes. Brissaud was lord of the land, and the poor kid who had run off with some ivory and pearl shell was long dead without a trial. It often came back to Flynn, sight of his white body. He had paid the extreme penalty, the will of Brissaud. The girl would be quite grown now. Marie — Marie Brissaud — she must be in her early twenties. Sometimes at night, or on the trail, Flynn tried to remember what she had looked like.

"When the Indian girls get looking pretty to you, that's when you better watch your step," Corporal — yes, he was still a corporal — Michael McCabe had said.

"Get any answer from that magazine to which you sent your poem, 'High on a Windy Hill,' this time?" Flynn had asked the last time they spoke.

"No, they never even had the courtesy to answer," the corporal had said, then added: "And I sent a two-cent return-postage stamp."

"I've heard it before, and more than once," Flynn had said. "That's how it is with an author, or a poet. Particularly a *poet*."

"Yes, and I suppose especially if he's Irish."

"Correct! Sad but true," said Flynn. "Weep for poor Oscar Wilde."

"And the filthy rotten tales they tell about him. The English never forgave him for outwitting them all at the dinner table. What was that poem again?"

> " 'I never saw a man who looked
> With such a wistful eye
> Upon that little tent of blue
> That prisoners . . . '?"

"That wasn't exactly the one, but it will do."
"How about:

> 'He did not wear his scarlet cloak
> For blood and wine are red,

108

And blood and wine were on his hands
When they found him with the dead'?"

"That's the one! Aye, my God . . . it would break your heart! Drove him away to Paris. *They* at least received him."

"Did you hear what he said when near death?" Flynn asked. "Some of his friends brought champagne and caviar. And Oscar said: 'I am dying beyond my means.' He couldn't pay his room rent. A Frenchman paid. Landlord marked it off the books. Just for the honor."

"The Lord will never forgive the English for what they did to the Irish."

"The day of reckoning ofttimes seems afar off, but come it will! And I dread even the thought of being English on that awful day!"

"Being English is something the Flynns and the McCabes need have no worry about."

"And amen to that. Hail Mary, and amen!"

And Flynn, Irish enough on his father's side, and practically a Catholic, perhaps even baptized — this was in controversy — crossed himself also, careful about it, right hand, not backward, like the devil.

If Flynn had ever thought he would have a nice, long rest at Vermilion, he had been mistaken. Young and long-legged, built for the snow and travel, it was in snowy travel they had needed him. He had recently been barely settled in a new post, at Fort Smith just below the MacKenzie boundary, on the Sixtieth degree of latitude on the map, although as it turned out the surveyors had been in error, had unwittingly taken azamuth on the ice, not hard ground, not computing its rise and fall, an easy thing to do there. Flynn admired the fellows who did the surveys. There were two of them, the Geologic Survey which told you what everything was — shale, basalt, water, good old dirt — and the Geodesic Survey which placed everything in position, how high the mountain, at what level the lake and lake bottom, and where the boundaries lay, the latitudes going around the earth, and the longitudes which were wide apart at the equator and closed to a point at the North and South poles. With one boot on the pole you could touch all the longitudes there were, but nobody had accomplished it yet. It was strange that survey crews came to his mind so repeatedly — the dead mink trapper, of course — because at South Nahanni, where he hoped to climb the Butte, or Twisted Mountain, 4,743 feet, C. C. D. S. and basalt, C. G. S., the two surveys, and get a nonpareil view of the storied valley, *le Vallon de la Mille Fumée.* How was that for French? He was learning it from the Crees.

Flynn had talked to an English biologist who was wintering at North Athabasca. He was quite conversant in French, and he said: "I'll tell you for a fact, Sergeant, Cree French may not be Parisian French, but if you're in Paris, it will get you what you want if you have enough money in your pocket." Which, of course, could be taken a number of ways, but on the whole it was encouraging. A man *without* money can get nowhere much in *any* language! He was there when the message got through saying he was needed at Telegraph Creek, a town away over in British Columbia. It was a quarter of the continent away, but who would think he'd be where he was, climbing a mountain to get a view of the Valley of the Thousand Smokes? The fact was, he had gone far off his route, which had been all right if he had had an excuse, a trap robber even, but all he had was a mind's vision of a golden-haired, brown-eyed girl, an entrancing combination. His mind and imagination were always at work.   cop.3

There was nothing for it but to head back, across the grain of the country to where he should have been in the first place, which was good old Vermilion. The corporal was gone. A constable was in his place. Flynn did get to visit with the Straws and see how young Jack was doing with his trap lines. God, that kid was *wild!* He had caught an otter. Got him in a Number Four Newhouse, set for wolves instead of the beaver it was meant for, and dang if he didn't come up and catch this otter, which was a male and a big one, way over twenty pounds. The pelt wasn't ice cut at all, which was rare. It just went to show you, one never knows what he might get in a trap, including himself.

Flynn had stayed all night at the Straws and went on, saving the dogs via a long trip through the Cassair Pass, actually just low hills and, of course, far too late in the season for any steamboat down the Grand Cañon of the Stikine, which was stopped with first ice. Flynn reached Telegraph Creek via Dease Lake (the town) and Telegraph, close to sixty-odd miles, by stage, actually a tandem wagon with cages for dogs. Telegraph was one of the real old towns of the North — going back to the Siberian telegraph-cable in the 1860s and lately revived when the Atlantic cable was believed to have broken down for good and all. There were now towns such as White Horse and Dawson on the route, which had not been the case in the 'Sixties. The telegraph was still a go across the Bering Straits to Siberia and on to Moscow, Suez, and points south.

At any rate the telegraph company staged a party for him. He'd brought his dress-scarlets — always on such journeys, you never knew, what with girls and all — and he was given a gold twenty-one jewel watch and a German hand transit with the E and W in reverse, and a mirror and sights reading vertical and horizontal, so he wouldn't get lost any more. Everybody, including some very decent women, got sort of lit up on champagne. It was quite merry, seeing the Atlantic had found one end of its cable, but the tsar was going ahead with the line anyhow, giving the world its first complete global service, even Australia. "The Bering Sea link is *quintessential!*" said the mayor of Telegraph, and everybody drank toasts to the tsar.

Well, that ended about the longest swing Flynn had ever made out of his district, but it was all fixed up. They wanted him to establish a police presence there and Shesley Crossing Inklin on the telegraph line north. It was a natural relief, no work at all, and both telephone and telegraph worked all the time — that's what gold could do. There were relay stations about every ten miles with a branch to Juneau, one to White Horse, one to Dawson, and a call for Mounted Police assistance at The Resort. Flynn didn't know what The Resort was, which surprised everybody.

"Go on up there," the inspector at Telegraph Creek told him, "it's right on your way home, and if they offer you a fee, take it. Those Yanks have nearly taken over the country, think they own it. It's a United States deputy marshal. He needs help."

"Good God! Is that in U. S. jurisdiction now?"

"No, a U. S. deputy marshal wants a man put under arrest, taken back to Juneau. We don't want their jail-birds. Charge him mileage if you like. I'm not sure what it is, but they have this fellow."

Flynn went north part of the way by narrow-gauge railroad, starting and ending at a place with no purpose he could see. What they had been doing was testing deep gravels for gold and had struck some oil, nothing important but it started quite a rush. Then, on Fallows Creek, gold in wide but lean deposits was found, a sufficiently large deposit to build a theatre. No Gillette, Mary Mannering, or anybody like that came, but a Louise Elliott had, said to be the famed Maxine's sister, playing her celebrated "Cowboy and the Lady" which Flynn saw and liked fairly well, giving him a chance to wear his scarlet jacket and nineteen-carat weave chevrons, attracting a good deal of attention. But duty called, and he went on north to this place, which was a hot springs hotel. It was named Taku, which he kept hearing about, though it was way over the mountains from his district. It was right near the Alaskan boundary. Many stampeders had taken that route to White Horse years earlier, and since then a railroad had been built up from Juneau, Alaska, and the famed Alaska-Juneau Mine, said to be the largest, lowest grade, and most productive gold mine on earth, if you could figure that out! It was in shale at low pitch, a wide strata, no timbering or very little, self draining, and gold in grains like flax that hung to the copper mercury plates, just about the opposite in all points than Uncle Frank's mine in Bullfrog which had showed how much *rich* ore counted!

Juneau had been a rip-roaring camp before Dawson was ever heard of, but anyhow they wanted in on it, so they started a railroad that climbed up Taku Inlet, no more than twenty-five miles from Juneau by ocean and sixty miles from the boundary by narrow-gauge railroad, the Juneau, Taku, Warm Bay and Yukon International, quite a name considering its less than hundred-mile length. The hot springs, which had so much sulphur in them the smell would knock you down, were popular with the stove-up miners from the Klondike. The diggings there had left them with terrible joint conditions or stiffened muscles, and they would come over and take the baths. They drank the water, too. And like many resorts, there was gambling. A deputy U. S. marshal named Stuben Baker had come over — they called him "Studebaker," after the wagons — and he wanted Flynn to collar this fellow, a gambler known as Doc Gibson, who was on the Canada list under the name of John "Swiftie" Flynn.

"Flynn!" said Sergeant Flynn, "that's getting too close to home!"

"No relative, I'll wager," the deputy U. S. marshal assured him. "He skipped bail on a bunco charge and is on the old R. C. M. P. list."

He had the list. Flynn was unsure, so he used the phone and called White Horse. There was trouble with the relays as usual, but the answer came back to wire Telegraph Creek. Before he had the chance a call came back to proceed, arrest him, he was on the old Soapy Smith list — they always paid the late Soapy that honor — he answered the description and was wanted in Juneau as an escaped felon. So Flynn got an order from the provincial commissioner, a sort of combined judge and notary, to have the U. S. deputy marshal sign and give him the old heave-ho.

The fellow was fifty-odd, an old sharper. They'd taken a double Derringer off him, so Flynn asked: "Ever know a big Indian named Survay?"

"Guilty." Quite a surprise. "I could have killed that man!"

"You frightened him terrible," Flynn said. "Black powder. He's been seen to light a cigarette and . . . pop! . . . off goes the black powder."

"He came for me," Doc Gibson said. "It was in self-defense. I got him with the powder. Other barrel had buck. I had no idea what happened to him, it was so many years ago."

"When I see him, I'll give him your regrets. Address? Alaska jail."

"Don't bother. Why, that 'breed is seven feet tall!"

The deputy marshal gave Flynn a twenty-dollar gold piece, newly minted, for his trouble. They were sitting there, waiting for Flynn to get off and take the handcar back. It was tied to the train. There were two men to do the work, but Flynn decided what the hell? — his dogs were in a police shelter back at Warm Springs and he didn't look forward to rattling back, sitting on the outside shelf of a handcar — he deserved a vacation. He was the ranking officer as far as Telesqua was concerned (a dingy cluster of huts and depot trading post on the B. C. boundary) and so he was finally empowered to declare himself on leave. Accordingly he decided to let the handcar go and ride on down to Taku Inlet and take the ferry to Juneau, a camp he had heard much about and which had just become the capital of Alaska territory.

"Oh, we have it, and don't have it," the deputy marshal told Flynn. "Washington passed the bill, but they hung on at Sitka, refusing to turn over the books. Our office is in Juneau, but the court records are in Sitka. A real mess. They have the Russian archbishop, and that nice warm wind off the Sandwich Islands, what else could you wish for?"

"Which do you prefer, Sitka or Juneau?"

"To tell you the truth, we ought to be moved up to Cook Inlet, one of those towns where they're surveying the railroad. Or Valdez." He pronounced it Val-*deez*. "Copper. Kennecitt. Bigger than Butte Hill. Straight shot up to Fairbanks. Mark my words, they'll move it again. Juneau is better for the marshal's office. Our court is in San Francisco. That telegraph of yours is closer. Cable line across the inlet."

"I thought the town was on the mainland."

"So it is, but so is Devil's Paw Glacier. Where they're building that line of yours, they can get to Skagway earlier than Juneau. This is one hell of a coast, man. It all moves. Glaciers. What we need is the wireless. Some Dago has one that works up to a hundred miles. Telegraph! I'd lay money they head for Canada. White Horse. On to Dawson and Fairbanks. You know more of that than I do. You that came up from Telegraph Creek. Inside valley. Straight north. No line will tackle the water and the glaciers. I wouldn't bet on Dawson. New gold won't grow. What else they have? I'd bet it will be cut across to Fairbanks and the Peninsula. The cable could cross north of Nome. I wouldn't be surprised to see them swing south and follow the Aleutians with a cable to Siberia at the tip of Kamchatka and across the Sea of Okhotsk. It's very shallow and would be a straight shot to that railroad at Vladivostok, the Transiberian line. And Japan. Avoid the glaciers. Of course I don't know. I just look at the charts. The naval station has a stack that high. You can bet money they won't lay cable in any glacial country. Glaciers *move*, awfully slow, but nothing can stop them. You can hear them here, grinding at night. You need a globe of the world. Out of our class, Flynn. Out of mine, anyway."

"If wireless works, cable will be redundant."

"I don't know what that word means, but it sounds like you do and are right. We live in a small world."

"Well, I'm not selling my snowshoes."

"Snowshoes? You really travel on them? In that blood-red suit?"

"No, I leave that home. Lately I've been favoring a parka and blanket-lined pants. Moosehide mucks. Toughest leather there is. From the waist down I can turn a hound's tooth. I brought these dress scarlets because people in town expect it. Regular damned champagne ball down at Telegraph Creek! I'll go back by way of White Horse. Up there they think they'll be the great city of the North."

"And I wouldn't be surprised. East end of the cañon, straight shot to Fairbanks. Poor old Dawson. Small world, Flynn, and growing smaller."

"Yes, Marshal. Listening to you shrinks it considerable."

"If the mine closes, as it will . . . no metal is ever planted to grow when it's gone. But we have fish. This is the damnedest fish country you ever saw. Crab. No lobster. Not fit to eat. Trout, fresh water. Halibut. Salmon red as that coat of yours. Get it on hooks from four hundred fathoms. Not the river run."

"Abalone?"

"Well . . . I guess so."

"I had abalone steak in San Francisco when I was taken there by my Uncle Frank. I was fourteen years old. Bull-

117

frog, Nevada. Had some stock in a gold mine. Highgraders. He bought some. You know they set me up a beer just like I was twenty-one. Most beautiful ore you ever saw. Some of it looked like agate, solid layers of gold. This highgrader sold us a bagful. Uncle Frank went straight in to San Francisco and sold every share he owned. Sold at something like a hundred and six and next we knew it was down to a dollar. All you hear now is Goldfield. Goldfield, Nevada."

"Your uncle have any stock in that?"

"I wouldn't know. Doubt it. Bullfrog scared him out."

"Think it would be the other way around."

"You know what the Indians say . . . 'a trap waits for the otter that follows the same trail twice.' "

"Right. Quit a winner. Damned few do it. Our prisoner, here."

"Don't rub it in," Doc Gibson interjected. "They're likely to give me a hard time in Juneau. Federal court. And it isn't as if I really did anything serious."

"Like peppering a man with a Derringer pistol?" asked Flynn.

"Yeah, well, he was looking for it. The other barrel was loaded with buck. I never get any credit for that!"

"Got money for a lawyer?"

"No. Want to lend me some?"

"I know your credit is fine, but I'll not be around long enough to collect. Couple of days and then off to White Horse by dog team."

Flynn was four days in Juneau, wearing his scarlet coat and the stripes. The good old R. C. M. P. made a sergeant look like a general. Gold chevrons! They had him at the Capital Club. He made a speech about how Juneau and White Horse would be the twin capitals of the North. He bought some really fine cashmere-silk underwear at the Alaska Commercial. Also a new Winchester .405. Ten percent off. Trade discount.

He thought, oh hell, why not? . . . and visited the prisoner, Doc Gibson. He was in a cell reading a Seattle paper.

"Anything about you in there?" asked Flynn.

"Say, glad you called."

Flynn said: "No, Survay isn't bailing you out. And you can be damned glad you have those bars for protection if he knew you were here."

"Oh, that god-damned 'breed! My point of view is I saved his life. I could have given him the buckshot and never been jailed. They had their gut full of him up around Savot." That was the name of the timber camp where they got the long-grain cedar, best boat material there was when it came to tackling the rapids. In Northern speech The Rapids always meant the White Horse where good pilots, back in the Big Rush, could make more money than from a claim on bonanza and, actually, without the risk. At least The Rapids gave it to you in about one minute, not coughing your lungs out for years.

Flynn had brought Doc Gibson some cigars. He was quite a likable fellow. Well, so he'd heard, Soapy Smith had been also.

Flynn had the dogs to worry about, so he returned to the Hot Springs with the new gun, got the team out and saw, as he feared, they'd had too much to eat and drove by a circuitous route to White Horse, avoiding the historic old gold rush camps and The Rapids, coming in by the back door, the eastern side of Lake Atlin. It gave him a chance to work some of their fat meanness out.

He cut quite a figure in White Horse if he did say so himself. The superintendent and *two* inspectors were there, to watch over the première city of the North — Dawson was expected to continue its descent into the second rate — with a road surveyed from both Edmonton and Hazleton. Hazleton was the northernmost city on the new National Railroad.

"How about Telegraph Creek?" Flynn interposed.

"Oh, yes," he was told, "the communications must not be left out. The Atlantic cable is all but defunct. The only cable line has to be the logical one, the route followed by man into the continent." (Who in his right mind would compare the long, deep Atlantic cable with the short jump over the Bering Straits?) "Not only Europe but the teaming Orient, Japan and the South Pacific lie in our course."

It did make sense, and White Horse was *positioned*. At any rate Flynn made his *acte de présence*, tall and admirably garbed, at White Horse, with its electric lights and shows. However, duty called, and he left in his new silk-cashmere underwear, .405 Winchester, and his old English Enfield revolver — not much to look at but deadly if aimed. It had not been his experience that the R. C. M. P. was a fast-draw, Wild Bill Hickok sort of an organization. It was instead a damned far-flung problem of live and let live, where ancient conflicts had to be let to work themselves out with the help of friendly persuasion and fair play. There was surely enough land to go around!

All good things come to an end. Neither Flynn nor his dogs wanted fat instead of muscle, so he departed on a route that was new to him, via Johnson's Crossing and back to Hay River. It came as rather a surprise to

120

him when he saw the familiar onion steeple of the Russian church and the white-painted, simply-marked sisters' hospital and school, only from a new direction. He paid his respects in the chapel, where he knelt for a prayer, and then to the sister superior.

It was from the sister superior he got news of the girl, Marie Brissaud. She had sent a very nice card to her from Quebec. In fact, she was expected with the first great snows to return about Christmas, a gift from *le bon Dieu*. Winter, not summer, was considered the time for travel in the far North, at least on those so-called barrens, actually an Eden of loneliness.

The sister superior said: "I would only hope she will pay us the honor."

Flynn said he hoped so, too, and if she did, would the good mother superior pay her his respects and that of the Mounted Police? He added, unfortunate as the first occasion was, he wished she would visit the poor boy's grave and offer a "Hail Mary." He crossed himself. The sister superior smiled and thanked him. It would be done. If he cared to stay . . . but now his duty called. There was little rest for the *few* who were to give order to the *many* in the Great Land. It was a nice speech. The sister superior dipped a knee, showing she thought so, too.

He stopped at the Straw place, found out Jack had done just fine with his otter pelt. He had supper and was on to what was again his home base at Vermilion when he learned that he was wanted at Fort Saskatchewan. The inspector there had heard of him and wanted to be filled in, chiefly about this fellow and that, and those fellows at White Horse who believed themselves the western Ottawa and now with some *reason*. The telegraph line was a bonus, and it was right on the projected road from Fort Saskatchewan and Edmonton. The inspector had no doubt of that. In the final shakedown Edmonton was to be the true center of the West!

Flynn saw the shows, dallied a while, went north again through the late odor of the tar sands, and was in time for the first great blizzard. The Mounted was moving him farther north. He was still a sergeant but with a foot on the rung for inspector when the new posts were opened.

"God knows where they'll send you," said Watson of the Geological Survey.

Flynn said: "Good heavens, Watson, it's the footprint of a gigantic hound!"

They both laughed, having read the book, the best Sherlock Holmes yet, best by far, but in Flynn's case truer than he might ever have guessed. . . .

Chapter Ten

So winter came again, winter and the great snow, and after that the *truly* great snow, the one that came from slightly south of west, which in any logical land should have been warm and fine but in this instance, while not cold, cold as the North deems cold, was cold enough, the sort which blows and packs, crusts, and then comes again, snow over snow over snow. And the wind shifted to the north. Flynn was, as usual, on his winter patrol, bent quartering against it as he went and looked forward to reaching Frenchman's Creek and the cabin where, luck permitting, someone had not already burned the fuel supply.

It cleared. Sun skirting the horizon gave a long view of the trans-MacKenzie country, range after range, bluish, gray, and what at a later date would be the midnight sun. There was always a fog distantly draped along the earth in the one area he was looking, a north-south range of mountains, for the vapor was never wholly gone from *le Vallon* — the Valley of the Thousand Smokes. He looked at it through his basswood snow glasses. A wind blew the wolverine fur of his hood, the fur that never gathered frost but softened the light still more through what seemed a glossy black. He knew, deep inside his sailcloth parka, when the snow came for it made a dull, sad, husky sound. It was not all new snow, but also snow picked up by the wind, the wind drift. A wolf howled. A dozen — or a hundred — answered, lost like the view, in distance. He liked the city, but God! — he liked this, too. It was the one place where a man could say his soul was his own.

Yes, all Flynn had to worry about was himself and his dogs, but not necessarily in that order. A man had to think of his dogs first, because if he didn't — well, they came through together, or not at all!

The wind had blown hard for a long time and made a cake of snow that broke in foot-wide lumps when he got off his sled, managing to urinate without the wind shifting and blowing it back at him. *High on a windy hill, facing the wind, the missus pisses.* Not Flynn. Back to the wind. The corporal's poem! Someone should publish it.

Flynn made a fire from carbide, dry pine needles, and pitch. In the quick flame he brewed strong tea, ate pemmican and last night's doughgods — frozen fish that could be made in a pan on the trail or in luxury on a sheet-metal stove. Many fine shacks had sheet-metal stoves. And fuel. You always left the woodbox full, an unwritten law of the North.

Flynn's course led downward by a series of terraced northward steps, a good place to go arse-over-tip, as the English said, and sprain, even break, your ankle on a hung-up snowshoe. In this the short oval "bear paw" shoe was better because you had to take short steps, slightly bowlegged, even though Flynn liked the long ones with their ski-ends not woven but a solid piece of oil-translucent hide, a sort of ski really where each step had to be a long, sliding one, so he could actually ride down a sudden declivity always remembering: "Look out for that bottom step, it's a doozie!" Time and again a gully would have a narrow channel, hidden by snow.

The spring flood watercourse presented gray dirt banks with a heavy overhang of snow. When it opened out, you saw the distance at low places called crossings, a very great distance amid the mists of a thousand hot springs, the far, far land. Its immensity could still stir him. Ruthless, cruel — but God, how he loved it all. Here was real privacy.

Flynn could see the steam from the hot springs where both summer and winter the Indians went to build their sweathouses. Yes, believe or don't believe, winter at twenty below zero was an Indian's bathing time. They would immerse themselves in water that at certain times would boil eggs and right beside it would be an ice-cold spring. The Indians would leap from one to the other, and cover themselves with dry grass in the sweathouse. Although an Indian might not bathe often by white man's standards, when he did, by the gods, it was a bath! There were more of those hot springs over to the east, away off beyond the big MacKenzie River where they ran the steamboats and the Marion where they dug the dark medicine rocks that gave off a strange glow on the blackest night. These black medicine rocks, almost black as Fort Murray tar, were now to be melted — heavy, hard, black stones that gave off a soft glow in the dark. Flynn had read of radium and Madame Curie even before the geological fellows told him radium occurred in the North in the medicine rocks.

Often at night the aurora made it brighter than day, the Northern day, that is, the time of the midnight sun only in reverse. When it got too cold, even the scents froze, and the sound of a rifle shot, for example, was absolutely silent until the *ka-wak* bounded back to you, very sharp, very short, and a rattle instead of an echo, a sound like breaking wood or the tear of a harsh starched cloth. No gun had the range or velocity at forty below as at forty above. There were men who could actually listen to the *ka-wak* of their gun and tell you the temperature, that is within five or ten degrees.

Flynn again stopped for a time. God! it *was* a big country! You saw what you thought was the horizon but after a while, out there, only another rim. It wasn't a horizon after all. The British said *an* horizon, Yank or Canuck a horizon. Flynn practiced thinking *an* horizon, because he liked the way Englishmen used the language, but it wasn't any *horizon* he saw, only a rim of blue-gray translucent hills because far and away, barely visible, there would be another blue-gray line, translucent almost to the sky, the bend of the world. Because the world was round, it sloped from view. Sometimes it was a *stellar* event, associated with the stars. The news fellows, those who wrote up the theatre, always talked about people such as Maxine Elliott, "The Girl with the Midnight Eyes," as *stars.* Flynn recalled how he had schemed to see her when she played in Vancouver, but it had come to naught. At the last minute he'd been sent to Dease Lake.

It was there, at Dease Lake, that he'd had his first look at Survay and heard him tell how that gambler had shot him with a Derringer loaded with extra coarse black powder — there'd been a wad between the charge which was capped and only some of the powder had time to burn, so it was not really an explosion. No good gun load explodes. It doesn't go all at once. It burns. Slow-burning powder may take a fifth of a second, while fast-burning powder causes an explosion, taking only one twentieth, or something like that. The slow-burning powder is better because the bullet has started to move, and the rest of it makes it gather speed and go faster, with a greater range, hence the longer the barrel, the longer range. The black powder in the big pellets took quite a while and with the short barrel of the Derringer it wasn't burning at all up front, only that under the percussion cap which was fulminate of mercury, and the pellets of that big powder became the charge, the real projectiles, like No. 3 goose shot. Those pellets had hit poor Survay and buried themselves just under the skin, spreading because a Derringer barrel has no length or choke. The choke was when shot was brought together, or at least not let to spread out. The longer barrel gave a longer range so bucks, or whatever, weren't able to fly through it. But the damned Derringer. No barrel choke. It spread right away, at about four feet, and covered a whole fourth of Survay's neck, chin and cheek, and luckily just the corner of an eye, making it always bloodshot, sort of a blue-black. Flynn had wondered at the time what Survay would say if he knew that the fellow was now in Juneau, probably still in jail if not out on bail. But all that was in the past, before he had been given the writ for John Survay's arrest. He now carried that writ in the document folder inside his parka.

It was time to be moving again. Flynn unrolled the whip and gave it a crack to get the dogs up. "Moosh!" he called, rocking the sled to get started. The dogs barked. Partly by Flynn's power the sled got going. There was still a slight decline, which helped. A grove of bleak, black-gray dwarf trees had to be avoided. Always a bad spot because of the wind drift and extra snow. It was there that the dog attacked him.

Flynn first saw the shadow move and shouted. At once he thought it some great, dark wolf, grizzly gray and black. It lunged and had Nanuck by the throat. But Nanuck was quick as well and, flipping over, used the line to his advantage. Flynn snowshoed forward, driving a cloud that partly obscured the rest of the string, but his long, Cree snowshoe prow got in the tangle. Still, it may have saved Nanuck from death. The dog looked large as a man, a man in a gray fur overcoat, the sort teamsters wear, the "dogskin" overcoats of horse drivers, bewhiskered men all covered with frost in winter.

It took him that time — a second or two of baffled, half-waiting time — to get turned and going and become part of it. His rifle was gone. He saw the stock sticking out of the snow. It was in his brain that the damned barrel would be filled with snow now. The brain has its compartments and at times of surprise, shock, explosive thought, the different parts register. At all events some seconds had passed. It takes time to fight the snow. Flynn was able to drive the bent end of one Cree snowshoe between the rolling animals, the attacker free of any harness snap, Nanuck tangled and restricted. The great attacking hound was familiar to him. *Good heavens, Holmes, it's the footprint of a gigantic hound!* The words actually came to him from some compartment of memory, while other compartments were functioning elsewhere. And he knew the hound. Baskervilles be damned. It was *Mach de Fer*, that god-awful brute that was said once to have tried to kill his own master, Black Jack Survay, the man who fed him!

Flynn let himself pitch forward over his snowshoes. The leverage tore the tip apart, a fortunate move that perhaps saved his life. The two dogs were parted and *Mach de Fer*, partially propelled by the showshoe, saw Flynn and came for him — not for Nanuck but for *him*. Flynn was briefly aware of the open mouth and fangs while on his back, rolling, and he acted by reflex to poke his right hand forward, making a fist and driving it down the animal's throat. Oh, he drove it hard, and the dog's weight added to the force, coming down on fist and elbow braced in the snow. Flynn doubled his fist. They rolled and, instead of attempting to escape, Flynn lifted himself so the dog's weight made the fist go deeper. He rolled and drove the fist harder still, buckskin mitten with padded wool glove inside. It gave some idea of the size of that dog — Flynn's gloved fist just fit. With force it went down the dog's throat, more than half way to Flynn's elbow. His sleeve was all blood and slobber. The dog was on him and his elbow on the snow, the firm earth far below. Flynn could smell the dog's rotten-meat breath, and blood ran out on his sailcloth parka.

Flynn stayed with his shoulders deep in the snow and let *Mach de Fer* use his own weight to close his windpipe. In a dog that was a long way back, and Flynn was slobbered almost to his elbow. It came to him that he didn't want to go too far, into the stomach. He resolved to remain still, and let inertia do its work.

Inertia! It wasn't what he thought it meant, a lazy boy lying in bed. The geological fellow said it was accumulated force. A boulder on a hill represented so many tons of inertia. You turned it loose, and the inertia took everything before it, as in Mark Twain's story about prying loose the boulder that rolled down and straight through the cooperage house, sending the barrel makers

129

running in all directions. They were the recipients of all that inertia, waiting years and years. For inertia is energy, and energy cannot be destroyed. Flynn knew about inertia, and this hellish hound did not.

He had to control the weight because he could lose glove and mitten. He had to wait, wait, set like a bulldog in the ring once he gets the vise grip, never letting go. Time — "the sweet comforter" — Shakespeare. Thoughts, like birds, flew through his brain. He was aware of other dogs, a sled, and people, but he kept his fist right where it was as he felt waves of a shudder passing through the animal's body. And still he waited. Waited.

A man was shouting at him and beating him with a club of some kind. Flynn rolled so *Mach de Fer* would get the beating. He could feel new waves of shuddering pass through the animal. He didn't actually want to kill him. There was a rifle being aimed. He rolled so the hound's body was over him, but his fist remained.

The girl's voice was in his ear: *"Non, non, non!"*

Flynn almost lost his mitten and glove in getting free. It came out all slobber and blood. Blood dripped from the canvas of his parka. He cursed the dog for fouling his parka — sailcloth, cleansed by the gales of the ocean, and now there was bloody slobber on it.

He realized that considerable time had passed. The girl was aiming a rifle at him. It came to his brain, if not mind, to say: *Shoot!* as had happened to that poor boy with the pearl shell, but it was only in his brain. He had no real idea of saying it. The dog lay with slimy blood from his open mouth staining the snow. The girl was standing with a rifle in her hands. It was a light-caliber, lever-action piece, no more than a .25 but deadly when fired. He held his hands wide because a woman with a gun is one dangerous combination. There's no bluff in a woman, so he had heard. A woman means business.

"*Non! Non!*" he said. It was all the French that came to him. It was the girl from the mission, Marie Brissaud, the girl who had brought in the poor, dead boy. Survay had been involved in that, too, but not present. Survay probably had had *Mach de Fer* kill that poor kid. That's all he was, a kid, killed for some trifling ivory, pearl shell, maybe a few real pearls worth one good black fox pelt. "Dead, dead for a ducat, dead!" *Hamlet.* Quotes always came to him. His mind today was far away, floating down Vesuvius Bay. So much ran through Flynn's brain, not his mind so much as his brain. There was a difference, a spiritual difference. The mind! *Toujours l'âme!* He said: "*Non, non,*" watching her hand on the rifle. "The dog, you see, is alive."

Uncle Frank once said: "Kid, let me give you a piece of advice." He was always giving Flynn a piece of advice! "Never tackle a red-headed woman or a bulldog." Only Marie Brissaud wasn't red-headed, and *Mach de Fer* was a long way from being a bulldog. Better advice just came to him — never challenge a woman with a rifle. Had Marie actually killed the poor kid at the mission? *Non. Non.* Flynn was sure that was not so.

He bowed and saluted. "I was attacked. Thank you for saving my life." He found himself, knowing little French, choosing his English carefully. Keep talking. People won't shoot you if you're talking. "I should have desisted. But for you I might have smothered that poor dog. The dearest thing *Frère* Survay has. A very sad thing. But perhaps all will learn from our lesson. *Amor vincit omnes.* Love and friendship will yet be triumphant.

131

For me, a policeman, to encourage, even enforce, peace and friendship is my *duty*. If I have failed, *je vous en prie pardon*."

She lowered the rifle. It was silver plated with mother-of-pearl inlays, the very material which had cost the boy's life. The poor lad, so cold, for some reason hung in Flynn's mind — so cold and helpless, his sad brief voyage from life to death, even now, in the dark box between the snow and the frozen earth — but he drove the thought away. His buckskin glove was wet and freezing from the slather of *Mach de Fer* and a frosty foam of freezing black blood. It had been a close call. Flynn could actually feel the dog's shudders of coming death when he, with some difficulty, managed to withdraw his hand without leaving the glove behind.

The dog was up on front legs now. He was looking at Flynn. There was no attacking about him, just mutual understanding. Which would he follow, with the chips down, Flynn or Survay?

Flynn looked over at Survay in the background beyond Marie Brissaud, holding a piece of babiche. "Oh, by the way," he said, "John Survay, spelled with an 'a,' " — he reached inside his parka and found the writ in his document folder, "you are under arrest."

Did that leave Survay nonplused? He stood up straight, almost dropping the babiche, and said: "Eh?"

"You are under arrest for the suspected homicide of a trapper, John Doe, alias Runt Macklin, on or before April third last. Place, the Geophysical-Geological Survey cabin, Number One Thirty-Eight, Tole Creek, on or about longitude One Hundred Twenty-Two degrees Twelve minutes west, latitude north Sixty-Five degrees Thirty-One minutes Twenty seconds." Flynn put the paper away.

That left Survay with his mouth agape. "He? Kill heem trapper? In shack?"

"Yes. It was your trapping ground. So you printed your name on the wall. I'm doing my duty in pointing out the alternatives. Now, if you printed your name on the wall to show your claim of rights to the geological fellows, it was perfectly reasonable. All I want is the truth. The facts. It could be your dog that ran down the trapper. I'm duty bound to point out the alternatives."

"Oh, you make big mistake! He say this was survey cabin, Canada government. I say no, this Survay house, belong to me. I print my name on wall in big print letter lak I learn in school? This man . . . he's dead?" He crossed himself. "I pray for heem! But Survay no kill heem! I kill heem, I sign name? I crazy fella I do this? You talk lak Irish damned fool."

"No, but perhaps he got to the cabin and wrote your name!"

"What you think this tom-fool story, Marie? I kill man and then sign my name? In big print? Survay not big fool. I kill this police, you see him no more. Lak wind, poof! Drag him off, leave him for wolf. Maybe two mile, three mile off. You arrest me, so I make you look lak monkey hang by his tail before judge. Ho-ho-ho-ho! You, Sergeant, you tak off parka, you show ver' fine stripes on arm. You bring this damned fool charge you be no-theeng. You be feeding dogs, assistant . . . what-you-say? . . . constable. You, Constable, clean out dog pens." The big black-speckled face opened an astounding mouth and eyes. Survay made motions of donkey ears with his mitts. "Hee-haw, hee-haw . . . my name, she's Maude! You ask yourself, big jackass fella, you tell those story. Kill man, sign for him, lak for beaver permit?" Tears

133

actually ran down his cheeks from laughter. "What you say, Judge, I have heem man for send crazy house! Marie, you listen this crazy police. People never going believe when I tell about heem crazy police!" It was funny, his wild jig, flinging his huge mucklucks out from the knees then going bowlegged, the while flapping his mittens like ears. Then he became serious. He made the sign of the cross again. "Before Mother of God, her holy name, I not do this thing."

It *was* pretty far-fetched. Flynn had never heard Survay called either a thief or a killer, only violent and mostly to himself. What Flynn really wanted was to be taken to *le Vallon* — the Valley of the Thousand Smokes. All the tales he had heard! The factor there was three hundred years old? Beyond belief! But the pearl shell and ivory, that was the real thing. No word of gold. In that country, if you lied, it always involved gold.

At any rate he didn't want to arrest Survay, at least not yet. Survay had endured enough without standing up to some charge that couldn't be proven. Flynn felt a bit guilty about meeting the fellow who peppered him, taking him across the boundary to Juneau where he'd probably get off, whatever it was he'd done, and Flynn still had the gold piece. For no good reason the gold piece, the look of Survay's face, and then the dog, open mouthed, tongue lolling, bloody saliva dripping from *Mach de Fer* — it all seemed to Flynn enough satisfaction for whatever the North had suffered.

His glove was still slimy from saliva, blood, and whatever that ugly animal had had for his dinner, rotting meat from the smell. Flynn would have to wash and dry the glove, but for now a long hand-rubbing in the hard, cold snow had to serve. He looked at *Mach de*

Fer, and *Mach de Fer* looked at him. He'd have to watch that dog. Dogs never forget.

"Tell me true of *Père* Brissaud," he said to Marie. To show sincerity he took off a mitten, crossed himself. "In the name of God."

It was the right move. It brought things down to a serious level. She said: "True, he's very old. The valley keeps him young. They say five hundred years old? *Non*, but very old. Years of French rule. Years of the great sails. Years of the Cree brigades. *Le Vallon?* Volcanoes? No, warm springs. Boiling springs. Geysers, yes. Sulphur springs. Great stinking water . . . Indians . . . healing. The Indians come always . . . all tribes. Only some Crees cause trouble, but they are a trading people. They love to argue with *Père* Brissaud. A ground ever warm. The castle . . . the great house . . . only a fire on the hearth and one in the cooking kitchen. One digs in the earth, and it is warm on the coldest days. The vegetables grow to great size in the midnight sun of summer. We have the fine *Parisien* foods. Grown here for more years than any except *Père* Brissaud has. . . ."

"Which are? Honor true!" Flynn said it with a smile.

"Who can tell? Some say *three* hundred years. *Non*. But who is old enough to know? He was with the great whaling ships. Ships of sail . . . not the steam with the harpoon fired by gunpowder. The springs warm the ground in winter, and great bones are found. The great elephant. Tusks taller than two men. Some of it porous and flawed, but much filled with quartz stone. Also mother-of-pearl. Such beauty! The great tuskers have long been dead. Even before *Père* Brissaud came. Pink ivory. Even blood red, from hot springs, and used for the chess men. The miners were there, but he would not allow them to stay. The Indians rose up and drove them out when *Père* gave the word. He is of great age . . . since the days of the Great Company at Churchill . . . since the long Cree canoes . . . canoes, one to another, in lines a quarter mile long, carrying the goods of Mother England to the swamps, the tundras, and the great mountains. But they are gone now, the traders. Only *Père* Brissaud remains. We get the vegetables of France from roots and cuttings. They grow to strange shapes and flavors in the long twilight. The endive, in stalks like rhubarb, only tender . . . clean breaking as ice. Only the olive oil, the wines, the brandies must come from France. From Spain. From China. Liquors so very old they came by sailing vessel around Cape Horn." She paused and considered him for a time. "Very well. You have been kind to me, *m'sieur le police.* I will invite you to be my guest at *le Vallon* . . . as you say, the Valley of the Thousand Smokes!"

He took time to examine his dogs, their feet which were all-important, particularly after a long stop, and his lead dog, Nanuck.

Marie said: "Of what good is a lead dog after he has been beaten?"

"He does not seem to be beaten. Remember, but for my good nature and the rules of the police, old Jaw of Iron there would not be standing and breathing at this moment. Ten seconds more and you would have one hundred kilos of dog, freezing. This I have done for you . . . for the holy sisters . . . for the great *Père* Brissaud. This, *mademoiselle,* is a gift from Sergeant Flynn of Her Majesty's" — he quickly changed that to — "*His* Majesty's Royal Canadian Mounted Police."

They were always changing the damned name. He

wished they could make up their minds whether it was His Majesty's, or Royal, or just Canadian Mounted Police, but after all, he was only a sergeant. It amused him to think that perhaps — just a joke, and a silent one — he could succeed as the master of the Thousand Smokes. How old was Brissaud? One hundred? Two hundred? Three hundred years?

She seemed to guess his thoughts. "The waters of *le Vallon* are very, very healthful. And ah, *m'sieu le police*, the vegetables! Like so. Did you know that here, close to the pole, the light of a sun from beyond the horizon *reflects*, and the Northern Lights, as you say, they make green plants green? And the ground always warm? The Indians live to be very old in the warm springs and the . . . what you call Northern Lights."

"And *Père* Brissaud is four hundred years old."

She smiled but a little, saying in a quiet voice: "You will make up your own mind. Do you, *M'sieur* Flynn, remember the day of your birth?"

Chapter Eleven

Marie, the dog whip still in her hand, stopped her team at the gate. It was instantly opened by an ancient French-Indian. He smiled at Marie, and they exchanged friendships. The stockade contained many houses, built of logs or stone, cache houses on pillars, and a very large two-story structure with a crow's nest to which wings had been added from time to time, providing a rather charming planlessness. Flynn was interested in the logs, which were not native surely, more of the kind one would find in Manitoba, say, or British Columbia, a variety of cedar by the appearance, clear timber with hardly a knot.

When Flynn appeared and stopped, two slim half-breed boys came running. He was cautious to get Nanuck by the back strap.

"Don't feed them much," Flynn said. Then, following blank expressions, he added: "No *heap-machewin.*"

Marie waited for him at the castle, as the main structure was called. It took strength to open the door until assistance came from inside — an old Indian. He smiled at Marie, bowed deferentially, and received a kiss on the cheek. They passed halls, ante-rooms, and a second door to what was evidently the great hall, very high ceilings, with two stairways, a balcony, and a huge fireplace with a fire to match of logs and coals. There was a luminous glow from the fire and a few lamps but chiefly from the great windows which were covered with caribou or deer skin, scraped and cured until they were translucent — an amber glow everywhere in which strangely no piece of furniture, great table, chairs, smaller tables appeared to cast a shadow.

Marie said: "You are going to ask how they got a mahogany table here?"

It was mahogany. Flynn had seen enough furniture to recognize Circassian mahogany which came from far-off Central America. It was obviously very old and ill used. The scarring reminded one of a saloon bar on which hob-nailed lumberjacks had danced but refinished, renewed, polished again and again with beeswax.

He asked: "This is the great table?"

"Perhaps. It is very old. It was used for . . . mundane things. *Père*'s father was a partner in the Great Company."

Flynn had heard that Brissaud came from a family with influence in the eastern provinces, and gossip among the force said that was the reason for the commissioner's suggestion that it would be well enough if the men in Division N let the old factor run the valley in his own way. A door opened, interrupting his scrutiny of the table. A man had entered, and for the moment there was only a shadowy impression of him in the well of darkness at the deep end of the room, while the thud and floor-tremble raised by his moccasined feet indicated someone of considerable size. Light from the fireplace struck him. After the image of *Père* Brissaud that had been built in Flynn's mind, this man was a shocking disappointment. He was large, though far short of the nearly seven feet that had been attributed to him. His shoulders were massive, his trunk thick throughout. It was a ponderous strength. He was a huge bull of a man rather than the rangy forest traveler Flynn had pictured. He seemed perhaps sixty — not the great age one expected. His face was heavy without being ugly. He might even have been called handsome in his way. He had a good crop of whiskers that had recently been trimmed down. The man stopped to look at the three in the room, then he came on, his walk displaying confidence to the extent that it was almost a swagger. At his waist was a Hudson's Bay knife with a foot-long blade.

"My dear!" he said to the girl. "We've been expecting you for . . . days."

He had a resonant voice, but something about it — its note of possession — grated on Flynn's nerves. Flynn glanced at Marie, and her expression was reassuring. She was a long way from being this man's property. There was almost a challenge in the way she faced him.

"I go and come as I like."

"Of course," he said, lifting heavy shoulders. He turned to look at Survay, and any benevolence instantly disappeared. He looked more massive, probably through a flexing of his muscles. His big fists were closed. "Something's wrong." There was nothing about the words themselves, but he managed to make them sound brutal. "I suppose you're in trouble again."

"His lead dog killed a man," Marie said. "A trapper down on the Severence."

"And then you let the police follow him here."

Flynn was not in uniform, but he *knew*.

Marie said: "It was I who brought the sergeant here, *M'sieu* Rambo." She addressed Flynn: "You once men-

140

tioned our brigades. *M'sieu* Rambo has led them during recent years."

The men shook hands. Flynn had thought this man was *Père* Brissaud. He wasn't, and he didn't immediately release Flynn's hand. He moved for a certain grip and bore down, showing his strength, trying to crush bone and tendon. It was a childish trick. He was far stronger and heavier than Flynn, but he lacked a certain wiry quickness, and Flynn deftly escaped. He looked in the man's small, bright-blue eyes wondering just why he'd tried such a thing and decided it was chiefly for the purpose of asserting himself.

The girl was watching them, tense for the moment as though expecting it to flame into open conflict, but there was nothing like that. Rambo was satisfied with himself, and there was no change in Flynn's face.

She said: "I'm going to the Eagle's Nest."

There were some stairs in the shadowy end of the room. Rambo waited for her to get out of sight. He started to say something under his breath to Survay, but the 'breed's voice was in ahead of him, chattering in a mixture of French and Cree.

"Keep still!"

Survay stopped instantly, but Flynn had caught the gist of what he'd started to say — that it wasn't his fault, that he'd done as Rambo had wanted him, that it had merely been the devil's luck a Mountie had found his trail. Rambo's intense blue eyes shot over to Flynn. "I suppose that goes down in your little book. I suppose that will just be so much more proof of what you've always thought of me. You've heard of me before, haven't you?"

Until then Flynn hadn't been sure, but now he began

to make connections. "You must be Moose Rambo. You used to be head of the Athabasca brigade. The company entered charges against you. They claimed you sank a York boat after a quarrel with the district factor."

"A lie. A damned Scotch lie. He wanted to get rid of me . . . MacTavish! . . . because he'd cheated the company of a dozen cross-fox skins, and I knew it. Am I still on your wanted list?"

"I don't know that you ever were."

"You see? It was a lie, or MacTavish would have pressed charges. I have no apology to make. If I had things to do over, I'd do just the same . . . except maybe I'd break that MacTavish's rooster neck. Maybe I'll do it yet."

"He's been dead for two years."

"Good. I'm glad to hear it." Rambo turned once again to Survay. "You back-shooting weasel!"

"It was notheeng! Only what I have to do. Hear me! Do not tell *Père* that . . . ."

"Trying to make the police believe I told you to kill him? That's what you're trying to do, isn't it?"

Survay didn't know what to answer. He gulped, making his pointed Adam's apple roll far up and down.

"Answer me! That's what you were trying to do!"

"No."

"You've always hated me. Ever since I threw you in the river for cheating old Kinapitic out of his traps. So now, when you back-shoot a man and get caught, you'd like to take me to hell on your lead string. Who told you to do it? Who really told you to do it?" Survay waved his head back and forth in negation. It infuriated Rambo. He took a long stride, swinging his hand, open palmed, and smashed Survay to the floor. "Tell the truth! Who was it sent you to kill the trapper?"

142

Survay staggered to his feet. "I try to tell. . . ."

"Sit at the table!"

Survay crouched on one of the chairs.

"Stretch your hands out."

He reached, laid his hands palms down on the scarred table top. Before Flynn realized what Rambo was about, he'd drawn the heavy H. B. C. knife from its sheath and drove it through the back of Survay's right hand, nailing it to the table. Survay screamed and reared back, but the knife blade held him. Struggle only made the pain worse. He crouched back in the chair, bent over the knife, his hand twitching around it.

Flynn was there with a long stride. He reached for the knife handle. Moose Rambo saw him and spun around, slamming his hand away.

"Turn him loose!" Flynn said.

"You're not in the police barracks now."

"He's still my prisoner. . . ."

"Inside this valley you have no authority."

Flynn's hand dropped to the butt of his Enfield. Rambo expected the action. His hand had been resting on one of the chairs. He swept up the chair with a swift movement, flung it waist high. It was a heavy chair. Flynn had the gun half way from its holster when it struck. Its weight stunned his movement for a second, knocked him off balance.

He tried to bring the Enfield up, but Rambo charged, swinging one massive arm in a chopping movement, knocking the gun free. It struck the floor. Flynn had a fleeting impression of blue-steel glimmer as it bounded away across the rough plank floor. He tried to set himself, but the advantage of weight and momentum were on the side of Rambo. The man's charge carried him backpedaling. His shoulders slammed the wall. He was pinned there against the massive, axe-flattened logs. He twisted from side to side, but Rambo's bull strength had him helpless. He was conscious of the heat and sweat of the man's body, the smoky odor of his hair.

Rambo was a grappler rather than an open fighter. That's how it always was with men who had learned to dominate a York boat crew. Weight and strength were an advantage in close quarters. His left hand came up, thumb driving to the nerve center in Flynn's armpit. The pain had a sudden, paralyzing effect. Instantly Rambo went for an armlock with one hand, using his other elbow to pin Flynn's throat to the wall. He laughed, a deep, guttural sound. "See, Mountie? I could break your neck. That easy." He rammed down. "That easy."

Flynn knew better than to fight the arm. Instead he turned enough to get one moccasined foot planted against the wall. Using that for leverage, he twisted at the waist, driving his hip into Rambo's abdomen. It was unexpected, and for the moment Rambo was off balance. He reeled back one step, and Flynn was free.

Flynn set his heels, his left hand feinted, and the right came up in a smashing arc, landing at the point of Rambo's jaw. Rambo wasn't ready for it. It snapped his head to one side, slapping sweaty black hair over his forehead. He staggered a step, heel catching in the rough floor, spilling him backward. He caught himself, hands flung back, a sitting position. After the first baffled moment his eyes were in focus. He expected Flynn to charge on, and he was ready to double his legs and swing both feet to the groin. But Flynn motioned for him to get back on his feet and continue the fight.

"I say, that's sporting. What-ho, old top!" Rambo said,

imitating his idea of a British fop. "I suppose they teach you that down at the training barracks." His hand was on a Colt revolver. With a practical movement he twisted it from the holster. "This has a hair trigger, Mountie. I don't want to kill you."

"I don't want to be killed, either," Flynn said softly.

"Go back and sit down."

Flynn returned to the table, seating himself across from Survay. Rambo paused to pick up the Enfield, thrust both guns away, the Colt in its holster, the Enfield in his belt sash. He couldn't resist a swagger as he walked back. "I don't give most men a second chance. Third chance, call it, because I could have killed you there along the wall."

"Why didn't you?" Flynn asked in a flat voice.

Rambo shrugged thick shoulders. "You're a guest. The lady's guest. Besides we don't often entertain Mounted Policemen. I'd like to have you hear what the bushwhacker has to say. I don't like bushwhackers any better than you do. Maybe not so well. We don't have any prison down in Regina, or wherever you send them."

Actually he had stopped talking to Flynn. He was standing with his stud-horse legs spread and anchored the way he'd learned standing in York boats on the mean rivers of the North.

Survay then started to plead. "No, I lie! You nevaire tell me to kill. You. . . ."

"That's better. Did you hear what he said, Mountie? I want to watch you write that down in your little black book. *Monsieur* Rambo had no part in it. Tell the rest of it!"

Survay looked up, frightened and pleading. His fingers twitched in pain from the knife nailing him to the table.

"Tell him who really sent you."

He whispered: "*Père . . . Père* Brissaud."

"Tell the rest of it."

"I tell. . . ."

"Why did Brissaud send you? Because the trapper had been running his mink line up the Severence? Is that what he said?"

Survay nodded and got out the word: "Yes."

Flynn didn't believe a word of it. Survay's eyes proved it. They searched out Flynn for understanding. Flynn looked Survay straight in the eye. He nodded. Survay's terrible speckled face showed gratitude. Flynn was a friend! Maybe his only friend! It is well for a man to have one friend! The one man who tested his mighty lead dog, *Mach de Fer.*

Rambo started to pace the room. Now that he'd wrung the words out of Survay, they seemed to agitate him. After a couple of steps he turned on the balls of his feet and came back. For so big a man he was surprisingly graceful, trained to get his bulk around in the smallest possible space on pirogue and canoe. He looked at Flynn. "You heard what he said."

"Was that why you wanted me to live?" Flynn asked the question without his face showing anything. He might have been convinced or not, there was no telling.

"Partly. Sure, I might as well admit it. I don't want old *Père* to go on a rampage and have the blame dropped on me."

"You must think there's a good chance of me leaving here alive."

"There's nothing for us to fight about. You wanted to handle Survay by your soft police system, but *I* had to get the truth out of him."

He was watching Flynn for the effect of his words, but as usual there was nothing to be read. Flynn could have made some remarks about the value of testimony wrung from a man when his hand was nailed fast to a table, but instead he encouraged Rambo by saying: "I naturally had my suspicions of *Père* Brissaud, or I'd never have come here."

It was what Rambo had been waiting for. His attitude changed still more. He yanked the knife from Survay's hand, wiped the blood from it against a leg, thrust it in his belt sash, then seated himself, lowering his voice in a confidential tone. "Don't get the wrong idea. About me and Brissaud. This isn't so damned easy for me. *Père* is a great man. *Was* a great man. Saved my life once. I came here with the Mounties on my tail, then I just stayed. Lived peaceful. But he's getting old now. Has the idea he's ruler of the North. Got stiff necked about the trappers down on Rainy Lake. I tried to hold him down, and now this comes up. Maybe tomorrow it'll be somebody else. I'm second in command here. You're not solving a hell of a lot by dropping this 'breed through your trap. You see my position?"

A gun exploded. Its unexpected concussion had an impact that stunned, and for a moment Flynn had no idea where it came from. He turned, his hand instantly dropping to his empty holster. The bullet had smashed splinters from a thick spruce log near the door. A scent of burning powder came to him, then he saw Marie descending the stairs. She came with a slow, cat-like tread, Colt revolver in her hand, a tiny trail of black powder smoke still coming from its muzzle. Forty-Four caliber, a lot of gun for such a small girl but, after seeing her swinging a dog whip, Flynn wasn't surprised.

147

"I told you to keep him here," she said to Rambo, jerking her head at the 'breed.

"He's here, isn't he? I don't like the smell of bush-whackers."

"Bushwhacker!" A great hollow voice repeated the word, making it roll around the walls of the big room. "So he is a bushwhacker!"

A man followed her down the stairs slowly, a step at a time after the manner of men with one stiff leg. Flynn watched as the firelight brought him into view. He was old perhaps, but there was an ageless quality about him. He might have been sixty — seventy — ninety. Flynn had noticed it often that way with big, powerful men who had lived much of their lives in the open. Such men never get old the way city men do. The outdoors, the wilderness — it does something. It had done something to *Père* Brissaud.

He reached the foot of the stairs and limped on, driving a diamond-willow stick each step he took. He was tall, one of the tallest men Flynn had ever seen, but his excellent proportions kept one from particularly noticing. He had a remarkable breadth of shoulder, a spine straight as a Blackfoot spear, a narrow waist. His arms were long and easy swinging. Perhaps he was no heavier than Rambo, but where Rambo was a bull brute, *Père* Brissaud had the lithe leanness of a caribou in winter. He carried his head erect, as though proud of its proportion. His nose was large and sharp ridged after the manner of many French; his eyes were set wide, and there was something of the bird-of-prey about them. He wore tiny gold rings in the lobes of his ears. At first thought the adornment was preposterous but, after seeing them once, it would have been impossible to imagine

Père Brissaud without them.

He was dressed like any woodsman or trader, Scotch wool and moccasins. He kept coming, a ponderous limp, covering the distance in space-eating strides. That left leg was not crippled. It seemed to have been stiffened through age. No one spoke while he crossed the big room. There was no sound except the thump of his diamond-willow stick. He was watching Survay's face all the way. He stopped a couple of strides away and thrust the stick at him.

"Bushwhacker!" he said again in his hollow voice. "It is true what she told me, Survay? You are a killer? You are not fit to live with us here at *le horizon du nord!*"

Survay wove his head in what started to be a denial, but Brissaud was not an easy man to whom to lie. Survay seemed to have forgotten the knife wound in his hand. Now the hand hung at his side, still bleeding, the red drip-dripping from the ends of his fingers.

Brissaud waited while seconds moved past, then he went on: "So. She told true. Of course. You have then killed a man. The poor trapper, Dimke."

Survay seemed eager to confess and have it over with. Fear had already done what it could.

"You know what we have always done with your kind." Brissaud no longer sounded angry and not contemptuous either. He spoke on a note of sorrow. "A gun, a cartridge, a pound of meat, and the clothes on your back. You will leave like that by the north trail. We will never see you again, Survay."

That was all. Brissaud swung his huge frame around on the pivot of stiffened leg and walking stick. Flynn had expected more. It was a small punishment, on the face of it, and seemed to bear out what Moose Rambo

had said — that Survay had only done Brissaud's bid-
ding.

Brissaud was looking for someone. He changed ends
of the diamond-willow stick and hammered it on the
floor. "Champlain!"

Champlain, a big, red-faced Frenchman, must have
been just outside for he stepped through the door almost
instantly. He still wore his long, red stocking cap, and
there were a few flakes of unmelted snow on it, showing
the temperature of the house.

"*Oui, mon bourgeois?*"

"Champlain, you hear what I have said?"

"*Oui.*"

That was the end of Brissaud's dealings with the half-
breed. He gestured for Champlain to take him out,
turned, looked at the wall where the bullet had scarred
through grayish whitewash. It pleased him. He chuckled.
The chuckle grew. He tilted back his head and shouted.

"Oh-ho! You see thees? You see thees bullet she has
fired?" A moment before there'd been only a hint of
French accent in his speech, but now he sounded like
a gleeful *voyageur.* "You see, *m'sieu le police,* what my
Marie can do with gun? Like so? Thees man stood there"
— he pointed to Survay's position with the stick — "and
my Marie up there, and the gun, without aiming, phoof!
You see how it graze hees shoulder by so much palm
of hand? It is true no woman in all North shoot like
my Marie. Sometam I, *Père* Brissaud, will let her shoot
pine nut from my head in pitch dark room."

He kept jerking his head back with minor bursts of
laughter, stamping his way back to the big chair which
he turned to half face the fire. He sat down, one forearm
on the table, the diamond-willow stick upright in the

other hand. He spoke to Flynn.

"My Marie has tol' me of you, *m'sieu*. Sit down, if you please. Here, at my right, so the firelight may shine on you. My eyes are not the hawk's as once they were."

It seemed natural for Flynn to do what Brissaud said. The man commanded without seeming to command. It was one of the marks of his personality. Minutes ago, before the man appeared, Flynn had hated him because of Marie. Now he'd almost forgotten it. Brissaud sat erect, his shoulders against the straight, carved back of the chair, grayish hazel eyes meeting Flynn's. He nodded the way men do when they've been confirmed.

"So, you are a sergeant in the Mounted Police. Your kind does not give up. You sit there, with nothing showing on your face, no anger, no resistance. You have seen your prisoner leave. Punished in our way. But you have not given up. You sit there because you must. You wait your time. Ha! . . . thees I can see in your eyes, *m'sieu*. But today is today, and tomorrow is something else. This poor bushwhack killer you will still follow to the last frozen mile of the North to find his bones, to cross him off your police book."

"I could arrest you for that," Flynn said, jerking his head at the door by which Survay had left.

"Did I hear right? That you could arrest me?"

"Yes, I could arrest you."

"Technically, as you say, you could arrest me. But to take me out. That would be the problem, no? To take me through the stockade. To take me *outside*." His eyes flashed, and with one of his unexpected changes of mood he tilted his head and laughed. The laugh was stentorian, amazing. He seemed delighted with this visitor of his. He beat the table with fist and forearm until it shook

151

along its massive length. Then he stopped, heaving for breath, and wiped the outer corners of his eyes.

"*Dieu!* Alone he would do thees. *Magnifique!* And I believe you, *m'sieu.* I believe you are such a man of your word that you would try. Against these walls, these stockade, these forty men of mine now here." He had fallen into the French accent but, as the excitement ran out, he spoke careful English again. "No. You must not let youth and bravery carry you so far. No man will take me from this valley of mine. This land I love. This *horizon du nord.* No man. No thousand men. Not while I breathe, *m'sieur le police.* You perhaps suspect me? You think I would send this man to kill your poor trapper for the few mink he caught? No. I would not. Not *Père* Brissaud."

Marie had been standing by the great fire, her attention hanging onto every word of Brissaud's, every inflection of his voice. When he stopped, she crossed the room on soundless moccasins and stood beside Brissaud's chair. Light from the fire struck across her face and raised glints of color from her hair. It was the first since Assumption that Flynn had seen her without hood and parka, and she was lovelier than ever. She wore a dress of soft-rubbed, cream-colored buckskin with fringes and intricate beadwork. Some squaw had probably spent the better part of a winter making it. The skirt was cut short, like a young girl's, and it fit her with tailored smoothness, accentuating her slim waist, the lines of her body just reaching the fullness of womanhood. At sight of her, on the trail, Flynn had noticed her hair, but now, with the parka hood gone, he could see the masses that covered her shoulders.

Brissaud looked up at her and moved one elbow so she could sit on the arm of the high, mahogany chair.

He laid his hand on her waist. Her waist was so slim, his hand so large.

Brissaud said to Flynn: "And you would have to get me away from my Marie, too. You would fight for your poor old *Père*, would you not, *ma chérie?*"

"Of course."

"Oh-la! Then I would need no others. Have you seen her, *m'sieur le police,* with her dog whip and pistol both? Ah, that is the sight for a man! A woman for Brissaud's heart. A woman of the North!"

Brissaud liked to talk, and he was the kind of a man Flynn could have listened to with pleasure were it not for Marie's sitting on the arm of his chair, his hand resting possessively on her. He heard only part of the things Brissaud said as he talked on and on. Moose Rambo had left, returned, and now was standing with his back to the fire. He was smiling, as though he knew exactly what was eating through Flynn's brain.

After half an hour Brissaud stood up, excusing himself, calling Louis Champlain, who took Flynn up some stairs along an unheated hall to a room in one of the long, dark wings of the building. The room they entered was dark with only a little glow of arctic twilight finding its way through a tiny, parchment-covered window. Champlain groped, located a grease-dip lamp, and lit it.

"Your stove, *m'sieu,*" he said, pointing to a little sheet-metal heater. "Would you lak me to start fire?"

"I'll manage."

Champlain left him, and Flynn looked around. There were two rooms separated by an arch. Sitting room and bedroom. The furnishings were split log, willow, woven rawhide, but all in good taste and comfortable. The one item from outside was a sepia print of Saint Teresa in a gilt frame.

The room was cold, but Flynn still wore his mackinaw. He sat down in a woven-willow rocker, stretched his feet, and realized for the first time how tired he was. Fatigue was an ache in his muscles. He closed his eyes.

He fell asleep without realizing it. When he awoke, he had to drag himself through several layers of consciousness, shaking the buzzing sound from his ears. No one else was in the room. The grease dip was burning down to a low, red flame, so evidently he'd been asleep for a couple of hours. He listened. The big house was silent and, if there were sounds in the winter twilight outside, they failed to penetrate the thick, axe-hewn logs.

Flynn got up and glanced down the hall. No one was there. He came back, added a chunk of hard tallow to the grease dip, and built a fire in the sheet-metal stove. The pitchpine kindling burned with a quick, hissing flame like kerosene, turning the metal white hot and enabling him to melt water from the ice in a brass pitcher. He stripped, took a sponge bath, then put his clothes back on.

A bath! . . . the Mounted Policeman's ultimate luxury. The soap was brownish Castile. The towel he found was rough as a file. He beat his arms for warmth. He was Flynn once again! Let him get a fresh start and look on his situation from a proper distance.

He didn't dare let Survay escape or die, because he'd probably be the only witness against *Père* Brissaud. He'd been gone a couple of hours. There was still time to catch him, get him down to Fort Campbell where Constable Nevers would keep him in jail, and let Flynn return to complete the job which was . . . ?

He stepped into the hall, closed the door. It was windowless, dark. He groped his way, counting fifty-four steps, then there were some stairs. He descended, found a door, opened it. It led outside. There was a flat wall of snow, high as Flynn's waist. No one had gone out that way for weeks.

He stood contemplating the stockade enclosure. All was quiet. No movement or sound. There seemed to be nothing to stop him. But why should he leave? He had come willingly. Not at gun point. It was his dream come true. Flynn — of the Thousand Smokes!

At any rate he wanted a private look around. He was in no mood for more sleep. He went forward. He half expected to be challenged at that moment, but the night retained its winter stillness. There was a triangular area between two wings of the building. Beyond he could see a criss-cross of paths. He took long, unhurried strides, reached a packed pathway.

"No, *m'sieu!*" It was Louis Champlain. He came, very casually, from the shadow of the log house behind him. "No, *m'sieu.*" He rattled the lever of his rifle in warning. "Go no farther." Champlain had been standing, letting him pass within a couple of strides. He advanced now, an old-fashioned rifle under his arm. "I am sorry, *m'sieu le police.*" He sounded almost apologetic. "You are not to leave. Perhaps it would be bes' if you stay in your room, *m'sieu.*"

In other circumstances Flynn would have been pleased with this Louis Champlain. He had courtesy and authority in perfect mixture, both unshakable. It was expected in a policeman. He'd learned to appreciate it.

"Ever think of joining the Mounted?" Flynn asked.

"I am French! Is not your Mounted Police formed to

fight the French? Fight half-breeds? And rob both for thees Scotch your railroad bring in?"

"I suppose Brissaud told you that."

"Perhaps, and perhaps not. You would not want me to talk of *mon bourgeois* behin' hees back."

It occurred to Flynn that the big *voyageur* was getting the better of it. A gun always adds weight to the spoken word.

"You will go back, please," said Champlain.

"Right! And I'll not cause you any more trouble tonight."

Champlain nodded seriously, seeming to take him at his word. He did not even follow Flynn to the door.

Chapter Twelve

Flynn climbed the stairs. Light reflected faintly, showing the way. Once in the hall he saw that his door was open, and the light came from his own lamp. A shadow moved across the light and recognition jolted him. It was Marie. He paused in the open doorway, looking at her. She had poured two cups of strong green tea from an earthenware pot and, sensing him there, she turned and smiled.

"Your tea," she said, not even appearing to notice the snow that encrusted his moccasins.

"How did you know I'd be back?" he asked, giving his voice an easy, laughing sound as he stripped off parka and mackinaw.

"I only guess. Women, they say, always guess right about when men come back."

He took the cup. Its contents were scalding. He put it down again.

"*Père* does not have company often. Oh-lon-la! You should see the feast he has ordered! Four women cooking, *m'sieu.* I know how hungry you must be, but I could not spoil your appetite with food. So, for now, nothing but the tea. You know that here, among our French *voyageurs,* among our men of the great rivers, one is judged sometimes by the size of his appetite, and you must uphold the glory of the police."

"I suppose *Père* eats more than any of the others."

"Of course."

"Then I dare say I'll drive him from the table in disgrace."

"It will not be so, *m'sieu!*"

Her eyes flashed when she said it. She was feline in her defense of the man, even when joking like that. He looked down at her, at her lovely young face. It was impossible that there was anything between her and *Père* Brissaud. She was as fresh and good as the spruce forest outside. He realized it was the failing of lonely men like himself to idolize women, but still he knew he was right about Marie.

The easy humor had left his face. Seconds passed with no sound except for the snapping of wood in the sheet-metal stove. She knew he wanted to say something and tried to help him.

"Yes?"

"Who are you?"

"I am Marie."

"Marie . . . who?"

"I call myself Marie Brissaud because a girl must have two names, so the blackrobes say."

"Are you Brissaud's wife?"

She shook her head, whispered. "You have not heard? He has a wife, or what is called a wife, although she has been among the living dead these twenty-five years."

He wanted to ask her more, how she felt about *Père* Brissaud. It wasn't easy. "You love him as a daughter?"

"Yes."

"And more than that?"

"Perhaps," she whispered. Her brows were drawn to-

158

gether, thinking about it. "Perhaps I love him a great deal."

"Where are you from?"

"You ask now as a policeman?"

He took a deep breath. "No, I'm sorry. I'm asking as a. . . ." He didn't know how to finish. "I'm just asking."

"I do not know. I have been here for . . . long tam."

"Were you too small to remember?"

"I was a little girl. I live . . . across Grande Portage, down great river. I hated them!" She spoke the last words between her teeth. "Do not ask me, *m'sieu.*"

"I'm sorry." He knew she remembered a great deal more and had spent a long time trying to forget. "Who brought you here?"

"Do not ask me!" She was almost crying. "Do not ask me questions. Why must people ask me questions? Once I feared *Père*, and now I love him. That is all that matters."

He reached, seized her by the arms. He expected her to resist. She was passive in his hands. She waited, looking up at his eyes with a strange, unfathomable expression. "How do you love him?" She didn't answer. She didn't even seem to hear. Her eyes were unchanged. He shook her back and forth. "Tell me! You're not really in love with him, that old man . . . ?"

"Please!"

She hadn't answered the question, and it was like an admission of something more. It was like an old wound being reopened, a bullet that lays embedded and starts aching with the cold dampness of spring, like Uncle Frank's wound from Little Round Top. He was still holding her by the arms. It gave him a true sense of her size. Her arms were soft beneath their covering of rubbed

159

buckskin. He'd lived too long in a raw land of men. He'd forgotten what a girl was like. Rediscovery was a shock.

"Please!" she whispered. "Your hands. You are hurting me." She wasn't the same girl as out on the trail. It was impossible to imagine her swinging a dog whip. "Please!"

He didn't relax his hands. If anything, his fingers sank deeper. He drew her toward him. She came willingly, like iron to magnet. She was close, looking up at him. The top of her head was barely even with his neck. He was conscious of her hair, the fresh spruce odor of it. She tilted her head down, denying her lips to him, though her hands clung to the front of his rough, wool shirt. It was like that for the time required to breathe a dozen times.

"Please!" There was a new intensity, an urgency in her whisper. She was looking beyond him at the open door. "Please! Your tea. It will be cold, *m'sieu.*"

He let her go. She stepped back, high color rising in her cheeks. A wisp of hair was across her forehead, and she brushed it aside, still looking at the door. Flynn saw *Père* Brissaud standing there, looking at him, his face gaunt and savage.

"*M'sieu!*" Brissaud addressed Flynn, his voice an explosive whisper. "You are my guest, *m'sieu.*"

Brissaud meant he'd have killed Flynn otherwise. He drove the diamond-willow stick to the floor, started on as though expecting to hurl Flynn from the room, but Flynn stood his ground. Marie leaped between them, faced Brissaud.

"Please, *Père!* It was my fault. I came to him here. And I could have gone or called for your help."

Père came to a stop. He heard her. It took a while

for the words to register. He filled his lungs with a mighty breath and slowly exhaled. "So. *Ma chérie.* Sometam the old forget."

"You are not old . . . !"

"Sometam the old forget. I should not be here . . . unless you call for me."

"I didn't mean that."

"It was well said. So well said I would not have you change it, now that you have stop' being truthful and would again be kind. I have always known that sometam you would choose. You are wild and free, lak the creatures of the forest. I would no tame you if I could . . . any more than you tame those wolf-dogs of yours."

The emotions of *Père* Brissaud had swung from anger to sentimentality in that short space. Light from the grease dip shone on a tear that followed a crooked course down his cheek. He turned away with one gold earring jiggling, making quick reflections, and backed into the hall.

"Forgive me, *ma chérie,* that I forget you are young."

"Wait, *Père!*" She ran after him down the hall. "Wait . . . !"

Flynn could hear her pleading with him as the diamond willow faded away in the castle's vast silence. Perspiration had gathered along his hairline. He wiped it away with the heel of his palm, noticed that his hand was shaking. He sat down, lit an English oval cigarette, smoked, drank tea. It helped him. He wondered about the feast Brissaud had planned.

The fire died, and his open door let in a chill draft from the hall. He didn't close the door or rebuild the fire. A man gets so he doesn't feel right in a warm room after he's spent years along the unmapped rivers and frozen sled trails of the North. An hour must have passed before Louis Champlain came to the door and said: "The food is ready, *m'sieu.*"

Then *Père* was going to stage his banquet after all! Flynn followed Champlain down the stairs to the big room. A dozen candles were burning in a master holder, shining on the brass, silver, and china spread across the great table. Only five places had been set. After hearing it called a feast, he'd expected something more. His eyes swept the room and came to rest on Brissaud, Moose Rambo, and Marie who stood by the fire.

"So you are here, *m'sieu le police!*" Brissaud cried. "We have been waiting for you." There was no sign that he harbored the least resentment. He bent, lifted a decanter that had been heating by the fireplace, and filled a heavy bronze tankard with steaming liquid. Then he lifted his own tankard and pronounced a toast. "*Ma'mselle! Monsieurs!* To the fire on the hearth and to the fire that burns in all of us, stronger than the cold of the North."

The words could have had a double meaning. Flynn met his eyes without being sure. The four men lifted their tankards in unison. The liquor was a mixture of brandy, water, honey, and spices. Flynn was not used to drinking except for the occasional Scotch at headquarters, and it had an impact that drove the breath from his lungs. He fought to inhale. He glanced around. Moose Rambo had downed his drink without a change of expression and was watching him, black whiskers parted, showing his yellowish teeth in a smile.

Brissaud slapped his hands. It was signal, and squaws came from the kitchen, carrying platters of roasted meat. The smell of it after his long fast made Flynn's knees weak. The liquor hadn't helped. It sent a quivering heat through his veins, but the effect was like paralysis.

"Another?" Moose Rambo asked, once more lifting the decanter from the hot stones.

His action was a challenge and, because Flynn disliked the man, he accepted it. "Sure," he said, controlling the lines of his face. "One more." He held out the bronze cup, let Rambo pour it full. He noticed that everyone was watching. He lifted it, drained it.

"Oh-ho!" Brissaud roared, stamping his moccasins and hammering with his diamond-willow stick until dust rose from between the floor planks. "Behol' this policeman! He is *un homme du nord* also! Still will *Père* Brissaud drink you two for one. Two for one, *m'sieu le police!* And eat! . . . *that* shall also be two for one."

The second drink only added a little to the first, making the drugged feeling settle more heavily, like a dull barrier separating Flynn from the rest of the room. He had no actual memory of sitting down at the table. He merely realized that he was there, seated next to Brissaud who was at the head, with Moose Rambo at his left. Champlain sat beyond Rambo with Marie at the foot. The table had been intended for fourteen or sixteen so, although one side was vacant, the spaces between them were wide, and distance was an excuse for Brissaud to make full use of his voice when he talked.

Occasionally Brissaud paused to ask a question, and Flynn always managed to hear it, despite the buzzing the liquor had left in his ears, and to answer it in spite of the numbness of his body. There was meat on his plate. Young caribou loin roasted over an open flame, tender and delicious. He ate, and the food started bringing him back to normal. He looked around, actually noticing things for the first time.

There was no uniformity in the service. Three of the dishes were china, extremely old with vitreous surfaces patterned by minute cracks. The rest was silver or silver plate, with some of the big platters in bronze. Even Flynn, who took little interest in such things, could tell that the metallic ware had both taste and antiquity, a combination that would make it prized by the shops and museums of the great cities.

There was enough food on the table for twenty. In addition to the caribou roast, which was easily a quarter of the animal, the squaws had carried in dishes of roasted grouse, roasted fish with wild cranberries, a loin of bear meat, boiled new peas, and French endive, white, thick as rhubarb, grown in cellar darkness, a specialty of fine hotels. Bread was bannock, grayish and hard.

Père Brissaud ate in huge mouthfuls, building a heap of rib bones on the table before his plate. He was talking. ". . . On this very table, *m'sieu le police!* This table, the table of the *Grande Rendezvous* in Fort William . . . I have tol' you already? *Oui.* Here again, where it should be, among trapper and river men, beyond railway and road, at our *horizon du nord.* I have heard my father tell of it . . . this table. A partner of the Great Company he was, *m'sieu.* In the great days. Like kings they traveled, those partners of the Nor'west. From Montreal and across the Great Lakes by canoe when it was still a wild land of *les sauvages.* Land of the Huron and the Chippewa. While from the Athabasca, the Slave, the Churchill, and all the rivers of the North came factor and *voyageur* to meet at the rende z vous at Fort William on *Lac Supérieur* . . . to feast and drink at this very table as we feast and drink tonight.

"Now is the south country chained and enslaved, with

fences holding the lands of Manitoba, with railroads cutting the high mountains where MacKenzie saw the Pacific. But here, in this valley north of the three rivers, it will remain as *le bon Dieu* made it, and here will I live out my time. No dog on leash is your *Père* Brissaud. Nor that girl, Marie, who will perhaps rule this Valley of the Thousand Smokes after me."

Marie laughed. "You will live to be two hundred years old, as the stories about you say."

He lifted one hand, let it fall. "No, Marie, I look as I always have. As sometime the bark of a tree seems solid like eternity while the core crumbles red."

A door opened, letting in a draft that set the candles to dancing. It closed again, and an Indian almost covered by a blanket capote came dragging moccasins across the floor.

"Munimuk!" *Père* Brissaud cried. "So at last it is you."

Munimuk kept walking until he reached the table. There he turned and pulled the capote back letting candle light fall across his face. He was old, older than a man could guess. His skin had become smoky black. It was wrinkled, like the skin of a withered potato. His hair, turned clam-shell gray, was stringy, pulled in braids that hung forward across each shoulder. He picked up a plate that had been left for him, chose a few tougher pieces of caribou, then retreated, and sat cross-legged on the floor.

After a time he started to talk: "It was in the year of *muche meenisa* when chokecherries rotted on the bush, *oh keche ookemawit!* The year of *uniska kinapitik* when I could count on fingers of *quatre* hands the white men north of *trois rivières.* . . ."

He rocked to and fro, eyes almost closed, chanting

his words, a garble of English, French, and Cree, telling the story of the North, of the white men, of the Crees and their cousins, the Assiniboines. He told of the great fur brigades when pirogues, York boats, and canoes were as many as the ducks of autumn, breasting the great rivers. He chanted on and on, scarcely noticing the meat on his plate, telling of the Valley of the Thousand Smokes, of how it had been sacred to the Indian's religion, believing it was the birthplace of the aurora which was the dance of the warriors who had died in battle, fighting those eaters of roasted snakes, the Sioux. He told more, of the traders who swapped muskets for beaver, and of other traders who traded only the devil-in-a-bottle that made a Cree kill his brother, and of those traders who brought smallpox that wiped out villages.

"But there were also great white men, greatest of all was you, *oh keche ookemawit,* you who drive away those devil-traders like squaw drive mice from teepee."

Père Brissaud rose and acknowledged the praise, but the ancient Indian was not through. He sat erect, forefinger raised, and with something like youthful fire in his eyes. "*Wache!* I come to tell you more. Of *kinapikwa.* Of snake! It is well that white man learn wisdom of the Cree, but when the Cree learns wisdom of white man, that is not well. *Muche-muche.* You savvy?"

Unexpectedly Moose Rambo struck the table with his fist, a booming blow that made dishes jump. "Good Lord! Do we sit here all night and listen to this?"

"*Wache!*" cried the Indian, rising.

"How often do we get a visitor from outside?" Rambo asked. "The Mountie. . . ."

"You are a *kinapikwa,* too, oh black-whisker. You. . . ."

"Be quiet," Brissaud thundered, "both of you!" He

166

turned to Munimuk, "What sort of riddle do you speak, old man? What's this about Crees learning the wisdom of white men?"

Munimuk was on his feet. His capote was tossed back, his skinny forefinger still pointed up. "Kamwit. He I talk of. Kamwit who would be chief, perhaps, if I did not live, and if my grandson, Wapinaw, did not live. Kamwit who learn to read the ink tracks that talk in white man's village at *École de* Beaupré. Kamwit I talk of who has learned so much he thinks bad Cree is better than good white man."

Moose Rambo squeaked back in his chair, roosted on its hind legs, hooked thumb in his sash, and laughed. There was a jeering twist to his lips. He'd have spat had he not been at the table, and he was almost spitting anyway. Instead he speared a piece of bear meat with a vicious drive of his fork and paused to speak before thrusting it in his mouth. "So I suppose young Kamwit's going to kill us all!"

Munimuk went on, ignoring Rambo for the moment. "We have been happy. Crees . . . *voyageurs* here since years of *noot akutawin keskwawin.* As you say, the cold and hungry madness. Since days when you build this house. Since days when you come and drive away trader with devil-in-bottle. It has been good for Cree here. Plenty food, plenty gun, trap, cloth, plenty medicine to cure sick eyes. *Kuk-ap-attis!* Now he comes. Young man filled with thoughts from white man's school, to breathe hatred into more young men." He pointed his skinny finger across the table at Rambo. "You know, *ka-ke!* You know because you are one that come many times, talk to Kamwit. You know what he does, so why have you not spoken?"

"Get your dirty hand out of my face."

"*Wache!*"

"Enough!" Brissaud said. "We will not quarrel at table."

"*Wache!*" Munimuk suddenly stood up.

"Sit down!"

But the ancient Indian did not sit down. He turned, moved across the floor, dragging his moccasins. He opened the door and stood with the cold air rushing around him, swinging his blanket capote.

"Do not forget! Munimuk has spoken."

He closed the door, taking a long time about it. Rambo let a laugh jerk his shoulders, and his black whiskers parted, showing his teeth in a grin. "*Key-as ke-wina!*" he muttered, naming the man a liar in Cree.

"He is not a liar," Brissaud said. "Wrong, perhaps, but not a liar." Brissaud sat with elbows propped on the table, staring off at the fire. "You have visited Kamwit?"

"I've seen him," Rambo muttered. "I see them all. You haven't been getting around well lately. Somebody had to do it."

"Of course. Kamwit is a troublemaker. What is he up to?"

"Nothing. The young men like to gather at his lodge and hear him talk about Montreal. It's made old Munimuk jealous. He's afraid the young men will want Kamwit for chief instead of that lazy Wapinaw. You can't believe there's any chance of Crees warpathing after all these years!"

For the first time in half an hour Flynn broke his silence. "Trouble in paradise!" he said softly.

Marie let her fork drop to the table, and she cried: "No, *m'sieur*, there is not!"

Chapter Thirteen

Tom Flynn went to sleep at almost the same instant he stretched out in his spruce-filled bunk. When he awoke, he knew that five or six hours had passed. He got up in the cold, dark room, groped for the water pitcher, learned that ice had once more formed. He fumbled through the dark, managed to pull out the parchment-covered window, scraped snow from the ledge, and ate it. The liquor had left him thirsty.

Below him the timbered valley stretched away and was lost in the mist. Nothing moved. No lights down by the river. Snow quenched the burning in his throat; he had no desire for more sleep. He sat down in the woven-willow chair, lit and smoked English oval cigarettes.

He'd been there perhaps an hour when the thump of Brissaud's diamond-willow stick could be heard moving along the hall. Brissaud was walking faster than usual, and for that reason Tom Flynn waited till he was past and then followed to the hall. Brissaud was talking to somebody. He sensed it was Marie even before hearing her voice in answer. They were speaking French, and it was hard for him to catch the words. Kamwit was mentioned. A door opened. It closed cutting off their voices, and he knew they were descending to the big room. He followed, waiting a moment before letting himself through to the head of the stairs.

Brissaud and Marie were crossing below, dimly revealed by the ruddy glow of logs crumbling to coals in the fireplace. A man was waiting for them, an Indian. In the half darkness he could tell nothing more about him than that.

"Where is he?" Brissaud asked, and the Indian answered something that brought a syllable of annoyance from Brissaud. He turned to Marie, still speaking French, and said something about keeping a watch on the Mountie's room.

She turned without a word and ran with long, soft steps across and up the stairs. By then Brissaud and the Indian were out of sight. Flynn stood where he was, quite still, shoulder resting easily against the wall. He'd have let her pass, but she saw him and came to a stop.

"You!"

"I sleep badly in strange beds. Especially when there's excitement in the house."

He moved toward her, and she started to back down the stairs. He reached, took hold of her arm. It was different from the time before. She twisted with unexpected feline strength and was free from his grasp.

"Go back to your room!"

"No, ma'am."

"Go back!"

He smiled at her, an easy, thoughtful smile breaking the hard lines of his face. There was a gun at her waist. He expected the movement, and it came. Her small hand swung up, weighted by a .45 caliber Colt. It was a long-barreled gun, designed as an Army pistol down in the States, heavy, and though she knew how to use it, it took her longer to draw than otherwise. His hand closed, preventing her from cocking it. She ripped back and forth, but her strength was no match for him.

He twisted the gun from her, half cocked it, glanced at it. It was a six-shooter, but there were only five loads, that suicide chamber under the hammer being empty. With a deft movement he rolled the cylinder so the empty one was next in line, then he handed it back to her.

"Put it away where it belongs."

She snatched the gun from him, revolved it on her trigger finger using what an American would call a "road-agent's spin," and once again pointed it at his heart.

"Now go upstairs!"

"You devil!" he whispered with a touch of admiration in his voice.

"I mean it, *m'sieu*. I do not want to shoot you, but you must go upstairs."

"No. I think I'll let you pull the trigger."

"You will make a mistake by laughing at me."

He walked toward her, and she backed away, keeping the same distance between them. She finally came to a stop with her back to the door through which Brissaud and the Indian had disappeared.

"No!"

He watched her intently but kept coming. There was no cartridge under the hammer. He wondered if she'd pull the trigger. Then he saw her eyes and knew that she wouldn't. He stepped around her, reached for the door.

"Ver' well!" She let the gun swing down and opened the door herself. "You don't care much for your life, do you?"

"I like my life a whole lot. I just knew you wouldn't shoot the gun."

"Then you knew more than I did," she whispered.

The door opened into a big, drafty hall. A grease dip sat on a bench, its flame blowing bright and dim. Beyond was an open door and the arctic twilight. Someone was coming, moccasins creaking on the packed snow. It was Brissaud with the half-frozen body of a man in his arms. For the moment he did not notice Flynn and the girl. He breathed from effort and laid the man on a split-log bench. It was Survay.

Brissaud stepped back, and his eyes came to rest on Flynn. "Ah! You have the good nose for blood, *m'sieu*." He shrugged. "I was hoping you would not know."

"Why?"

"Because you of the police suspect so many things, so many lying things."

Flynn walked over and looked down at the dead man. He'd been hit on the left side near the base of the ribs by a big bullet, over two hundred grains and soft nosed for it had obviously started to expand when it struck his heavy, buckskin parka then crushed a couple of ribs like a sledge, angled up to pass entirely through, coming out beneath the left armpit. The moccasin and sock of his left foot had been removed, leaving it bare.

"Big bullet," Flynn said in his impersonal, policeman's voice.

"The Thirty-Five Winchester is indeed a big bullet, *m'sieu*." It could have been a Thirty-Five or any of those grizzly calibers. Brissaud went on: "He was given his gun, and a single cartridge. If he chose to do the easy thing and use cartridge on himself . . . so. It is his privilege."

Flynn made no comment, though he knew it was not suicide. There were some powder-burn markings but only the light ones that a bullet carries across moderate

172

distances. He'd seen suicides. Too many of them. Calibers like an old-time .35 throw so much flame from burning black powder that they often ignite clothing at short range. Somebody wanted to get rid of Survay. Dead men don't testify.

Flynn turned away. He noticed that the Indian was standing in the door, watching him in his quiet way. He was in his middle twenties, unusually squat and heavy set for a Cree. His eyes were quick, narrow, intelligent.

Flynn said: "You're Kamwit."

It was just a guess, but the man was Kamwit all right, the troublemaker that Munimuk had been telling about. Kamwit didn't confirm or deny his identity. He merely stood flat footed on his moccasins, waiting.

"Where did you find him?" Flynn asked.

"No savvy." Kamwit shook his head and made a negative sign with crossed fingers. "No savvy English much."

"You savvy English all right. Or was Latin all they taught you at *École de* Beaupré? Where'd you find him?"

"No savvy." Then Kamwit started to answer the question jerkily, Indian fashion, in chopped-off sentences. "Me, squaw, both in lodge. Eat. We hear it. Bang! Like big rifle, half mile away. *Waniskak.* Go out. Look. So I fin' him. He like this." Kamwit indicated a man lying in a half-curled posture. "So. Rifle I find in deep snow. So I hitch dogs and bring in on toboggan."

Kamwit might have been lying or not — anyway there's no trying to cross-question an Indian.

Moose Rambo was there. He approached with his usual, heavy-legged confidence, turned the dead man over, pulled up the parka. When Flynn went back to the big room, Rambo followed. "Think the Indian shot

173

him?" Rambo asked.

"No."

"Shot himself?"

"Of course not."

"I didn't think a Mountie would fool that easy." He had something in his hand, tossed it over. It was a lump of lead. "Here. I found this hanging between his shirt and parka where it came out on the right side. Thought maybe you'd want it for exhibit A."

It was a deformed bullet. Flynn let it roll over in his hand, appraising its weight. It had mushroomed to twice its original diameter, but the base was still round, and he could tell it was a larger diameter than a .35 Winchester. Heavier, too. It was a .405 or a .45-70. Either caliber was common enough in that country.

"What does Brissaud shoot?" he asked.

"You don't think that *Père* would do his own killing?"

"What does he shoot?"

"Generally a .405 Winchester. He has a dozen or more guns."

"Where does he keep them?"

"In the Eagle's Nest."

Flynn turned and climbed the stairs. It wouldn't prove anything anyway, but it was his job to find out. The Eagle's Nest was a gabled room perched on the top of the house. There were no coverings on its windows, leaving it cold as outside. A telescope on a tripod occupied the middle. There were books along one wall, calf bound and extremely old. At the other side of the room were the rifles in an open case.

He took them out one by one — a .25-20, a couple of slide action Remingtons in .30-30 caliber, an old-time H. B. C. fusil, and two lever-action Winchesters, both new .405s. He sniffed the muzzles. One still carried the banana oil smell of solvent, but the other had recently been fired.

The circumstances were enough to warrant arresting old *Père* and taking him to Fort Campbell. If he was guilty, he'd probably confess. Emotional types like *Père* don't keep secrets very well. If he wasn't guilty, then getting him away might save his life. Actually Flynn was less convinced of his guilt now than he had been before. The whole thing was too pat, too nicely tied up and delivered. Moose Rambo and Kamwit were up to something, and it didn't take a great deal of imagination to guess what it was.

There was a box of .405 cartridges in the case. He checked the gun to make sure it was loaded, carried it with him to his room where he put on his mackinaw and parka. Then he went back downstairs. Moose Rambo was still standing with his back to the fire. He was watching.

"Going somewhere?"

"I'm arresting *Père* Brissaud."

Rambo nodded. He made a pretense at sadness, but there was an elated glint in his eyes. "And Marie?" The man wanted her left at the castle, that was obvious.

"I have no charge against her," Flynn said. He gestured with the rifle. "You took my service pistol, remember?"

Rambo nodded. He felt along the mantel, found it, handed it over. Flynn slid it back in the holster.

Rambo said: "This is tougher on me than you might think, Mountie. *Père* Brissaud is my best friend. He saved my life one time . . . I guess I told you. I wouldn't want him to know I'd practically turned him over to you."

"And you wouldn't want Marie to know."

"Her, either. So I'd like to have you do me a favor. Toss that gun on me and back me through the door."

"You go to the devil."

Flynn walked on, entering the hall, leaving Rambo standing. Kamwit stood near the dead man. No sign of Brissaud or Marie. There was a gun strapped just beneath the skirt of Kamwit's parka. His hand started toward it, stopped. His eyes kept shifting from Flynn's face to the muzzle of the .405 Winchester.

"Where did he go?" Flynn asked. "Brissaud."

"In kitchen. Down porch. Nex' door."

Flynn circled him, stepped outside. The sharp, misty air felt good to him. A light was burning in the kitchen, shining around the closed door. He pulled the babiche latch string. The door was iced, and it took a sharp drive of his shoulder to open it.

He stopped, eyes shifting around the room. Light of a grease dip fell on a squaw who was hunched over a stone and sheet-metal stove, coaxing water to boil. Brissaud stood half in shadow a step beyond. He was carrying a gun, and there might have been time for him to draw, but he made no move to do so. He merely looked at Flynn with open surprise.

"This your gun, Brissaud?" Flynn asked.

Brissaud took a stride forward and drew up when he saw the muzzle aimed at him. "Oui, m'sieu. My gun."

"I believe this is the gun that killed that mink trapper."

"No. Not my gun. Not. . . ."

"Stand back."

Brissaud had reared very tall, shoulders back, fire building up in his eyes. Then he conquered surprise and spoke with a voice unusually soft, scarcely more than a whisper. "So. It is that way, m'sieu!"

"Yes. I'll have to put you under arrest."

"You plan to take me out and hang me on your English rope?"

"I'll take you out. That's my job. If you're guilty, maybe they'll hang you. I'm not a judge."

"I see. Your task . . . to arres' the French, the Cree, the half-breed. I think at first perhaps you are different. But no. You are a Mounted Policeman. An Englishman. . . ."

"I'm an Irishman, and your being French has nothing to do with it."

A smile touched Brissaud's lips. He still believed the Mounted Police had been formed for no purpose except to rob his people for the benefit of the railroad emigrants. "Who gave you the gun?" he asked.

"Rambo told me where to find it."

The news jolted Brissaud. He'd evidently had no suspicions of Rambo. The man was second in command, and *Père* had always trusted him. "So. You talk well. Perhaps you are lying to me."

"And perhaps not."

"He'll help take me from this valley? . . . this traitor Rambo?"

"I'll take you out alone."

"Ho! Ho-ho! Ho-ho-ho!" Brissaud tilted his head far back, the laughter booming in successive bursts, each louder and of longer duration than the last. He ended by wiping tears from the corners of his eyes. "So. One tam you said you would take me out . . . alone. And now you are here to do it. You are brave, *m'sieu le police!* Always have I admired the brave. But this time you are also the fool. You will not take me out."

"Put up your hands."

"You said what?"

Brissaud didn't seem to comprehend. He bent forward, diamond-willow stick braced, watching as Flynn drew a set of handcuffs from inside his parka. They swung back and forth, catching the light on their nickeled surfaces. Brissaud hissed in a voice suddenly raw with anger: "You would tak me outside lak thees. Chained lak. . . ."

Brissaud stopped. He was listening. A door had opened into some other part of the house. A draft came through, making the grease dip flutter. Flynn moved, trying to make things out in the shadowy limits of the room.

Marie's voice came, low and deadly: "This time I will shoot, *m'sieu!* Lower the hammer of the gun. Put it on the table!"

He remembered the empty cylinder and kept the rifle in his hands. She was coming toward him, taking form in the shadow, her step light and sure as a lynx cat's. The Colt was in her hand. She raised her voice a trifle: "Put the gun on the table!"

He saw her finger tense on the trigger. Suddenly he realized that this was the second time she had cocked the gun and that would cause the empty chamber to roll past. He started, intending to put down the gun. It was too late. She misinterpreted the movement. Her revolver came to life with a roar and lash of burning powder. The bullet struck between his hand and the rifle stock. There was a pain like white fire, and the gun leaped away from him.

He reeled back. There was a stool behind him. He fell over it. He got to one knee, looked down at his hand. The bullet had scorched skin just over the artery in his wrist and gone on, glancing from rifle stock to inflict a flesh wound. Blood was slowly weighting the sleeve of flannel shirt and mackinaw.

He noticed that the girl had run to him, gun still in her hand. He came around with his good hand and took the pistol from her grasp. The next instant it was dark. The squaw had blown out the grease dip. He could hear the girl feeling along the floor for the pistol. He got to his feet, groped in that direction, ran against the table. Things came to light in the darkness — glow of a fire through cracks in the cook stove, twilight through the open door from outside.

"Marie!" he said. No answer. "Marie!" He hadn't heard her go. There were running moccasins outside, but no one had passed the open door. "Don't be a fool, Marie. I'm giving *Père* a chance to save himself. They're after his hide . . . Rambo and Kamwit. Marie!"

Someone was silhouetted in the door, squat, bowlegged. That was Kamwit. A man shouted a word in French. There was a rifle report. It cut off the sound of his voice, leaving the ringing cold-weather echoes. Too many things were happening. Kamwit was out of sight, inside the door. "Light the lamp!" he said, wondering if the squaw was gone. "Ishwao, the light!"

She didn't answer. Flynn strode to the stove, jerked off a segment of the sheet-iron top. Flame came up, lighting the room. He looked around. Light struck Kamwit's face, giving it more than ever the hue of tarnished bronze. His arms were folded. He was expressionless. "Gone. Factor and young Ishwao, both gone. Just me . . . you. Mebby-so we talk. Savvy?"

"All right. What do you want to talk about?"

Kamwit took his time. Other Indians came to the door, tall, young men, more typically Cree than Kamwit. There were six of them.

"We talk," Kamwit said. "Mebby we help-'em Mounted Police." He could speak English with any white man in the North country, but one would never have guessed it by his terse utterances, his way of filling gaps left by words with the intricate-fingered maneuvers in sign language, hands repeating each thought expressed by his tongue so none of his Cree audience would be left in ignorance.

"I could use a little help," Flynn said.

"Good. *Ka-meyo!* We help. We help catch killer. Survay? No? I see-'em big *bourgeois* kill Survay. I see-'em damn good."

So far Flynn could believe him.

"I see-'em! Testify in white-man court. Swear out warrant. Even Mounted Police must serve Injun complaint. So say big book from Ottawa. Heap savvy?"

Flynn savvied plenty. They'd taught this fellow more than Latin and Shakespeare down at Beaupré. He knew his rights. Of course it might seem to a court just a bit extreme that the big *bourgeois,* one hundred years old, was away over there shooting a mink trapper! "Sure. Me savvy."

Flynn stripped off his parka and mackinaw. His arm was still bleeding. There was a clean dishtowel hanging nearby. He got it, tore wide strips with his teeth, bound the wound. His steps brought him close to the door where the Crees were grouped. "Tie-'em!" he said to one of them, a tall, mean-faced man with frost scars on both cheeks showing he'd traveled far from that tempered valley. While the scar-cheeked man was tying a knot, Flynn was able to see beyond them across the stockade.

Shooting had brought lights up in the cabins, but no

one was coming the half mile to investigate. Closer, though, he caught movement — furtive movement from shadows close to the big house. Kamwit had brought others besides these at the door. The plan was easy enough to read. Kamwit and Rambo would be there to take over when Flynn arrested Brissaud and took him downriver. He acted as though he suspected nothing and asked Kamwit: "Can I depend on you to testify against him in the spring?"

"Sure. Me testify."

"I'll need my dogs and sled."

Kamwit spoke to the tall, scar-faced man: "Wuniskak. You go up dog pens. Tell-'em keep dogs ready."

Flynn nodded as though he was satisfied with everything. He slipped mackinaw and parka back on and started for the inside door.

"You arrest now?" Kamwit asked.

"Right now."

He went through the door and closed it after him. There was a dark segment of hall, after that the big room. He started climbing the stairs. Somebody was following. He spun around and saw Rambo. Flynn waited as the big man climbed slowly.

"What have you decided to do?" Rambo asked.

"I'm taking Brissaud out with me."

"You'll need some help."

"I'll make out."

Rambo took another step, placing himself on the stair just below. His eyes looked narrow and cruel. "You're taking Brissaud. Get that . . . Brissaud."

"Say what you mean!"

"I mean that you're leaving Marie behind."

There was a moment's pause as the two men faced

each other. "I'll do whatever seems best in my judgment," Flynn said.

"I said. . . ." Anger flared through the man, but he checked himself. "Don't make it too tough on yourself. Or on her. I won't have you disgracing her under arrest."

"What if she wants to go?"

He measured his words, letting them fall slowly through tight lips: "Don't try to take her out."

Rambo stood on the same step, powerful legs set after his boatsman habit. His eyes followed as Flynn climbed the stairs.

Chapter Fourteen

Flynn paused in the upper hall. He climbed to the Eagle's Nest. He found his way along the hall. It was getting on toward winter dawn. A glow of amber light came through a parchment window. There was movement.

"Marie! Put the gun down. I know *Père* isn't guilty of murder. It was Rambo and Kamwit. But they have the house surrounded. Our only chance is to get out of here . . . all of us together."

He heard the surprised inhalation of her breath. She took form, one shoulder and the side of her head silhouetted. She came toward him, a lynx-soft tread, gun drawn but not pointed. "Is this another of your tricks? Who surrounds this house?"

"Those men of Kamwit's. Old Munimuk was telling the truth."

She believed him. Brissaud came limping forward to say in his hoarse, booming voice: "What folly is this you would have us believe, *m'sieu le police?*"

"Kamwit and his men are here. Kamwit swears he watched you kill Survay last night. He's waiting for me to arrest you before taking over."

"Ho! So this is how you would make good your boast to arrest me, take me from this valley single-handed. But you are not clever. You are being a fool!"

"The truth doesn't need to be clever." Flynn walked

to the end of the hall, managed to pull the parchment window free, and looked down on the area behind the house. "Come here!"

Brissaud stood for a while, leaning on his diamond-willow stick. Then he came forward, driving it hard, no change on his fiercely cut face. He still believed Flynn was trying to trick him. The two men stood shoulder to shoulder, watching the shadows below. At first there was nothing, then movement became visible. Little movements, the furtive movements of waiting men. Here and there gun metal made reflection in an arctic day that was just starting to gray out the stars. Flynn could sense tension mounting in the old man's rangy body. He veered around on his diamond-willow stick.

"You saw them, Marie?"

"Yes."

"You think . . . ?"

"I think Munimuk was speaking true."

Père needed time to think it over, get used to the idea of treachery after so many years. He commenced talking, to himself more than anyone. "It has been so long. I cannot understand. Why would they come here with their guns? Why?"

"What will you do, *Père?*" Marie pulled his sleeve, trying to wake him from his indecision.

"I will see for myself what they want. I will see for myself whether they have the bravery to face me."

Flynn tried to stop him. "They mean business out there. You'll. . . ."

"*M'sieu!* I, *Père* Brissaud, have known these Crees since they have been papoose on mother's back. I have carried medicine to them when they had the eyelid scale that would make them blind. They would not now raise a gun against me."

"But I just talked to Kamwit. He'll kill you if he decides he has to, though right now he thinks there's a chance of taking over peaceably and not running the risk."

"And so, what would you have me do?"

"You're still under arrest. I'm taking you out. How many white men are there in those cabins by the stockade?"

"Eighteen . . . twenty . . . depending on the traplines, m'sieu."

"That'll be enough . . . if they fight."

"They will fight!"

Flynn once again drew out the handcuffs.

"And what now?" Brissaud asked.

"I'll have to put these on you. I don't want to make Kamwit suspicious."

Brissaud stood straighter, his shoulder muscles seeming to thicken, his head haughty. "And you think that I, Brissaud, who have commanded here longer than you have years would sneak out, like a chained bear, for those Crees to spit at? You think I would show myself thus? No, m'sieu le police. I will walk out, oui, but thus, lak man!"

He wheeled and started away at a long stride, almost forgetting his stiff leg, labored up the narrow stairs to the Eagle's Nest. He came down carrying the rifles, an extra revolver, ammunition, and looked at Marie. "I had forgotten you, chérie."

"What do you mean?"

"It is not right that you should face danger because of me. Perhaps, after all . . . you, m'sieu le police . . . you will tak her through stockade . . . to safety? Then . . . !"

"I am not going outside," Marie said quietly. She chose

one of the rifles, a slide-action .30-30, pumped it, spinning out a cartridge which she caught with a deft stab of her hand and thrust back into the magazine. "There will be trouble? So! I will stay here."

Père was going to command her, then he thought better of it. He shook his head. "No. You would be taking a greater chance than ever to show yourself. Who knows what that Kamwit would do if he captured you? Then, indeed, he would have a hold on Brissaud, no?"

The old man was right. Flynn could see that. He agreed: "Yes, best we stay here and hold the house."

Père smiled with a grim twist of his lips. "So, *m'sieu le police*, you no longer wish to chain me!"

"I dare say you'll do as you please whether I want to chain you or not."

"Oh-ho! At last you have come to understand *Père* Brissaud!" He dropped the heavy .405 Winchester in the crook of his right arm and went to the stairs, looking down on the big room. It was dimly revealed by coals in the fireplace. "Rambo!" he spoke quietly and waited for an answer.

"Don't call Rambo," Flynn said wearily. "He planned this with Kamwit."

"No. No, *m'sieu*, I do not believe. . . ."

"You don't believe anything, do you?"

"Eh . . . so. You have told the truth each time. You tell the truth now. So Rambo is traitor. But Louis Champlain? Where is he? Or do I have no faithful man left?"

There'd been a shot outside while Flynn was in the kitchen, and that might be a possible explanation for Champlain's not coming. Brissaud turned from the door, closed it. He looked at Flynn and over at Marie. "You

186

must forgive me for last night," he said with unexpected softness.

For a moment neither of them understood what he meant.

He repeated: "You must forgive me. For the things I said in your room, *m'sieu.* You cannot understand how much Marie has meant to me. Sometam I have been a great fool. An old fool. I have dreamed it would be so always. I should have known that the young belong to the old only for a short while, and then they go. Youth calls out to youth. It is the way of life."

She came to him. Light from one of the parchment windows struck across her face, reflecting from tears that had filled her eyes. She seized his shirt with one hand, pressed her head against his massive chest. "*Père!*"

"No, my little one." Gently, but with irresistible strength, he pushed her away. "No, my Marie. It is true as I speak, and dreams have nothing to do with it. I am old, and you are young. I could see the first moment that this was the one. This policeman. I am fortunate to have it so. This policeman and not the black-whiskered traitor who wanted you."

"Oh, *Père.* . . ."

"No. No, Marie. Do not deny it. Do not deny anything. I am happy that it is so." It was like saying good bye. "You, *m'sieu le police.* You will be good to her. This trust I give you, now."

She followed him as he started away, opening the door, entering the hall. "*Père*, wait! Where are you going?"

"Stay back! But you, *m'sieu le police* . . . if I die, my Marie have all this. Castle, ivory, shell of pearl from ancient sea, worth great fortune. You I trust. Great

187

riches. For my Marie. You, damn' redcoat police, still you I trust. Swear on honor."

"I swear on my honor."

There was yet laughter in him. "You she maybe give ten percent. Ho-ho! This joke!"

She might have followed, but Flynn, close behind, had a hand on her shoulder. Had he ever touched her? She seemed to warm, and there were shudders of nervousness running through her slim body. It was too dark for him to see her face very well. He thought for a moment she was crying and then recognized it as only the quick, nervous inhalation of breath. He gently moved her aside, walked past, ahead of her into the hall and then down the stairs.

She whispered: "What are you trying to do? Tom . . . you can't go out there too."

It was the first time she had ever called him by name. It did something to him. It gave him a strange, warm feeling of surprise, even then at the brink of danger. He knew that she was concerned for his safety as well as *Père*'s. He should have known after those minutes in his room, but he couldn't believe it was true. It seemed so impossible that this girl could see anything about him to care for . . . impostor, driver of dray wagons. He stopped, looked back at her, silhouetted in the dim light that flickered in the hall. "I'll have to lay down a covering fire for him if they make trouble," he said. "It might save his life."

Brissaud had reached the short entrance beyond the bottom step, limped across it, seized the door, and flung it open. For a few seconds his form was silhouetted in the misty morning light. He filled the door. It was too low for him, and he stooped his head to pass through.

Snow was deep despite the fact that Flynn had twice
waded it. He strode out, ploughing his way, feeling for
bottom with his diamond-willow stick.

Flynn, following, was tense, waiting for a gunshot from
one of the Crees lurking in shadow, even though better
judgment told him it would not be that way. Kamwit
and Rambo hoped to reach their goal easily, without
risking any more murder than they'd committed already.
Flynn stopped just beyond the range of light, watching
Brissaud stride on.

Brissaud drew up at the distance of a dozen paces,
and there he wheeled around, his eyes piercing the shadows. He recognized a couple of the Indians and called
them by name. "Mookawan! You . . . Niska . . . Oowasis!
Why do you come here with your guns and stand outside? Have you not always been welcome in my house?
You and your fathers and grandfathers? I tell you, come
in, and sit on my floor, and eat the good *mejim* with
me!"

Flynn could not see the Indians, but a command from
Brissaud was not an easy one to disobey.

"Come here!" Brissaud shouted in his great voice.

Evidently one of them started to obey, for there was
a voice in Cree ringing across the V-shaped yard ordering
him back. It was a second before Flynn realized the voice
belonged to Kamwit.

Brissaud turned and looked toward the snow shed that
protected the kitchen door. "Kamwit!" he roared. "Kamwit, it is you they have followed here? You who have
led them against me. You, the boy who came to me and
pleaded to be sent to the white man's school at Beaupré."
He took in everyone with a sweeping gesture. *"Wache!"*
he shouted and went on speaking in Cree, pronouncing

189

the words with a practical inflection showing that the language was practically native to his tongue.

He asked them how it would be with the great brigades to the Saskatchewan, if Kamwit and Rambo were to rule from inside the big house, whether there would then be fair trade for their furs? With food, and cloth, and traps to keep them fat and warm through the months of long night? He stopped and waited for an answer. None came, but there was a tenseness that could be felt. The men had heard him and were thinking.

A sharp voice cried out, rattling words in Cree. It was Wuniskak, the skinny man with frost-scarred cheeks. *"He is a lunatic!"* Wuniskak shouted. *"Let him die!"*

Brissaud spun around, tried to locate him. His rifle was waist high. A gun exploded, sending a streak of flame through the deep shadow that hung beneath the kitchen snow shed. The bullet struck Brissaud. He swung part way around. He still held his rifle, but the diamond-willow stick was gone, and lack of it, together with the impediment of deep snow, made him lose equilibrium. He fell, plunging shoulder first, sinking from sight.

Flynn's rifle was ready, but Brissaud, in falling, was brought almost in line. It caused a couple seconds' pause. He sensed movement in the snow shed shadow as the Indian changed position. He pressed the trigger.

He'd fired a .405 before but, though Flynn was a big man, its recoil drove him back against the log wall. He pumped the action, turned back to the door, fired again, instinctively pointing at another powder flash. Guns were exploding from a half dozen directions, their bullets cutting riffles of snow above the place where *Père* Brissaud had gone down, others thudding into wall logs, carving splinters from door planks by Flynn's shoulder.

Flynn braced himself against the gun's recoil and fired back, without aiming, without needing to aim. After enough years of living and sleeping with a gun a man gets so he doesn't need the sights over distances of fifty or sixty yards. An Indian was hit. He let out a high-pitched scream ending in a rattle of breath as one of the big .300-grain slugs smashed the life out of him. Return shots were centered on the doorway now. Marie was behind Flynn, firing the Remington. The muzzle was so close he could feel the burn of powder lashing past his ear. He dropped to the floor, pulling the girl with him.

They were shoulder to shoulder, below the level of deep snow with high-velocity rifle bullets whipping overhead. He touched her shoulder, felt the currents of excitement passing through her.

"They've killed him," she kept whispering to herself. "They've killed him!"

"No. He's alive."

"You're just saying that. I know. I'm not a child. . . ."

"He's alive, I tell you. And he'll stay alive if he'll only keep down."

Shooting had slackened. Only one rifle was left, firing regularly, driving one bullet after another into the snow where Brissaud had gone down.

Flynn came up, peered across the snow, called: "Brissaud!" He took time to stuff cartridges into the magazine. "Brissaud, do you hear me?"

No answer or movement for a second. He had a sickening sensation, a fear that one of those slugs had found him out beneath the snow. He started to call the man again, more loudly, when the man's voice came to him, slightly muffled.

"Yes, *m'sieu.*"

"Crawl this way. Keep down. If they open up on you, I'll be in a position to lay down a covering fire." He waited for Brissaud to answer. "Do you hear me?"

"Of course." Brissaud was breathing with little grunts of effort. "It is thees shoulder. A scratch only. But I would tie heem up."

"Never mind about that. . . ."

"A moment. Then I will get that traitor Kamwit."

"They'll kill you if you show yourself. Keep down and crawl this way."

The man laughed and said: "Ah . . . so."

He was coming toward them, swimming through the soft whiteness, still breathing hard. After four or five yards an Indian noticed a disturbance Brissaud's movements caused in the snow's surface and fired, the bullet kicking snow and driving itself deeply in the wall logs beyond.

Brissaud was not touched, but the bullet angered him. He cursed, lunged to his feet. He wheeled, rifle in his hand, and commenced firing it from his waist. He did it with a practiced rapidity, its heavy recoil not seeming to affect him. Marie and Flynn were up again, blind-shooting toward the Indian ambush. Brissaud was a perfect target, huge, standing there in the light of a growing arctic dawn, but the unexpected hail of bullets put the attackers to cover, and Brissaud, his rifle fired dry, plunged on through the open door.

Flynn hurled the door shut, dropped the bar. Bullets tore the heavy planks, whisked on, filled the air with a whir of splinters. Marie was climbing the stairs. Flynn climbed after her, trying to get Brissaud to follow.

The big man flung him away. "Go upstairs! Do not worry for Brissaud. Brissaud will take care of himself. You, *m'sieu*, have made promise. You have promise to keep her safe, my Marie. Then do it. Their coward bullets cannot hurt *Père* Brissaud."

Flynn left him, climbed the steps, made the girl go ahead of him. Only two guns were still going outside, splitting the door planks. And then those two stopped. It seemed very quiet. From the top of the stairs they could hear Brissaud sliding cartridges through the spring slot of the magazine, muttering to himself as he did so. When that was finished he climbed, still muttering, using his rifle in place of the willow stick.

Light from a parchment-covered window struck him. One sleeve of his gray wool shirt was heavy with blood. Snow had gathered on it, and blood dripped from his fingertips, turning the snow dark red. "A scratch only. It tak more than such a scratch to stop *Père* Brissaud. We cannot delay for such things. I must go to the big room. We must hold that room from them, *m'sieu*."

He lurched away, still driving the rifle to the floor. The wound didn't seem to affect him.

There was more shooting outside now. An occasional bullet could be heard as it thudded into the logs below, but they were no longer shooting at the door or at the house. Some of the guns were at a greater distance. Flynn ripped the parchment from a window and looked out. Snow sheds and crazy-built wings of the big house gave cover to the Indians, hiding them from above, but he could see men crawling up through the river brush. They were *voyageurs*, the French and half-breed inhabitants of the valley at last getting into action.

It was dim, with little light finding its way through

the deep-cleft windows. Brissaud paused only a second, and started down the stairs. There was movement near the rear door, but he did not notice.

They hesitated, two Crees. Glow from the fireplace shone on them, on the rifles in their hands. Marie screamed a warning at *Père* and tried to bring the Remington up, but the big man was in her line of fire. One of the Crees dived for cover, but the other spun and lifted a rifle to his shoulder.

Flynn had not moved from the doorway. He swung his rifle up, fired from the hip. A man needs a little luck with a shot like that, but on the other hand one of those .405 slugs packs the punch of a swinging sledge. The Indian was hit. He was tall but not a heavy man. The bullet doubled him, fairly lifted him from his feet, carried him to the wall. He was limp and momentarily standing still. His rifle turned over in the air and fell with a flat clatter. Then he went down, arms drooping, legs crumpling under him.

His companion was hidden by shadow, and there was no sound. Just the ringing echo left trembling in the wake of the Winchester's concussion. Flynn heard the metallic scrape of a rifle being dragged across the floor. The other Cree had his belly full and was getting out.

Brissaud had not moved since the bullet lashed from Flynn's rifle, only a few inches at one side of his cheek. He stood about two-thirds of the way downstairs, erect, head haughty, neither fear nor anxiety showing on his face.

Flynn slid fresh cartridges in his gun. The air was filled with a stench of burnt powder. A new sound became audible, the sound of footsteps below. A man — a white man. There's a difference in the way a white man walks. Bold, confident — it was Moose Rambo. "Wait!" he said. "Put down your gun."

He came straight to the foot of the stairs, eyes meeting Brissaud's all the way. There he stopped and stood as was his habit, with his powerful legs spread, hands on hips just a few inches from the butts of two Colt revolvers.

"*Père*, you can't stay here. These Indians mean business. You'll have to come with me."

"With you, *M'sieu* Traitor?"

"Traitor?" Rambo acted as though the name shocked and hurt him. He looked beyond Brissaud, at Flynn who was faintly visible at the head of the stairs. "*He* told you that, I suppose?"

"Traitor! You are what old Munimuk said you were, and I was a fool not to listen."

"No, *Père*. I'm not a traitor. You're making the biggest mistake of your life if he gets you to believing that. You're my friend. You're the best friend I ever had. You saved my life once. Men don't forget those things. I've come here to return the favor now, *Père*. To save your life."

"And how would you do thees?"

"I talked to Kamwit. He doesn't want to kill you, but he will if he has to. He's here to take over one way or another. Anyhow, he told me. . . ."

"And Kamwit agreed that I could creep away lak whipped malemute!"

"Don't put it that way. He's giving you a chance. . . ."

"I make no compromise. With Kamwit, with you, with no man. This valley . . . I have been ruler here. It is word I do not like, but I use it now. I have been ruler. I will be ruler until I no longer breathe. You tell your Kamwit that. You tell your Kamwit to cross back through the stockade or else I will hunt him out and kill him with these two hands."

Brissaud descended as he spoke. He was still using the rifle as a walking stick, gripping it by the stock, driving the barrel hard against stair planks. As he approached, Rambo moved back and to one side, keeping his distance, placing Brissaud between himself and the stair door.

It was dark and hard to see. There was only a silhouette of the two men against flames rising from the fire. Rambo had turned, and there was a gleam of blued gun metal in his right hand. He hadn't drawn. He'd merely lifted one of the Colt revolvers in its holster.

Brissaud glimpsed the partly drawn gun and shouted: "You would then draw a gun on me, *M'sieu* Traitor?"

"Stand back!"

"Oh-ho! Ho-ho-ho!" Brissaud laughed, but there was no humor in it. Rather it was a shout of challenge. He stood on the next-to-the-bottom step, head and shoulders tossed back. The rifle was still pointed down, but he had lifted its muzzle a few inches from the stair. At that moment he looked like the giant that Northland fable had pictured him — a man seven feet tall who ran down caribou and killed silvertip bears with his hands. Then he sprang, swinging the rifle.

Chapter Fifteen

Rambo had expected something. He retreated, but Brissaud's length of arm fooled him. The rifle barrel was coming for his skull. He tried to aim the Colt, but there was no time. It caught him across the top of his head, a glancing blow. He reeled and plunged sidewise to the floor. He was down and out of sight, somewhere in shadow beside the stair. A heavy log balustrade ran down that side, protecting him from either of the rifles above.

Père Brissaud paused only an instant after the man went down. Rage and the spirit of combat made him a new man at that instant — the man he'd been when driving the thieves and whiskey traders from that corner of the North. He seized the bottom post of the balustrade, used it to swing himself around.

Rambo had taken the rifle blow and felt for his gun. It was gone. He didn't retreat as Brissaud expected he would. The rifle was still in Brissaud's right hand. He swung it again, but Rambo moved with an unexpected, cat-like quickness inside, taking its force on an upflung arm. Rambo set himself, and his fist came up in a smashing arc, connecting with the point of Brissaud's jaw.

The old man wasn't ready for it. His mouth was a trifle open. The fist snapped his head to one side, spilling gray hair across his face, and he went down like something flung from a catapult, the back of his head banging on the floor. His rifle was gone. His eyes roved, came to rest on Rambo. Old though he was, there were unsuspected resources of energy in his body. He came to his feet, lurched forward, reaching with long arms to grapple with his antagonist. Rambo was still out of sight, in shadow beyond the stair wall.

"Put down the gun!" Brissaud said. "Put it down, *M'sieu* Carcajou. Fight lak man. Like *voyageur*."

Flynn was running down the stairs. He had the .405 in his hands, but shadow and the peeled-pine balustrade made it impossible to aim. Brissaud was lurching ahead, and Rambo's voice came from the shadow. "Stay back! Stay back or I'll pull the trigger."

"You would not. You would not have the nerve, *m'sieu*, to pull trigger on *Père* Brissaud!"

"Stand back."

"No. . . ."

The gun flashed and roared. The bullet was driven at point-blank range. It struck Brissaud, hammered him back. He was off balance, hanging to the stair post with one arm. His eyes were shocked and off focus. He thrust himself away, lurched on, and the gun pounded again, its bullet smashing him through the chest, driving the life out of him. He went down heavily, face first across the rough floor.

Flynn had covered half the distance downstairs when he heard the first explosion. He spun, vaulted the balustrade, and was descending as the second explosion came. Rambo was directly beneath him. Flynn twisted in mid-air, attempting to land on his feet. Rambo sensed him and started back, trying to get out of the way. Flynn had left the Winchester above. He was trying to get the Enfield from its holster as he went down.

Rambo cursed, stumbled, overturning a bench. The Colt exploded once again, wild, driving flame and lead past Flynn's head. There was a bench beneath him. It turned as his feet struck it and flung him off balance, against Rambo's legs. No chance now to get the Enfield. He had to let it fall. The two men clinched, staggered against the wall, and once more the Colt exploded wildly.

They bounded from the wall, both men trying to gain equilibrium. Rambo was heavier, and his close-coupled weight was an advantage. He set his feet, whipped around, tried to press the gun muzzle beneath Flynn's ribs. Flynn seized the hand and thrust it down. Rambo cursed through his teeth. He set himself, ripped the gun loose, brought it around horizontally. Flynn saw it coming. It was like an explosion inside his skull. He had no memory of going down.

It seemed to be a long time — seconds, even minutes — but Rambo was still there, pinned between him and the wall, so no more than a bare second had passed. He acted by reflex, rising, driving a shoulder to Rambo's middle. It took Rambo off balance. His hand struck the wall, springing the gun loose. He made a grab for it, but it fell to the floor, bounded underfoot, was kicked, clattered away across the dark floor. Actually Rambo was better off without it. He could now forget about the revolver and fight the way he knew best — hand to hand, using the brutal tricks of the York boatmen.

He gathered his strength and with a mighty swing of both arms hurled his adversary loose. Flynn was still groggy from the gun blow. He reeled back a step or two, before bringing himself to a stop. The room spun across his eyeballs. He shook his head, trying to clear it. Through the buzzing of his ears he could hear Rambo laugh, a brutal, triumphant sound from deep in his throat.

"This is what you've been looking for, Mountie!"

Rambo set his moccasined feet wide on the floor, and his fist swung to the jaw. It landed like a sledge. Flynn's head went to one side. He tried to catch his balance and sagged forward to his knees. Rambo bounded in, swinging again, but he was too eager, and the blow struck Flynn above the temple.

Flynn seized the arm and hung on with blind, desperate strength. Rambo tore his arm away, leaving half the sleeve of his flannel shirt ripped free in Flynn's hands. He drove another left and right, the blows bounding off Flynn's upraised forearms. Despite the punishment consciousness came back. He knew enough to drive forward, meet Rambo. He clinched, and the two of them reeled to the wall.

The bench was there again to trip him. He fell backward, pulling Rambo atop him. As he fell, he doubled his legs, knees pressing against his chest. Rambo knew every rough and tumble trick of the river, and he realized what his enemy was about. He let go. There was no time. Flynn's legs recoiled, smashing Rambo in the groin.

Rambo was forty or fifty pounds heavier, but Flynn's shoulders were braced, and the trail-hardened muscles of his legs drove him back. Flynn twisted. His hand touched something. Gun metal. His own gun. The Enfield revolver. Police issue. British. A gun he'd never liked much — Colt .44 — there was a gun! He sat up, hand closed on its butt, finger on the trigger.

There was a shadow form silhouetted briefly against the fire. Not Rambo. An Indian. The squat, bowlegged figure of Kamwit. Rifle in his hands. The impression was only momentary. Kamwit's rifle exploded, digging slivers from the floor a couple of feet distant. Flynn fired a fragment of time later. The exchange became rapid and blinding, a succession of shots deafening in the confines of that room.

The rifle stopped, and Flynn pressed the trigger once again. Then once more, realizing as he did so that the Enfield was fired dry. He rolled, rolled over again. His position had been too clearly marked. He struck what he thought was the overturned bench and then realized it was one of the massive mahogany chairs.

He dragged himself to a sitting position, broke the Enfield, its ejector spilling empty cases. He fumbled in his pockets for loose shells and started feeding them in, groping. Punishment had slowed him. He had three of the cartridges inserted, was feeling for more. He suddenly remembered the girl. At the same second he had the impression of a light footstep behind him. He thought of her, even started to say something. Then he knew it wasn't Marie. He flung up one arm and tried to rise. Something struck him.

He was down on his back. He had a vague memory of firing the Enfield, turning, firing again and again, time after time, though part of it had to be dream because there were only three cartridges. He was down with the rough floor under him. For a long time, for an interminable period, he was suspended between waking and sleeping. Thoughts kept revolving through his brain. There were sounds. Indian voices. Moose Rambo. Then Marie — she screamed. And screamed again. . . .

The voice was a knife through the lethargy that coated his brain. He tried to force himself up, but it was no use. He lay on the rough boards, telling himself that he had to wake, that Marie needed him, and the black waves of unconsciousness covered him deeper, deeper. . . .

It seemed to be hours later. He could see the beamed ceiling overhead, revealed bright and dim by shifting fire-light. He started to move, but pain limited him. He lay back, eyes closed, trying to sort the nightmare memories of the minutes before unconsciousness had come. Brissaud had been killed. There had been a struggle with Moose Rambo in the dark, then Marie's scream. Over and over that scream of Marie's came back to him, almost as though she were actually there.

He thrust himself to a sitting position and kept himself in it until he was ready enough to look around. He was still in the big room. There were men gathered around, looking at him. Unfamiliar faces. Half-breeds, French *voyageurs.* He knew them — they were the men of the valley, the men he'd seen fighting their way up from the river.

A short, broad man of fifty came forward to run a rifle in his chest. "Don' try to get up."

Flynn didn't feel particularly like getting up. He held the bench on which he was propped, took seconds to answer. "I won't." His lips were thick and stiff. "What the devil?" he said, pointing to the gun.

"Ha! You ask the devil. Perhaps a man you have long been dealing with, *m'sieu?*"

He knew what they thought. He was a stranger, and it would be natural to blame him for an uprising of the Crees. Right at the moment he didn't feel like arguing. He looked around. The short, arctic day was gone. Light

202

no longer glowed through the parchment windows. A fire had been built and logs, thick through as a man's thigh, were burning themselves out. Considerable time had passed. The short *voyageur* held the rifle tightly.

"Who are *you?*" Flynn asked.

"Toscan. Bateese Toscan."

"Marie. Where is Marie?"

"That I would ask you."

It helped Flynn to sit and talk. He was steadier, and his mind was sorting things to correct order. He looked beyond the muzzle and met Toscan's eyes. "I'm Sergeant Flynn of the Royal Canadian Mounted Police. I came here to arrest a suspect. . . ."

He could see that he was getting nowhere. No matter how reasonable his explanation, this *voyageur* would not believe him.

"What of Brissaud? He is dead. Perhaps you would have us believe you did not kill him."

"Of course I didn't kill him. Moose Rambo killed him."

Toscan started to say something, but a younger *voyageur* became impatient and elbowed him out of the way. He had a red, excited face. He lifted his rifle to gesture as he shouted: "You theenk we do not have eyes, *m'sieu?* We have foun' hees rifle with hair and blood in front sight." He pointed at Flynn's scalp where it was bruised and the hair matted with blood. "It was you he struck, *m'sieu le police.*"

"You say there's hair in the front sight?"

"*Oui, m'sieu.*"

"Take another look at it and see if it's more like mine or Rambo's."

"It is yours!" He stopped waving the rifle, brought it down, banging its steel-shod stock on the floor planks.

"Now perhaps you will stop lying and tell true."

Flynn didn't feel like laughing, but he twisted his lips up in something like a smile. They still felt thick, as though moving them would break the skin open. His head was aching again. He knew nothing he could say would change things for him. He'd taken a beating, and the hopelessness of his present situation made him a trifle sick.

He looked around at their faces. They all hated him. It only made it worse that he was a Mounted Policeman. Ever since the Half-breed Rebellion these men of French and Indian blood had believed the Mounted was organized for purposes of tyranny to take their land, Red River land.

Flynn said wearily: "Then you think I plotted this attack against you?"

"Always you have wanted to destroy the *horizon du nord*, so your robber fur traders could make money here, trading poor rifles and wormy meal for our furs."

The old hatred. He couldn't change it. The Mounted — the government — one or the other had made a mistake once, and now it was being paid back with compound interest by these good people of the North. Knowledge of this kept him from becoming angry. He felt for his English ovals. The cardboard box was there, but the cigarettes were sticky from blood. He held the gummy mass in his hand, wondering where the blood had come from. He was still looking at it when Toscan took out a deer-bladder tobacco pouch and handed it to him with a thin sheaf of papers.

The kindness surprised him. He rolled a cigarette, ignored the pointing rifles to stand and light it from a candle flame. Men watched with alert suspicion as he inhaled. There was no chance of him escaping. The tobacco was strong, a mixture of trade leaf and "red willow" bark — dogwood — and it helped to steady him. "Aren't you doing anything to find her?" he asked, meaning Marie.

"You will tell us where to find her," Toscan said. "She is not at the Indian village. We have followed. Now you will tell us where it was planned to take her if your attack failed."

"Why don't you ask Kamwit?"

"Dead."

"And Rambo?"

"Gone. To look for her perhaps."

"You never thought that *he* might have organized this attack?"

"He is a good man we have known for many years, *m'sieu.*"

Flynn discarded the cigarette, trod it beneath his moccasin. "Put down the gun!" he barked at Toscan. "You're being a fool. You should be out looking for her instead of sitting over me. Are you afraid to get away from the warmth of your fire? Would you rather sit and talk like a bunch of squaws?"

"He is right!" The young *voyageur* was once again waving his rifle excitedly. "The Mounted Policeman calls for action, not cheap words. So we will give heem action! There are rafters in thees room, yes?" he spun on Toscan. "Why talk lak squaw? Give heem tobac, all thees while minutes go by. He will tell what he know when noose is aroun' neck. *Oui!* Babiche noose, that is good medicine for mak men talk."

Flynn looked around. He knew by their expressions that they wouldn't hesitate to hang him. A young half-

205

breed ran from the room and was back in less than a minute carrying a piece of plaited babiche. He tried to make a knot, but the babiche was stiff from cold. He squatted in the strong heat of the fire, working the moose thong, softening it until he was able to make a slip noose.

He stood, chose a rafter, tossed it over. The noose swung back and forth, and sight of it brought a sudden silence. For a few seconds it was so quiet one could hear the logs contracting in the fireplace.

"Good?" the half-breed asked, grinning around at Toscan.

Toscan did not answer. Instead he turned and said to Flynn: "You must understand how our justice must be."

"I thought it was a gun, a cartridge, and a pound of meat."

"For those in valley. . . ."

A new voice cut in: "Did you theenk, perhaps, we would be such fools as give one shell and pound of meat to Mounted Policeman? You are not men. You are wolves. You would not die. Hear me! . . . my father, a Cree half-breed, he die in rebellion at Battleford, and it was Mounted Police that keel heem. Why should half-breed French-Cree trust . . . ?"

"I'm not fighting the Half-breed Rebellion over again. I'm trying to get free so I can save a girl. Marie. But you're too dull-witted to understand." He spun and faced Toscan. "Here's a proposition. We'll pick up his trail . . . Rambo's. All of us. If I'm not telling the truth. . . ."

"No. No, *m'sieu le police*." He pointed at the noose which swung back and forth at the height of a man's head. "You have kill *Père* Brissaud, and so you must die. Die before one of your Mounted Police tak you away from us." He motioned to one of the men. "Jules! The chair. We will give heem the good drop. It is only merciful. One of the small chair top the other, perhaps. And the noose . . . a trifle higher. *Oui,* it is not well when the toes touch the floor." He looked at Flynn. "You are a Christian? Then, perhaps, a few minutes. Two or three. We would not wish a man to die without word to his God, *m'sieu.*"

Flynn said: "Champlain, where is he?"

"You know Champlain?"

"Yes."

"We fin' heem by south door. In snow. Wounded." He tapped the region above his heart.

"He's still alive?"

"Through the grace of *le bon Dieu.*"

"Take me to him."

One of the *voyageurs* cried: "The police, he only kills time!"

Toscan silenced him with a jerk of his head. "Perhaps, but every condemned man must be given the last chance to prove his innocence, it was the way of *Père* Brissaud." His eyes roved the other faces. "Is there one among you more wise than *Père* Brissaud? No. Then we will tak heem to Louis Champlain. Perhaps Champlain will open his eyes and talk."

Toscan lifted his rifle and gestured with the muzzle, signaling for Flynn to go in front of him, through a door, and down a dark hallway. Suspicious, and ready with their guns, the other men strung out behind.

"Thees door!" said Toscan.

Flynn pushed the door open and paused for a second looking inside a dimly lighted room. A young squaw turned and looked at him — then quietly lost herself in shadow. She'd been bending over a man who lay on a bunk. It took Flynn a few seconds to realize that the man was Louis Champlain. His face looked big boned and sharp by the rays of the grease-dip lamp. His complexion which had been ruddy was now grayish.

A breathless silence had fallen over the *voyageurs* as they followed Flynn and Toscan across the room. Toscan took Champlain's hand and said: "You know me, Louis?"

It took a long while for Champlain to answer, then his voice was barely a whisper. "Yes. You are Toscan. They tell me that *Père* Brissaud is dead. Is it true, Toscan, that our *Père* is dead?"

"We must all die some day, Louis."

"I have been told that he died by bullet."

"Yes."

"Then it is best that I die too, for I failed to guard him."

"No, Louis. . . ."

"I shall not live with him dead!" Champlain got elbows braced in the bunk behind him and tried to struggle to a sitting position, but with gentle strength Toscan forced him back again. "No, Louis. You must live and help revenge his death. Look! You have ever seen this man before?"

Chapter Sixteen

Champlain lay back, eyes seeking Flynn's face. "Ah!" The word was a long exhalation. "The policeman. So. You have caught heem. It is good. I knew it would not be well when *Père* asked the policeman to table. I knew the police hated and would kill heem."

Flynn had expected such a response. Louis Champlain would be no different from the others. The man was still speaking, lips barely moving, and the *voyageurs* crowded close, tense on each word as it came. Flynn recognized his chance — perhaps his only chance. The grease dip stood on a bench a short step to one side. He turned as though to say something to Champlain. In moving his hand swung close and heat guided his fingers. They closed on the flame, and the room became a void of darkness.

For a shocked instant no one made a sound or a move, then they were all plunging, shouting at once. A rifle slammed his arm. Flynn seized it by the barrel. The man fought for it, but Flynn had a quick, spring-steel strength, and he ripped it free. He pivoted and was by himself somewhere near the center of the room. The door was a dim rectangle of light. He moved through and was alone in the hall.

There'd be a way outside at the far end of the hall, and they'd be expecting him to take it. Instead he turned, ran with long strides to the big room. No one was there. He paused for a moment. The babiche rope still hung from the rafter. He saw his mackinaw and parka on the floor where they'd been stripped off him. He picked them up, turned, hurried through the door leading to the kitchen snow shed.

The sharp cold felt good when it struck him. It took away the trapped-rat feeling he'd had inside. He stopped, protected by deep shadow beneath the snow shed roof, listened. Men were shouting, moccasins thudding inside the house. A rifle whanged, and echoes seemed to make the sound come from all directions at once. He let a grim laugh jerk his shoulders. They'd be hunting him through every room in the big, dark house.

He took time to slip on mackinaw and parka, glance at the rifle. It was .30-30 Winchester, the standard lever-action gun of the North. He had some extra cartridges in his pocket, but they were all for the .405. He'd have to get along with the half-dozen in the gun's magazine.

One of the rear doors squeaked open. Four men came out, paused a few seconds to look around. They were about thirty paces away. One of them issued a command in French, and they split, two of them moving immediately out of sight, the others walking almost directly toward the snow shed where he stood.

There was a fifty-fifty chance of them not noticing him. His only good hiding place would be inside. He made no move, stood with shoulders against the logs, fingering the rifle. He wondered what he'd do if they found him. He was not going to be retaken, and on the other hand he didn't want to shoot it out with them.

They walked on, after coming so close he might have reached the rifle out and touched the nearest of them.

He could hear the whip of their wool and buckskin clothing, a word that one spoke under his breath, and even smell the slight, smoky odor of Indian-tanned leather. One of them was looking directly at him, but the shadow was deep, and seconds later they were past, turning the corner of the house.

Flynn exhaled, listened to the receding squeak of moccasins on packed snow, and moved away from the wall. He guessed their plan. Nothing complicated. They'd make a half circle of the house and meet the other two on the east side. There they'd probably talk it over and decide to post themselves as lookouts at the four corners. If that was the case, then the west side would be momentarily unwatched. It was fifty or sixty yards slightly uphill to the dog pens. With luck he'd have time enough.

He ran, crossed the triangular area between wings of the building, found the hard-trodden path leading to the dog pens. Malemutes started barking when they saw him. His own dogs — and others. There's something about running with your back to danger that is twice as hard as facing it, and he speeded in a moment of terror, expecting a bullet between his shoulders. But the bullet did not come, and in nine or ten seconds the woven-willow pens were there to protect him.

A man stepped from nowhere and was facing him. Flynn came to a stop, swung the rifle around, paused without pointing it. The man was unarmed. He was the half-breed dog tender.

"My malemutes, sled." Flynn spoke the Cree tongue, making the same thoughts in sign language. For some reason Cree always worked better than English in getting the dog tender to hurry.

The 'breed grunted, turned, called to his helper while

getting the fence thong untied. The Indian boy crawled from a tiny lean-to shanty, and the two of them ran in and out of the pens, leading out the police team. The dogs didn't respond well to fast handling, but Flynn kept talking, calling each wild malemute by name as he was led out, and they submitted, all except big Nanuck who lashed back and forth with his fangs, making the 'breed swing his shot-loaded whip in self-defense. Finally it was Flynn himself who got the big lead dog in his place.

Nanuck was already hitting the tug, muscles trembling under his heavy gray coat, but Flynn held him, taking a look at his neck and shoulder, cut in three places, but Nanuck's thick underhair had been protection, saving the tendons and arteries of his throat. Flynn went to the shed, glanced in the grub can. There was dried caribou for the dogs, some pemmican for himself. Not so much as he'd have liked, but enough to get by for three days. His rabbitskin blanket was in the hamper. There were the usual extras — a whip, some mending babiche, snowshoes, his duffel.

He seemed to take a long time checking things over. Actually it was only fifteen or twenty seconds. He had a last look at the dogs, then he cried "Moosh!" and swung his dog whip. For a while the malemutes were barking, jerking individually at cross-purposes. He grabbed the handles, rocked the runners free of their set, and started the sled forward. With movement the team settled down to a steady pull, and they were traveling swiftly and smoothly around dog pens into the open.

Tom Flynn made no effort to keep out of sight. Hiding would be useless. He went boldly, straight down the trail toward the stockade gate. A man shouted. One of the *voyageurs.* Flynn answered, turning as he ran, shouting a few words in Cree.

"Halt!" the stranger cried.

Flynn kept going the same pace, waving his whip hand high.

"Halt!" the shout came again.

Flynn was a hundred and fifty paces off. A gun exploded, making a high, ricketing sound across the cold air. No bullet. It had been fired in warning. Flynn shouted: "Me . . . François!" choosing the name merely because it was so common, knowing the *voyageur* would let identity of every François he knew run through his mind before shooting to kill.

The trail dipped, giving the protection of second-growth spruce. After that the stockade gate was scarcely a hundred yards away. Flynn watched as the old gatekeeper shuffled into sight and stood on bowed legs, hunched forward as a lifetime of canoe paddles and portage bundles had bent him, trying to recognize the man and team that advanced through twilight.

"Open up!" Flynn shouted, not slowing his pace.

The man did not move. He was carrying a rifle, but his mittens were on, and the gun was neither cocked nor pointed. He had no idea of using it, carried it merely from habit. The team came to a stop against the gate, and Flynn trotted forward. Light showed no trace of antagonism on the old man's face.

"I am old, lame," the gatekeeper said. "Such shooting! Often shoot at target. Marie. . . ."

"Have you seen Marie? Tonight?"

"Oh, sure. Her team. Wolf team. That damn *Mach de Fer.* Make Survay leave behind. Say her team."

"Survay didn't take his old team?"

213

"This *her* team. He have to leave with old dogs. Yes-terday."

"He didn't take the team he came with?"

"No. They say not let him. Take old team. He don't like, but he say all right. He get out damn' quick. He's in trouble, no?"

"Who took the team?" He grabbed the man and shook him. "The one Survay and Marie came with?"

"I say, Brissaud not let him have this team. Survay, he take old team. Those dogs LeBois sometime drive. You know, gray Huskies? What you say wolf team, damn' *Mach de Fer*, these dogs Moose Rambo take. He take Marie. She don't want to go. He say: Go! Place too much shoot. Take her team! Wolf team! Survay's team! Moose Rambo, too! He say okay. He drive. She don't want to go, but he say *go*."

"Moose Rambo was driving them?"

"*Oui*, Moose Rambo. Now I remember. The wolf team and *M'sieu* Rambo. Sometimes he drive that wolf team. And *Mach de Fer*, that dog of the devil. . . ."

"He had the toboggan."

"*M'sieu* . . . you are choking me, *m'sieu* . . . !"

Flynn still held him. "Which way did they go?"

"So . . . like so." He gestured northwest, speaking an excited mixture of English, French, and Cree, talking about the country of desolation.

Flynn let him go. He could see men running down from the house. The old man opened the gate, and Flynn helped maneuver through with a hand tug over his shoulder. He was on the hard-packed trail outside, and the old man was already getting the gate shut. He shouted at his dogs, urging them for-ward, swiftly following the trail as it swung into timber,

214

covering him from view.

Snow was falling, settling softly into the toboggan track. It came more and more deeply, but Nanuck had his nose out, following the spoor of *Mach de Fer*, the wolf.

Flynn unsnapped the hand tug and fell behind. "Go it, Nanuck," he said through clenched teeth. "Go it, you devil. Catch that wolf dog, Nanuck. Catch him tonight. I won't let the harness bother you next time you meet him."

For a distance of five or six miles the toboggan followed the good trail, then it swung sharply to the west, breaking trail where snow had settled deep and soft among the spruce. Flynn paused to lash on his snowshoes. When they were fast to his feet, he stood for a moment, listening for pursuit. There was no sound, except for nervous movements of his dogs and the quiet hiss of snow slanting through spruce needles and settling to rest.

Onward, Nanuck followed the wolf trail without being guided. It was slightly uphill, and the sled sank more deeply than the toboggan, taking away some of the advantage of the broken trail. Flynn kept watching the trail, reading things from it. There was only a single set of snowshoe tracks. Long, narrow webs, the kind Crees make for the long trail rather than the circular bear-paws in favor for thick timber and trapline. The man did not take a particularly long stride, but he sank more deeply than most, so Flynn knew he was close-coupled and heavy.

Even without the gatekeeper's word he'd have guessed it to be Moose Rambo. He studied the toboggan trail. It was the same toboggan Marie had used, but it sank in a manner which showed that it carried at least a hundred pounds more weight than on the journey in. So he had Marie a prisoner.

Snow was falling harder, blowing a little, and here and there it filled the trail ahead. Spruce was thinning out. There was a hillside with a gray strata of rock jutting from the snow, and Rambo's tracks went around it, found a V-shaped gulch, and the climb became steeper.

Hills now made rounded summits, visible through the storm and fading mist on both sides. There'd be a plateau country beyond and, after many hours of travel, the MacLeod Hills. The gatekeeper's words came back to him — what he'd said about the "country of desolation." At first Flynn had thought it only a general term for the great barrens, but the barrens lay to the north and east. He recalled then that the eastern, rocky escarpment of the MacLeod Hills was frequently referred to by trappers as Point Desolation. There was no other place that Rambo could be headed.

The gulch was more narrow, steeper; and the trail twisted in snake coils through rock and jackspruce. Then even the jackspruce vanished, and the toboggan quit the gulch bottom and slanted steeply up the northern side. Up there the mist was gone, carried on the gale that roared down from the great barrens. Flynn lowered his head and quartered into it, letting the wind carry the long wolverine parka edging across his face. The cold was too strong for a blizzard, too strong for hard travel, but there was a blizzard anyway, and he did not slacken his pace. He slogged ahead, the monotonous, long-striding snowshoe pace as hard pellets of snow came in repeated gusts, whipping in like birdshot. No stars. Only the grayish darkness without landmarks. Sometimes he was blinded, without sense of direction, but he kept going, on and on, trusting to his instincts and the nose of Nanuck who still somehow found spoor of the wolf team.

The country was slightly rolling with here and there a gully half filled with snow. Such places swamped the sled, and Flynn half carried it as the dogs wallowed back deep to the opposite side. His legs, and the faltering of Tazin, his wheel dog, against the breastband told him it was time to stop. He found a place sheltered by scrub willow in a draw, trampled a circle in the snow, and went to the grub can.

He paused with his hand on the cover and looked at his team the way a dog driver always does, for any half-wild malemute is likely to jump his master when the sharp odor of meat strikes his nostrils. They were crouched, tails fluffed over feet, all except for Nanuck who stood high, arrogant of fatigue, watching with intense, amber eyes.

Flynn let the old smile break the bitter lines of his face, and he spoke to the dog: "Some day I'll run those legs right out from under you, Nanuck. Someday I'll do it, you gray devil." A man would go crazy on the trail without some living creature to talk to, even though it might be a half-tamed malemute.

The dogs were trembling and greedy when the lid came off the grub can. Even as it was, frozen in rock-hard chunks, the odor of caribou jerky came to them. He broke the pieces loose, and doled it out, one piece to each, and they gulped down the frozen chunks to thaw and be turned to energy inside their pinched bellies.

They were still ravenous the way they should be. He took out a piece of squaw pemmican for himself and squatted on his heels, chewing the stuff. It was half fat, made leathery by cold, with here and there a sharp crunch of ice crystal from chokecherries.

He rested for no more than half an hour — only the time required to eat, examine the harness, go over each malemute's feet to pick away bits of ice, and look for the pink discoloration that first warns of cracking foot pads. By now the toboggan track was blown completely full, but it was still revealed, in reverse, by the drifting ridge that had built itself along the windward side.

If it had been clear weather, Flynn would have sighted the MacLeod Hills long before. Through the blowing storm they appeared suddenly as rolling, treeless summits, although there was still no sight of the high escarpment of Point Desolation. He guessed it as being eight or ten miles beyond.

Flynn stopped again, more for Tazin, the wheel dog, than for himself. He unsnapped the animal and put him in the sled hamper. Tazin had traveled with him for three years. Flynn could seldom bring himself to kill a dog, especially a faithful wheeler like Tazin. Sometimes an old dog seems to play out and then snaps back after a two-hour rest to run younger ones into the snow.

The night wore on as the trail twisted through deeper country. There was a deep, muggy gloom and then a brightness without sun that constituted the northern day. He traveled with eyes closed for a while, and day vanished. The wind was still coming across his right shoulder, but there was little snow left, and he had a good view of the escarpment ahead.

The toboggan trail was plainer now, only partly filled by snow. He put Tazin back in his place and took time to brush snow away from the toboggan track and examine it. He guessed by the depth of the new snow that Rambo was less than an hour ahead.

He stood up, pulse quickening, watched for a while, but the track snaked out of sight across the edge of a gulch. No sign of movement. It was ideal for an ambush. Flynn got the Winchester from beneath his robes, went on, gun ready across his arm.

Wolf spoor was strong, making Nanuck bristle to new life, the hackles rise along his neck. He barked, and Flynn quieted him. The toboggan had dropped over the gulch rim without hesitation, and its tracks were visible for a quarter mile, following the bottom.

The escarpment was close above Flynn. From a distance the cliff had seemed to be thousands of feet in height, but on closer scrutiny its apparent size diminished, and he could see that only a hundred feet of nearly vertical gray rock stood between snow-covered talus and the rim. He stayed with the toboggan track, watching each turn in the gulch for movement. The trail climbed the side, looped over a divide, and disappeared over the rim of a second gulch.

Nanuck snarled and lunged forward, twisting with head thrown high in an effort to free himself from the tug. It was a warning. Flynn glimpsed movement at the end of the far climb from the gulch. He ducked instinctively against the sled as air whipped past his cheek, and the report of a rifle came an instant later. A sharp *ka-whack!* — with echoes accumulating and rushing in behind it.

A second bullet whipped into the sled hamper, tearing bits of fur from the rabbitskin robes. Flynn could see the man, wolf team, and toboggan. The distance across was nearly two hundred yards and shifting wind currents had made aiming hard, and that had saved his life. Moose Rambo was more spread-legged than ever in snowshoes. He looked huge as a grizzly, standing with his back to the wind, his fur-edged parka flapping before him. The rifle was up, and he was trying to pick out Flynn's shape behind the sled hamper.

Rambo was an excellent target. Flynn had his rifle up —then he stopped. The toboggan was beyond, and he could make out the fur-wrapped form of someone seated in it. Marie. That's why the man felt safe to stand there in the open.

A third bullet whanged. There was a sound — a thud as it struck one of the dogs. Nippow, one of the swing dogs. It knocked him down. He twisted, tangling the harness, biting at his side. The others lunged and started forward, dragging the sled downhill. They wallowed over their backs in snow, dragging the mortally wounded Nippow.

Flynn tried to guide the sled while staying in the protection of its hamper. He was half aware of more bullets, but the deep snow was protection as well as hindrance. He was on his side, head lower than his feet, cushioned in billowing white. His rifle was gone. He stayed where he was and groped for it, finding it packed in snow beneath him.

He worked it free, saw that there was snow in the barrel. He didn't know how much. Sometimes snow in a barrel will cause a gun to rip itself apart when fired. He started turning, maneuvering to get the snowshoes under him so they would support his weight.

He'd gone farther down the slope than he thought. Neither Rambo nor the toboggan was in sight. His own dogs and sled were at the bottom of the gulch. He went down the steep drop, half walking, half sliding. The male-mutes were tangling themselves in harness, snarling at the fallen Nippow.

Flynn drove them away with his whip and looked at the dog. Nippow was dead. The bullet had struck him a quartering blow by the right shoulder and passed all the way through, tearing a big chunk from his side. The cold had already frozen blood hard in his hair.

Flynn cut the dead malemute free, rolled him over in deep snow, shortened the harness. Then he rested on one knee, getting his bearings. He'd seen a cleft in the escarpment, a narrow-sided gulch that was probably the only dog team route to the top. Rambo would go that way, and it would be suicide for Flynn to follow.

His eyes roved the wall of rock. There were other gullies breaking in here and there. He'd be able to climb afoot, leaving dogs and sled behind. And that was what Rambo would probably want — to force him to abandon his supplies.

It would be better to explore farther. This deep gulch that held him now would be protection for another half mile. He got the dogs to moving. The gulch narrowed and steepened. It was tougher going with no toboggan trail to follow. He ran into heaps of blocky slide rock over which it was necessary almost to carry the sled. Then, amid thorn and scrub spruce, the gulch fanned out against the base of the escarpment.

Chapter Seventeen

Flynn turned north. It was steady, brutal labor. Snow filled the air thickly. It came in spinning billows that turned everything misty and uncertain at distances greater than fifty paces. It brought something like a grim smile to his lean face. It was the best break he'd had — this snow that would give him concealment while following on Rambo's heels to the top. *If* it did not stop as suddenly as it started and leave him at the mercy of a bushwhack shot from above.

He swung the sled around and traveled a contour of the mountainside. It had been brutal work. Exertion is hard on a man in such frigid air. He set his teeth to keep from breathing deeply, to prevent the frosted lung sacs that would give him the dreaded black cough of the Arctic. Snow kept coming, swirling in on the wind, billows so thick he could scarcely see Nanuck in his lead position.

After a long, blind struggle around the slope, Flynn's sled jumped forward and slid to the bottom of a steep-sided gulch. Nanuck snarled and lunged ahead with new strength as once more he picked up the wolf spoor. The toboggan track was there. Flynn could feel it beneath his snowshoes.

The walls became steeper and in a hundred yards were sheer bleak stone on both sides. It was a harder climb than he'd expected. Farther. One of the dogs slipped, fell on his side, carrying a second one with him. Their weight and an unexpected lurch started the sled back downhill. Flynn wedged one runner with a snowshoe, but he couldn't stop its momentum. It twisted and turned on its side.

He managed to right the sled and get the cargo back, but he'd lost a precious thirty feet. He noticed that the air was clearing. Stars were coming through. He heard the baying of wolves. A gun crashed, high above, but cliff walls held the sound, making it seem right on top of him. The bullet struck projecting rock and whined away. There was another, another. Blind shooting, or at best Rambo was aiming at the shadowy movements of the dogs.

One of the malemutes was nicked. He snarled and spun in the traces. Flynn maneuvered the dogs into the shelter of the cliff wall. He hadn't yet cleared the snow from the barrel of his rifle. He did that now, using a steel wire from the catch-all inside the hamper. He took some babiche from the catch-all and fashioned a sling, placed the rifle around his shoulders. Then he started to climb, leaving the dogs behind.

At first it was almost vertical, from one foothold and ledge to another. After fifty or sixty feet the going became easier, but still he spent a great deal of time exploring false paths, turning back, hunting another.

No shooting, no movement above. A wolf was baying, but at a greater distance. He crossed the cliff edge, rested on one knee, scanned the broken rim. Rambo might still be there. There were many places for a man to conceal himself.

He went on, using hands and knees up a pitch of wind-polished rock then to surer footing on snow. The snow had been wind laid, and its crust bore his weight. From there he had his first good view of the summit. It was table land, broken here and there by other summits. In sheltered spots grew dense clumps of scrub spruce and brush. A quarter mile away stood a tiny cabin and beyond it a cache house on high stilt legs.

Flynn moved on to gain a better view. No smoke came from the cabin chimney, but a toboggan trail had recently been broken to it. He made out other things — the toboggan unhitched by the cabin door, shadow movements of the wolf team in some pens beyond. He wondered where the girl was, then he saw. . . .

She was standing beneath the cache house in an unnatural posture, her arms outflung. He waited for her to move. She didn't. She was twisting back and forth, her arms still stretched level with her shoulders.

He called her name. "Marie!"

She heard him, and her voice came across the wind and cold in answer. He couldn't understand her words. She was still twisting from side to side with arms outflung. He knew then that she was tied between the stilt legs of the cache house by babiche thongs that were invisible at a distance.

Flynn started on, among projecting rocks, finding moments of cover in brush and scrub spruce. Rambo. The man was scarcely fifty paces away. Flynn pitched face foremost, expecting a bullet, but the man hadn't raised the rifle to his shoulder.

Flynn lay with his cheek close to the rough snow, cursing himself. It was a hell of a pose for a manhunter, there on his belly. He raised himself to one knee. Rambo had disappeared. He was still coming, in cover of rocks and scrub spruce, his snowshoes making the regular hiss crunch of movement. Flynn waited, rifle partly raised to his shoulder.

"Mountie!" Rambo was hidden in scrub spruce. "Answer me. Or are you too yellow gutted to answer?"

"Here I am."

Rambo laughed. "So. Up here to blast old Rambo. But you won't do it. I'll tell you why. Because if you kill me, you'll be killing her." He waited. "Did you hear that, Mountie?"

Rambo went on talking, all the while moving closer through the scrub spruce. "Maybe you could kill me. You know how to handle a gun. I found that out. But you won't kill me, Mountie. Do you know why?"

"Say what you started to say!"

"All right. I have *Mach* on the loose. The wolf. He's always hated her. He'd kill her now that she's helpless. He'd do it, Mountie, if he wasn't afraid of old Rambo. You're damned right he would. Now do you see, Mountie? Maybe you can blast me, but when you do, you'd never stop *Mach de Fer* from tearing her white throat out. He'd do it in ten seconds with me dead, Mountie."

Flynn was crouched and tense, gripping the rifle. He remembered the wolf that first night on the trail — how the brute had looked, crouching in the snow, watching Marie with his savage, yellow eyes. He was cowering from whip and gun then, but a person never tames an animal like *Mach de Fer* — Jaw of Iron. Nothing, neither kindness nor brutality, will quench the will for vengeance in such a brain.

"Why don't you answer me, Mountie?" Rambo bellowed.

"What is there to say?" He was already edging back toward the cliff edge.

"Now you're talking sense, Mountie. What is there to say? You're damned right . . . what is there to say?"

"You got me, Rambo. I can't kill the girl." He was still on the move, talking to keep Rambo from being suspicious. He wanted to get below. There was one chance, and he had to take it. One thing Rambo hadn't considered. Nanuck. That great, rangy lead dog was spoiling to tangle. But Flynn didn't want Rambo to suspect, to be waiting with his rifle for Nanuck to show himself. And so Flynn talked. "All right, Rambo. Tell me what I'm to do."

"Drop your gun and come up here."

"So you can kill me?"

He was in full sight crossing the smooth stone, but Rambo didn't know that, hid where he was in the scrub spruce.

"No. Not kill you. I like you too well. I want to have supper with you. Biscuits and bacon, Mountie. You've had a long trip, Mountie. You must be hungry."

He could tell that Rambo was moving forward again. The hood of his parka popped into sight over some jagged stones, then the rest of him. He stood in full sight, deliberately making himself a perfect target. He swung his arms wide, waving the rifle. He roared laughter, stamped his feet while looking around, trying to see where Flynn had been hiding himself.

"Here it is, Mountie. Take your free shot. You been on my tail a long time. You earned it. You take your turn, and *Mach de Fer* will take his!"

Flynn kept moving back, the gray of his parka concealing him against the gray of wind-polished stone. It became steeper, and the bulge of it hid Rambo from view. He turned over, got hold of a rock crack with his fingers, and went down the cliff, clawing from one support to the next. His dog team was directly below. He could hear them although they were hidden by an overhanging cliff. He knew by the sound that Nanuck was lashing back and forth, trying to get himself free of the harness tug. He seemed to sense what was coming. Flynn hesitated an instant, leaped the final thirty feet. He came down almost atop the dogs, landing on his feet, cushioned by deep snow.

"Mountie!" Rambo was bellowing above. "Why don't you shoot, Mountie?"

Flynn got to his feet, climbed waist deep through snow, dragged himself up with one hand on the harness breastband. Nanuck crouched with tendons and muscles drawn hard and trembling like piano wires. Flynn located the snap fastener, freed him. Nanuck would have been off, but Flynn caught him by the collar, guiding him along the steep ascent.

"Mountie!" Rambo still shouted. "Mountie, you yellow gut. Have you crawled away with your tail between your legs? Are you going to sneak away and let me have her? Come on out. I don't need my gun, Mountie. Throw your gun away and I'll throw mine. All I need to rip you apart is my two hands."

The climb didn't take so long this time. Flynn knew the way, moving surely from one step to the next. He reached the edge, but this time he did not dare cross the smoothed, slanting rock. He circled for a distance and approached in the protection of a jagged reef that thrust itself waist high from snow.

Nanuck was fighting to free himself. With a lunge more ferocious than the rest, he broke away, circling the barricade. Rambo fired. Just the one shot. It had a deadly echo to it. Flynn cursed himself. He shouldn't have let the dog loose. Not there. Not with Rambo's gun waiting. That bullet had probably ended any chance of Nanuck's fighting the wolf, any chance of his saving the girl.

He crouched, listening. Seconds dragged past. It seemed like half a minute, though in reality it might not have been a fourth that long. Then he heard the snarl of fighting animals. Dog and wolf. Elation jolted him, and he couldn't resist the jeering cry that sprung from his lips.

"What now, Rambo? Do you still want me, Rambo? I'm coming. I'm coming to blast you, Rambo."

He could hear Rambo cursing. There was a steepening pitch then the projecting line of jagged stone. He pulled himself forward. No snowshoes, and the snow there was not so wind hardened. It let him sink to his knees. He reached above, got a hand hold along the reef, drew himself up.

His hood came in view, and Rambo's gun pounded, the bullet striking rock, sending fragments across Flynn's cheek. No chance. A second slug glanced and droned away across the abyss, leaving a momentary sulphurous odor of burnt rock.

He moved back, looked around. Farther along the reef became lower, disappeared in snow. He ran, sensed the instant of showing himself, pitched face down, pulled himself forward with elbows digging snow, pushing the rifle ahead of him.

He caught a glimpse of Rambo. Too unexpected. He was flat in the snow, and Rambo got the first shot. He was surprised, too, and the bullet whipped wildly overhead. Rambo spun, dived to the cover of leafless brush. Flynn's Winchester was back against his shoulder, and he fired at the man's vanishing shadow, knowing at the same instant that he'd missed.

Rambo had been turned, watching wolf and malemute as they fought, rolling over and over in the snow, half way between cliff and cache house. Then he was out of sight, down among waist-high bushes. Flynn pumped and pulled the trigger again, hating to waste the cartridge, but knowing he'd have to keep Rambo on the move to give himself the chance to advance.

He took half a dozen steps without drawing a shot, found protection between two drifts. Snow softer, harder going. He reached cover of buckbrush and spruce. He paused to listen. No sign of Rambo now. The brush seemed to hold darkness. It was like grayish fog. Through an opening he could see the cabin, the cache house with Marie still twisting back and forth, trying to fight free of the babiche thongs.

He could hear *Mach de Fer* and Nanuck. Then he caught sight of their movements. A gray form was on top. The wolf had a throat hold, the same death grip as that time back on the trail. They reared high. *Mach de Fer* was unrelaxed, but Nanuck was a veteran of a hundred battles, and with a deft maneuver he twisted the wolf backward. But it failed to pull him free from that death grip on his throat.

Mach de Fer came again atop the malemute, lifted him, slammed him down. Repeated again and again . . . . Rambo was watching from somewhere in brush cover, too. He shouted, sounding his old triumphant laugh: "Oh-ho! See, Mountie? Your cur's as good as dead already. So what now?"

His voice was unexpectedly close. Flynn had only one chance, to get him now before Nanuck was killed. He rose, parted wire-hard twigs before him, started through. A twig struck his parka, making a sharp, rasping noise. Rambo fired, aiming at the sound. Gunflame was close, slicing the half darkness. The bullet winged overhead, cutting twigs that still were rattling to rest after it was gone.

Flynn fired back, aiming at the gunflame. He worked the lever, fired again, again. The exchange was close, rapid, one shot coming atop another. Flynn pumped, and the hammer fell with a futile click. He hadn't fired a total of seven shots. He'd lost track, but there hadn't been that many. He pumped the lever again, saw no responding gleam of brass cartridge. The magazine hadn't been filled in the first place. He cursed, hurled the gun away from him. It cleared brush, clattered against an exposed rock.

The parka was a handicap. He stripped it off. Cold stung his unprotected head, but it let him hear better. He waited until the ring of gunfire left his ears and little sounds once more became audible — the snarl of battle as Nanuck and *Mach de Fer* sought a decision, the rush of wind through branches, the little, crunching sounds of snow as it packed beneath him.

He started forward, stopped. There was other movement. Rambo. Retreating or coming forward — for the moment he didn't know. Twigs, frozen hard as steel, made ripping sounds across Rambo's parka. He was coming, not going away.

Bushes hid him, then his shadow appeared, unexpectedly close. He was watching off where Flynn had tossed his rifle. Flynn had been standing almost erect. He moved instinctively, crouching to hide himself. It was a mistake. Rambo caught the movement, tried to turn.

Snow and the thick brush were a handicap. They tangled the rifle as he tried to aim. He cursed, ripped it free, pulled the trigger. Flame and explosion seemed to burst in Flynn's face, but the bullet made rattling sounds through bushes many feet away.

Flynn was in movement, driving headlong through brush tangle. Rambo glimpsed him and tried to bat the gun barrel to his head. It glanced from Flynn's upflung arm. They collided, and Flynn's momentum carried Rambo back. Rambo would have fallen, but brush and deep snow supported him. His gun was gone, fallen, barrel down in the snow with only its stock in sight. He made no effort to recover it. There was no time. Instead he wrapped massive arms around his assailant and drew him with crushing strength close to his body.

Flynn had felt the man's strength before. He'd intended to slam him down, to leave him tangled in brush. But Rambo had been too quick. Flynn worked his hands between them, tried to drive them forward, rip himself free. It had no effect. Rambo had reeled forward, and now he was set with stud-horse legs set wide. His arms grew tighter and tighter. His hands were locked in the small of Flynn's back. Rambo bent his knees, expanded the massive muscles of chest and shoulders.

He was breathing hard, breath hissing through set teeth. A laugh came from deep in his throat. He was speaking. Groups of words came with each hiss of breath from his teeth. "This is how I wanted you, Mountie. With my bare hands. I'd have had you in the castle but for those damned Crees. Cowards! I'll finish you now. *Now*, Mountie." He was applying more pressure as he talked. His strength was not the strength of a man. It was like the strength of a great grizzly.

231

Flynn was bent back farther and farther, his spine like a bow pressed to the breaking point. Air was gone from his lungs. Blackness with darts of white light raced across his eyeballs. He could feel Rambo's hands working in the small of his back, hunting a certain spot, a fulcrum over which he could give that little extra twist that would break the spine.

Rambo was still talking, grunting. "Sure, Mountie. Like this. Just . . . so. I've snapped men's backs before. But it has to be just right. Just right . . . then the twist. Ever see a man . . . with his back broken? He lays and kicks . . . like a dead chicken."

Rambo forced him back one, two, three steps. Flynn's hands were free. He swung his fists, a right and a left, but there was no power in the blows. They only brought a snarling laugh from Rambo's lips.

Blindly Flynn tried the old tricks, the things that had worked in the past. He tried to relax and slide through the man's arms, to shift his feet forward so their combined weights would carry them back. Both futile. Rambo had set himself, weight ready to compensate for any maneuver.

The rifle. Memory of it came to Flynn's brain. It had been dropped barrel down in the snow. Flynn swung his right arm in an arc to one side. The tips of his fingers brushed the stock. He reached again. This time he got hold of it.

He dragged it toward him. He didn't have strength to point it. Its length made it ineffective at such close quarters anyway. Only one chance. He rammed it hard with its muzzle in snow, swung the lever down and back, his finger on the trigger. Rambo glimpsed the action. He lunged back.

"No!" he bellowed. He knew the danger of a barrel hammered full of snow.

If Flynn had had his original strength, he'd have spun free then with the rifle as a weapon. But his back was paralyzed. Rambo made a grab for the rifle. He jerked it away, but Flynn's finger hooked the trigger, and the gun exploded with stunning, deafening impact.

It left him blinded with no sense of position. The barrel blocked by snow had caused the explosion to backfire, to rip the breech and place a long, ragged crack in the barrel.

Chapter Eighteen

Flynn got his bearings. He was down on his knees with no feeling in his right hand. There was blood on the snow. He lifted his arm, expecting to see the hand torn off. The hand was still there, but skin had been torn between thumb and wrist. He staggered to his feet. Strength was flowing back through his body.

Rambo. Rambo was there. He was rising, looking directly at Flynn, but at that moment he was too dazed to see. Powder had burned the whiskers on one side of his face, turning them from black to gray.

Flynn let him rise. He shifted his feet and swung a right aimed at the jaw. It missed the jaw, going high, mashing teeth through lips. Rambo went down, caught himself on an outflung arm. Blood was running from his lips, streaking down both sides of his chin. He felt along his waist, drew a long H. B. C. skinning knife. He rose, holding it underhand, keen edge up. He paused on one knee, steadied himself with his left hand on trampled snow.

Flynn took a backward step. The torn remnants of the gun lay in the snow, still smoking. He seized the barrel. It made a heavy club. He swung it in a short, horizontal arc as Rambo sprang. The barrel, striking him across jaw and cheek, stopped Rambo. He was stunned but not out. The knife was still clutched in his hand. He grabbed the gun as Flynn tried to swing it a second time, jerked Flynn forward.

They were close. Rambo tried to rip the knife up with a stroke that would have disemboweled Flynn. Flynn seized his wrist. They staggered, locked in each other's grasp, reeled out of the brush, fell with shoulders almost atop the reef. It was good footing there. No restraining brush or snow. Flynn's long, spring-steel body had the advantage now.

He dropped the gun, twisted away from Rambo at the same instant, freed his hand, and brought a smashing uppercut to the big man's jaw. It spilled Rambo backward. For an instant he was lying half way over the jagged reef. He had strength enough to save himself for a moment by rolling to the other side.

Flynn leaped after him as he staggered blindly to his feet. Rambo's parka was twisted, weighted by snow. He tried to lift both arms to protect himself, but the movement was too slow. A right and left caught him and sent him reeling backward.

The cliff was there, only a few feet away. He saw it, attempted to stop. His feet slipped from under him. He was down, sliding over smooth rock. He made a desperate grab, but there was no place for his clawing fingers. He hung for an instant anyway, fingernails making ripping sounds on rock, eyes staring, an awful fear showing on his brute face. Then he was gone, leaving only a scream that was carried away on the howling storm.

Flynn hung to the reef for a while, breathing, trying to steady himself. He felt his way to the edge, looked far below. A dark form was wedged head foremost between angular talus rocks, broken and not at all like a man.

He moved back out of danger, circled the reef as fast as snow would let him. No sound of dogs now. He caught sight of the cache house. Marie was no longer there. A weakness grabbed him. Nausea. His victory meant nothing. He'd won, and he'd failed. With Marie gone it would have been better had Rambo killed him.

He kept going, walking mechanically, scarcely knowing what he did. He found the toboggan trail, followed it. Snow was still everywhere in the air. He was bareheaded, without parka or hood. He didn't even realize it.

The wolf team was snarling in chorus. Then there was another sound. A dog. Nanuck. Nanuck was coming toward him, belly deep in snow. He was torn, and he left a dribble of blood here and there, making little, dark balls in the snow. But he wasn't beaten. Certainty of that brought a sudden surge of hope.

He heard Marie, then, calling his name. He turned, saw her coming, following the toboggan track.

He watched, half expecting her to turn into an apparition like those platters of roasted meat that starving men see floating toward them across the big snows. She didn't disappear. She walked directly to him for a while, then turned from the track, and paused to look down on something.

It was *Mach de Fer* — dead. His neck was broken. No vision. It was real. Everything was real. It had been many years since Flynn had wept, but he could have wept now.

He walked to Marie, looked at the dead wolf. He appeared bigger than ever, spread out on the snow like that, dead. Nanuck had finished him, Nanuck, victor in a hundred fights along the great trails. Two years ago Nanuck had snapped the neck of a malemute that

Flynn had just bought for three hundred dollars at the White River auctions, and he'd been angry enough to kill the big lead dog then, but it was a different story today.

He said: "I told you he'd kill that wolf sometime."

It was strange that he'd say anything like that, his first words after thinking Marie was dead.

She turned, smiled at him. "It meant so much to you?"

"It meant you'd live . . . or die."

"Perhaps." She still had the soft smile. She was lovely with the circle of wolverine fur framing her face. He realized then that she'd freed herself somehow and would have lived whether Nanuck had triumphed or not. It made no difference. Nothing made any difference as long as she was safe and waiting for him.

"You got away," he said, "from the thongs."

She held out her wrists. They were criss-crossed with wounds that the thongs had left. "Rawhide. You see? Rawhide always stretches when it is moist and warm." Moist and warm. The blood and warmth of her body. Still, there was no sign of pain on her face. "*Père* was killed," she said as though he didn't know.

He nodded, asked: "He meant a great deal to you?"

It took her a second to understand what was really on his mind. "You don't understand, *m'sieu*. It wasn't like" — she stopped for a long five seconds before whispering — "like the love I have for you."

He hadn't expected the words. At least not like that. With such simple directness. He reached. His hands closed on her shoulders. She seemed very small beneath the heavy covering of furs.

She went on, speaking in scarcely more than a whisper. "I didn't know before. He tol' me . . . that night . . . after he found us together. *Père* . . . he was my father. My real father. You see . . . he had a wife. His first wife. An invalid for half her lifetime, living somewhere, far away, in the south. My mother was his wife of the North. He never told me. He brought me there, but he never told me. He thought it might hurt me. You understand . . . ?"

"Of course."

She started to say something more, but he wasn't listening. He stood for a while, looking down on her. She was more lovely than he'd ever known. Her cheeks were flushed beneath their snow tan. Her lips were parted. Her eyes had a deep softness.

She was waiting for him. He knew that, but still he hesitated. He knew that this was the moment he would always remember, the moment that would stay with him after all the raw conflict and hatred were forgotten.

THE END

About the Author

Dan Cushman was born in Osceola, Michigan, and grew up on the Cree Indian reservation in Montana. He graduated from the University of Montana with a Bachelor of Science degree in 1934 and pursued a career in mining as a prospector, assayer, and geologist before turning to journalism. In the early 1940s his novelette-length stories began appearing regularly in such Fiction House magazines as *North-West Romances* and *Frontier Stories.* Later in the decade his North-Western and Western stories as well as fiction set in the Far East and Africa began appearing in *Action Stories, Adventure,* and *Short Stories.* A collection of some of his best North-Western and Western fiction has recently been published, *Voyaguers of the Midnight Sun* (1995), with a Foreword by John Jakes who cites Cushman as a major influence in his own work. The character Comanche John, a Montana road agent featured in numerous rollicking magazine adventures, also appears in Cushman's first novel, *Montana, Here I Be* (1950) and in two later novels. *Stay Away, Joe,* which first appeared in 1953, is an amusing story about the mixture, and occasional collision, of Indian culture and Anglo-American culture among the Métis (French Indians) living on a reservation in Montana. The novel became a bestseller and remains a classic to this day, greatly loved especially by Indian peoples for its truthfulness and humor. Yet, while humor became Cushman's hallmark in such later novels as *The Old Copper Collar* (1957) and *Good Bye, Old Dry* (1959), he also produced significant historical fiction in *The Silver Mountain* (1957), concerned with the mining and politics of silver in Montana in the 1890s. This novel won a Golden Spur Award from the Western Writers of America. His fiction remains notable for its breadth, ranging all the way from a story of the cattle frontier in *Tall Wyoming* (1957) to a poignant and memorable portrait of small town life in Michigan just before the Great War in *The Grand and the Glorious* (1963). His previous Five Star Western is *In Alaska with Shipwreck Kelly* (1996). His next one is concerned with a dramatic murder trial set in Montana in the 1890s.